"Campbell grounds us in such graphic grit, making these lives so bitterly, relentlessly real, we want to reach through the pages and pull them to safety—aware, alas, that many would firmly refuse rescue." —*San Francisco Chronicle*

"It's a hard-luck, hardscrabble life in the world of Bonnie Jo Campbell's stories, a landscape that's as fertile as it is unforgiving, where families crop up and wither with the weather but manage some piquant humor and moments of worthy reckoning along the way." —*Minneapolis Star Tribune*

"The stories in this collection are hard to read. They're supposed to be. They'll linger in my brain for a long time as I try to puzzle out all their layers of meaning." —*A Bookish Type*

"The varied and marvelous stories in *Mothers, Tell Your Daughters* are a different breed of narrative. They ask for, no, demand, slow contemplative reading and rereading, and they reward this effort with their wisdom, wit and grace; the abiding wonders of their language as it pirouettes from the profane to the lyrical in a sentence or a paragraph." —*Author Exposure*

"*Mothers, Tell Your Daughters* should be required reading for anyone who wants to perfect the art of the short story." —*Lit Reactor*

"Campbell writes with empathy and insight about characters often on the verge of emotional, financial, or physical catastrophe. And she does it all without melodrama." —*Newcity Lit*

"With grace and candor, Campbell adds some very necessary grime to the face of American fiction."   —*Ploughshares Blog*

"Campbell introduced us to the wily and wise-beyond-her-years Margo Crane, a modern-day female Huck Finn taking to the river in search of her lost mother. The strong and stubborn protagonists that the Michigan author excels at writing are back in her third short story collection. The working-class women in these stories are grief-addled brides, phlebotomists discovering their sensuality, and vengeful abused wives, all drawn with Campbell's signature dark humor and empathy."   —*The Millions*

"From the first word of each story, Campbell immerses you into the character's world. There is a hard line drawn between these characters, making them each unique."   —*Western Herald*

"The fierce women in the gorgeously ragged stories of Bonnie Jo Campbell's *Mothers, Tell Your Daughters* are like rusted razor blades—damaged but still sharp enough to draw blood. With each of these brilliant and unforgettable stories, Campbell solidifies her place as one of the finest writers of contemporary fiction."   —Roxane Gay

"Bonnie Jo Campbell is the real deal—a writer whose plainspoken characters I believe from the first word, even as I sometimes want to shout 'Oh God, No!' or even 'Why, Why, Why?!' I know why. I know these women. They are my cousins, nieces, neighbors. Some of them are me. What I don't know is how with such hard stories she invariably leaves me feeling strengthened. There is magic here. Read the stories and see for yourself."

—Dorothy Allison

"Bonnie Jo Campbell has some secret hocus-pocus going on here that births us for real real real humanity, yearning, leaping, chuckling, cussing, and embracing, while looking you and me right in the eye."   —Carolyn Chute

"Oh it's a dark, sticky, potent, relentless, and heartbreaking business between mothers and daughters, and Bonnie Jo Campbell likes it in there. She likes telling the truth—sixteen separate and powerful truths—about those unseverable bonds and the men who stretch them to their limit. These muscular, deeply affecting stories are about women you might have forgotten even exist, but I guarantee it, they will remind you—in all the best ways—of every shameful thing you have ever thought or done."   —Pam Houston

"Bonnie Jo Campbell is a master of capturing a roiling central mystery of life: the way love and hate, sadness and hilarity, power and weakness are so often inextricably, tempestuously fused. *Mothers, Tell Your Daughters* is an exhilarating book by one of our finest writers."   —Robert Olen Butler

"American fiction waited a long time for Bonnie Jo Campbell to come along."   —Jaimy Gordon,
National Book Award–winning author of *Lord of Misrule*

Mothers,
Tell
Your
Daughters

ALSO BY BONNIE JO CAMPBELL

ONCE UPON A RIVER

AMERICAN SALVAGE

Q ROAD

WOMEN & OTHER ANIMALS

Mothers, Tell Your Daughters

 STORIES

BONNIE JO CAMPBELL

W. W. NORTON & COMPANY
Independent Publishers Since 1923
New York • London

Mothers, Tell Your Daughters is a work of fiction. All of the characters are products of the author's imagination, and all of the settings, locales, and events have been invented by the author or are used fictitiously. Any resemblance to actual events, or to real persons, living or dead, is entirely coincidental.

Copyright © 2015 by Bonnie Jo Campbell

All rights reserved
Printed in the United States of America
First published as a Norton paperback 2016

For information about permission
to reproduce selections from this book,
write to Permissions, W. W. Norton & Company, Inc.,
500 Fifth Avenue, New York, NY 10110

For information about special discounts for bulk purchases,
please contact W. W. Norton Special Sales
at specialsales@wwnorton.com or 800-233-4830

Manufacturing by RR Donnelley
Book design by Brooke Koven
Production manager: Devon Zahn

Library of Congress Cataloging-in-Publication Data

Campbell, Bonnie Jo, 1962–
[Short stories. Selections]
Mothers, tell your daughters : stories / Bonnie Jo Campbell. —
First edition.
pages ; cm
ISBN 978-0-393-24845-6 (hardcover)
I. Title.
PS3553.A43956A6 2015
813'.54—dc23
2015022459

ISBN 978-0-393-35326-6 pbk.

W. W. Norton & Company, Inc.
500 Fifth Avenue, New York, N.Y. 10110
www.wwnorton.com

W. W. Norton & Company Ltd.
15 Carlisle Street, London W1D 3BS

1 2 3 4 5 6 7 8 9 0

To Susanna

CONTENTS

Sleepover   13

Playhouse   15

Tell Yourself   37

The Greatest Show on Earth, 1982:
What There Was   47

My Dog Roscoe   65

Mothers, Tell Your Daughters   85

My Sister Is in Pain   105

A Multitude of Sins   107

To You, as a Woman   127

Daughters of the Animal Kingdom   137

Somewhere Warm   155

My Bliss   173

Blood Work, 1999   175

Children of Transylvania, 1983   197

Natural Disasters   229

The Fruit of the Pawpaw Tree   239

Acknowledgments   263

Mothers,
Tell
Your
Daughters

Sleepover

Ed and I were making out by candlelight on the couch. Pammy was in my bedroom with Ed's brother; she wanted to be in the dark because her face was broke out.

"We were wishing your head could be on Pammy's body," Ed said. "You two together would make the perfect girl."

I took it as a compliment—unlike Pammy, I was flat chested. Ed kissed my mouth, my throat, my collarbone; he pressed his pelvis into mine. The full moon over the driveway reminded me of a single headlamp or a giant eyeball. Ed's tongue was in my ear when Mom's car lights hit the picture window. Ed slid to the floor and whistled for his brother, who crawled from the bedroom on hands and knees. They scurried out the screen door into the back yard and hopped the fence. Pammy and I fixed our clothes and hurriedly dealt a hand of Michigan rummy by candlelight.

"You girls are going to ruin your eyes," Mom said, switching on the table lamp. When Mom went to change her clothes, Pammy whispered that she'd let Ed's brother go into her pants. Her hair was messed up, so I smoothed it behind her ear.

"Too bad this show isn't in color," Pammy said later, when we were watching *Frankenstein*. While the doctor was still cobbling together body parts, Pammy fell asleep with her small pretty feet on my lap. I stayed awake, though, and saw the men from the town band together to kill the monster.

Playhouse

In the little courtyard of my brother's place I close the six-foot-high gate behind me. Coming over without calling first shouldn't be a big deal, since I usually spend half my life here. Since I was born, I've never gone this long—three weeks—without seeing Steve, and that's no exaggeration. Not to be a drama queen, which I'm not, but ever since his Summer Solstice party, I'm feeling sick and weird, and twice Steve hasn't returned my phone calls. Maybe the brats were undercooked or got left out in the sun, and that's why I've been shaky. We fought at the party, and I said, *Fuck you*, and carried a bottle of tequila down by the pink peonies—I remember that much—but then I woke up at home. Woke up in the shower, to be precise, with cold water running over me and my boyfriend, JC, yelling. No surprise that I can't stand for JC to touch me since that night.

Vines with glossy leaves obscure most of the privacy fence, and the beds of gladiolas and irises have gone crazy, so they crowd the flagstone path and paint my bare legs with mustard-colored pollen. This spring, I helped Steve unload a truckload of cow manure, which caused his neighbors fits, and I can still smell it. As I come around the corner of his house, pink fobs on a flowering bush thump me and wag as if mounted on springs. On either side of the door are hanging baskets brimming with dark purple wave petunias, and the smell is too much. I lean over a fountain of yellow daylilies and throw up. I'm thinking about going back to my car and wiping my mouth—there's a brown cloth glove on the back seat—but the security light comes on, followed by the light in the kitchen.

"Look, it's Janie," Steve says to the toddler on his hip, and at the sight of him and his three-year-old daughter, my heart swells.

"Hey, guys," I say. "Long time no see."

"And your aunt Janie has orange hair. What the hell did you do to yourself?"

"Hi, Pinky," I say. Her real name is Patricia, but nobody calls her that. Pinky has rosy cheeks and curly hair, dark like Steve's, like mine before I made the mistake of bleaching it. I can't stop smiling at the sight of my brother and my niece, and I wish I'd brought the kiddo a present, a book with pictures or something glow-in-the-dark.

"I finally decided to go to college. *Clown* college," I say and follow him inside. My hair looks bad, I know—I don't need to hear it from anybody else.

Pinky looks cheerful, as if she's being carried somewhere she likes going. At three she still always wants Daddy to pick her up.

"Hey, shut the door behind you. I got the AC on," Steve says. "Were you born in a barn?"

"Same barn you were born in, dude."

His one-story house is about as big as JC's house, where I've lived for two years, but Steve has a big back yard where he grills out in the summer. The lingering smell of what must've been brats for dinner threatens my stomach again, as does the sight of greasy paper plates in the garbage. I want to ask about food poisoning, but I don't want to start on something negative.

"Do you want a glass of wine?" Steve asks and puts Pinky down. "And seriously, what happened to your hair?"

"I washed it in the Kalamazoo River," I say and follow him into the kitchen, onto the yellow-and-white flooring that compresses under my feet—it feels weird if you're not expecting it. Right before Pinky was born, he installed cushioning under new vinyl, so it's more forgiving if she falls on it. He lays floors for a living, so he knows about all your specialized materials.

I accept the white wine in a wine glass with a couple of ice cubes, hoping it'll settle my stomach, and decline the cigarette Steve offers to roll for me. I've been trying to quit, though I already smoked three at work today.

"So what've you been up to besides ruining your hair?" Steve asks when we settle on the couch. In front of us, almost blocking the TV and crowding the furniture, sits a big plastic playhouse. This house within a house takes up a big part of the room, looks bright and safe with its gently sloping magenta roof above yellow walls with smooth window openings. Under the window facing us are stickers depicting fruit. I hate the way the playhouse makes the room feel crowded, but I'm not going to start bitching right off.

"I was just trying something out," I say. JC thinks my hair is a sign of me losing my mind. I've promised to color it black again, but the chemicals in the hair dye were sickening the first time, and I'm not ready to smell it again.

"Well, you stay away from Pinky's hair," he says, like nothing is off-kilter with us. Maybe his phone hasn't been working, and maybe he hasn't been ignoring my calls. The wine has a sour flavor. I prefer mixed drinks when it's hot like this, or just a few shots. Not as many as I had at the party.

Steve sits up suddenly, as though he's been pricked by an electrical charge. People always say Steve and me have a lot of energy. Our dad has the same energy, too, and he uses it to tinker with the electronics that entirely fill his trailer, except for the cot he sleeps on.

"Hey, Janie, you've got to help me with this playhouse. I tried to get the Bitch to do it, but she says she won't be around me and power tools. She says I have inner rage. I told her, *You used to love my inner rage, Bitch.*"

The Bitch is Pinky's ma, who still comes over to watch Pinky sometimes, though she lost her custody rights when she was convicted of cooking meth.

"Aren't you going to put that thing outside?"

"It was a hundred degrees today. My crazy kid'll sit out there and cook herself. I'll take it out through the slider when the temp drops." He nods at the sliding glass door as though he and the door have made an agreement.

"It's my fun-fun-funhouse!" Pinky says.

"That's what they call the one at day care." Steve turns to Pinky and speaks in an animated way. "It's *fun*, isn't it, your funhouse?"

With a great show of bending her knees and swinging her arms, Pinky jumps in the air about an inch and then runs to the playhouse and opens the saloon-style doors. She disappears inside. I wonder if ever in my life I was that young or joyful.

"Looks like it's all plastic. Why do you need power tools?"

"The roof came off when she pushed on it with the broom.

Some kind of factory defect. I don't need the roof falling on my kid's head," he says.

Pinky comes out of the playhouse and sits beside me on the couch. I put my arm around her and worry about whether she really would let herself cook in the name of having fun. She's lucky to have a dad who will protect her. When Steve leaves the room to get his cordless drill, I let out a breath I haven't realized I've been holding. When he returns, he opens his hand to show four three-inch galvanized deck screws. His hand is shaking just like mine.

I drain my glass and put it on the shelf behind the TV. At the party, I saw Pinky drinking out of glasses people left on the coffee table. You wouldn't think a kid that age would like the taste of watered-down mixed drinks and stale beer and wine. When I brought it up to Steve, that's when we got in a fight.

"Lean on this part," Steve says and taps the edge of the hollow roof before crawling inside on hands and knees. Seeing her daddy, over six feet tall, crouching in the playhouse makes Pinky laugh. She reaches in through the window and taps Steve on the head. He doesn't seem to notice her touch as he fusses with the adjustment on his drill. He contorts himself into an upside-down position, and Pinky jumps away as the drill engages, covering her ears at the grinding-whining sound. He secures the roof easily while I lightly push down with my forearm. After the second screw, I move to the other side, where a sticker reads *Gas*, and above it there's a gas hose—a length of shiny rope with a plastic nozzle at the end.

On the TV is a report about the fair tax. I've been hearing that phrase, wondering if it really is fair, and so I lean on the roof and watch the screen, but with the drill screaming, I can't make out what they're saying. When it's time for the fourth screw, Steve says, "Push down hard right here. This is where it's not lining up right."

As he engages the drill, I push my forearm harder against the roof, and suddenly I feel more than pressure. Something bad is happening; there's a screw grabbing me, going through my skin, and the drill's scream vibrates through my arm and shoulder. When I try to pull away, I feel tearing. "Hey, Steve, dude, could you back that screw out?" I pant, my voice like a robot's, trying to keep calm so I don't alarm Pinky. My heart is pounding, though, and sweat bursts out over my whole body.

"Did the screw go through the roof?"

"Yeah. Back it out." I push my arm hard into the plastic roof where it's pinned, trying not to tug against the screw.

"That fair tax is bullshit," Steve says, suddenly angry, shaking his head at the TV, though his view of the screen is partly blocked by being inside the playhouse.

"Yeah, could you back that screw out? Uh, right now, bro."

When Steve first reengages the drill, I feel a jarring, and for an instant the screw goes farther in, and maybe even hits my bone.

"Sorry," he says. He reverses the direction and backs it out.

"Fuck," I whisper and try to catch my breath. I lean against the wall and press hard on the wound to stanch any bleeding, but don't dare look at it.

"Shit, now it's sticking out in here." The drill grind-whines again. "I'm surprised it went through the roof." He reaches outside through the window above the gas pump and runs his fingers over the roof until he feels the hole the screw made. Without my weight compressing the roof, the screw no longer sticks out the top. His arm out the window makes me think of Alice in Wonderland grown too big for a house after eating some cake. "You notice the price here on the gas pump? Only two bucks a gallon. Now there's a happier time."

Steve pushes on the roof from below, assures himself it's secure. After he gets his drill back in its case and crawls out of the little house on his knees, he notices me grimacing. "What's the matter?" he asks. "That screw didn't go into your arm, did it?"

"Yeah, it did."

"Let me see it."

I clutch the arm tighter.

"Just come over here and let me look at it," he says and pats the couch cushion. When I sit beside him, he takes my arm and squints at the wound. "Looks like it just broke the skin."

"Really? You don't think I should go to the ER?"

"You go to the ER, you'll be paying that bill for years. You know that, right? Does it hurt?"

"No. But it felt weird when it happened."

"Looks fine to me. Look at it yourself. You think it did more than break the skin?"

"It felt like it did." I look. Turns out it's not bleeding at all. The wound looks like nothing, just a red spot. His reassurance calms me, as always, more than my own thoughts do.

"Well, I can't drive you anywhere, that's for sure. If I drive with Pinky after I've been drinking, it's child endangerment. I'm just saying, from my eyes it looks okay."

"You're probably right." I take one more look at the red spot.

"I just saw a news show about emergency rooms." He's shaking his head. "That's probably the biggest problem with health care in this country, people using the ER as their doctor. Costs taxpayers more than an average month's rent just to walk in the door, and that's before any tests." Both of us like to laugh at this world, but Steve's able to move right from joking around into his real opinions, and then he stands by them, while I find it easier to go along so nobody has to argue.

"I don't really have a doctor," I say. "Except at the women's clinic."

"My new funhouse!" Pinky announces. She's back inside, leaning out between the shutters, resting her elbows on the window ledge above the pictures of oranges, apples, and bananas, as though she is a chubby miniature shopkeeper from olden times. Clutched in one hand is a stuffed rabbit with a pink ribbon around its neck. I gave that rabbit to her for her birthday in April, and I feel ridiculously grateful that she likes it.

"That's cute as hell, her standing there in that window," I say.

Pinky waves, and we both wave back.

"Remember our playhouse?" I ask when I settle myself on the couch again with a second glass of wine.

"That was a great playhouse," Steve says. "But I still don't know how the Indians cooked inside their teepees without smoking themselves out."

The summer when he was fourteen and I was eleven we slept out there so we could smoke cigarettes and pot. In October, though, we tried keeping a campfire going inside and burned the thing down. There was an older neighbor, a friend of Steve's, a pot dealer, who used to hang out with us. Once when Steve wasn't there, the guy climbed on top of me and pinned me on the old rug. He was wearing shorts, so I was able to reach under and pinch his balls, and I kept squeezing until he howled and let go. It sounds like nothing now, but I was freaked out and shaky for days, and after that I never went into the playhouse without Steve. Steve thought it was hilarious, my pinching the guy's balls, and a few months later, after the guy stopped coming around, I, too, could see how it seemed kind of funny.

Pinky waves out the playhouse window again, and the motion makes me feel tearful for no reason, so I ask my brother about the fair tax. He's always kept up on politics and likes to rail against the conservatives. I'm pretty sure I feel the same way, but I'm no good at explaining why, especially to JC, who hates Democrats and Republicans alike.

"Oh, it's some Republican bullshit sales tax," Steve says. "If it's up to those fuckers, we got no taxes and no labor laws, no unions, no EPA. You know, I have to think about that environmental shit now, with Pinky in the picture." He's agitated, but when he looks back at the playhouse and waves at Pinky, his agitation falls away.

"She's got more hair than when I saw her three weeks ago," I say. "That curly black hair is really something."

"Strangers go crazy over it," Steve says. He has one ankle up over the other knee and he's flexing his foot against his carpeted floor. "People tell me at the grocery store how pretty her hair is, and at the doctor's office. And it's hard work brushing a head of hair like that. And I had to learn how barrettes work. I'm learning how to fucking *braid*. That's not the kind of shit a guy just knows." He stops drumming his fingers and lights a cigarette. When he offers it to me, I accept, and he rolls and lights another for himself. He keeps the window behind him cracked open, but blue smoke still hangs in the air. Steve's wavy black hair is thinning, though he's only twenty-six—could that have happened in three weeks?

"How's things at the Smart Mart?" he asks.

"Sucks dead donkey dicks, same as usual. This guy comes in this morning with a fucking sweat sock full of pennies, and they're nasty. He's counting out three dollars on the counter, and there's a line behind him, so I make this cardboard sign: *No sweaty pennies*. Right then Matt comes in and throws the sign at me and tells me I've got to clean the bathroom before I leave."

"Well, get your damned GED and get a better job."

When Steve says that, my arm aches a little more. I finish my wine and go into the bathroom to look at it in the mirror. The wound is still just a red spot, now stuck with fuzz from the couch. Maybe there's some swelling. I pee, flush, and come out, thinking I'll ask Steve to take a closer look.

When I get back, Pinky is leaning against the coffee table, holding my wine glass, looking like a tiny, chubby barfly. As she lifts the glass toward her lips, I grab her hand and peel off her fingers.

"Thanks for coming over," Steve says, and his eyes are watering like he's about to cry. His forehead wrinkles. "I've been wanting to tell you I'm sorry about what I said at the party, calling you a dumb cunt. I know you hate that word." He watches Pinky open the saloon doors and shut them carefully behind her. "I guess I was too high, and the Bitch was here, and we were fighting, and I was on those antidepressants that fucked me up," Steve says. "You'll be glad to know I got off those."

"Just don't start bawling like a dang baby," I say. But then I start crying out of relief, and once I'm crying, the pain in my arm—it really is hurting now—makes it hard to stop. I move over on the couch and hug my big brother with one arm. I'm not going to ask him why he didn't return my calls—we'll just move on from here.

"I guess it wasn't any of my business," I say. "What I said. I shouldn't have said that."

"What? I'm trying to think what you said."

"About Pinky drinking out of the glasses on the table. I was worried."

"Now I remember. You said I was a bad father."

"I didn't say that, did I?" I pull my arm away. "I wouldn't. You're a good dad."

"As if you know a fucking thing about being a parent." He shakes his head like he's getting pissed off again. "Now I remember."

"I didn't mean to say whatever I said. I was just worried."

"The Bitch was supposed to take Pinky for the night, but she decided to stay and party." He raises his voice as he goes on. "I would've asked you to watch her, but you were too drunk already. And you getting so drunk and sloppy at the party when Pinky was here didn't help. I don't need her seeing that kind of shit."

"What shit? She knows people drink," I say.

"Do you even remember getting home that night? Roger said you fell on your face right at your front door. He was worried about you."

"JC was pissed at me. I know that. I was already fighting with him, and then he finds me on the front doorstep at three a.m." I lean back on the couch. JC said somebody rang the bell, and by the time he got out there, I was passed out alone, with puke on my shirt.

"I'm sorry to say this, Janie, but JC's a dick. He bosses you around like you're one of his kids. And he's like a Tea Party member or something, isn't he?"

"You don't really know JC. He's a good guy. He just—"

"He's a dick, Janie. All men are dicks," Steve says. "Trust me, I am one."

"He's pissed at me now because I don't want to have sex with him."

"Why the hell won't you have sex with him? Seemed like you were all ready for action at the party."

"I don't know. I just don't want to." I'm never going to tell

Steve that JC and I usually have sex on a regular schedule twice a week, Friday nights and Sunday mornings. He'd think I'm a freak, but I just like to know what's going to happen ahead of time. Since the party, though, the thought of sex makes me sick to my stomach.

"How old is he now, anyway? Forty?" Steve asks.

"Thirty-eight."

"He's too damned old for you. Pick on somebody your own age. Go with one of those guys you were screwing at my party. Roger's a good guy. He's got a decent job."

"What do you mean, *screwing*?" I ask. Through the window of the funhouse, I can see Pinky addressing the stuffed rabbit over some serious issue. When she sees me watching, she closes the shutters.

"Just what I said. *Screwing*," Steve says quietly. He rests his eyes on the TV, but he is weighing his words carefully.

"I didn't screw anybody at your party. You know I'm not like that."

"You didn't used to be." Steve shakes his head, though he's looking more intently at the TV now, bouncing his leg with a lot of energy. "You seriously don't remember what happened with Roger? And that friend of his, Mickey?"

"What are you talking about?"

"You were humping your bottle of tequila down by the peonies, and they were out of booze, so I told them to go down and harass you."

"Sons of bitches better not have taken my tequila," I say and force a laugh. I do remember the peonies close to my face. They weren't pretty anymore, but were splayed on the grass, as though the tired stems couldn't hold up the big, ragged flowers anymore. I also remember the splintery leg of the picnic table with the paint peeling off. Now that Steve has said it, I remember somebody yanking the tequila bottle out of my hand, though I was holding it tight.

"That guy Mickey took pictures on his phone," Steve says. "Don't worry, when I saw him showing Roger, I took his phone and deleted them all."

"Pictures? What pictures?"

"Not the kind of thing a brother wants to see."

"You say Roger took me home? Why didn't you take me home?"

"I couldn't drive you because Pinky was here. Anyway, Roger wasn't as drunk as I was."

"He doesn't even have a driver's license, does he?" I say. "You're fucking with me, aren't you? Stop fucking with me, Steve." I get up and roll myself a loose, crooked cigarette and sit back down. "I've been feeling shitty. I was wondering if maybe we ate some bad meat or something."

"You got some meat, all right. Mickey was pissed when I erased the pictures, but I figured you didn't want them getting back to JC," he says and glances to make sure Pinky isn't listening before adding, "And a brother doesn't want to see his sister with some guy's dick in her face."

"It had to be somebody else." I look out through the sliding glass door and can only see the patio, but I know the peonies are only about a hundred feet beyond. Anybody could've seen me lying there.

"Oh, it was definitely you. The first picture was Roger licking the Tasmanian Devil tattoo on your boob. No mistaking that."

An electric sensation zaps my left breast. Steve gets up and puts something special on the VCR for Pinky and tells her it's a half hour before bedtime, and Pinky scrunches down in her tiny armchair, a miniature of the chair an old man would use, only pink. Cartoon bears tromp across the screen.

"Fuck," I say under my breath. I can't stop shaking my head. "I couldn't have."

"Don't rag on yourself. You were drunk. You were fighting with JC. You were finally relaxing, having some fun."

"But you said I was passed out down there."

"I figured you must've woke up when things got interesting."

"You're saying I had my shirt off with a stranger."

"Roger's not a stranger. You've seen him plenty of times over here. He's a good guy."

I've always been shy about undressing in front of JC and never make love with him unless I've taken a shower and brushed my teeth.

"After I erased the pictures, I went down and put your damned clothes back on you. And you weren't helping. It was like dressing a damned corpse. Give me a squirming kid any day. At first I felt bad for you, but then I was just pissed. Some money and pot came up missing while I was screwing around trying to get you dressed. Maybe you shouldn't drink so much, Janie."

My arm aches so badly now that I can't stand it. I should do something, something to change everything. Stand up and scream, make the whining-grinding sound the drill made. Quit drinking, cold turkey, right now. Or maybe tomorrow. Go to the ER and see about this arm. But I don't like to make a big deal out of nothing, and this has to be nothing. I'm waiting for the punch line that'll let me know this is just Steve's joke. When he gets up to put Pinky to bed, I curl up and fall asleep on the couch to the murmurs of him reading her a story.

I wake up later to lonesome crying that feels like my own, but it's coming from Pinky's room. The little house is dark except for the TV with the volume turned way down. My arm is throbbing, and when I stand, pain rushes me in a wave, and I'm smelling grease from those brats again. There's a note on the counter saying Steve's gone out to get juice for tomorrow's breakfast, he'll be right back. Pinky's room smells of baby powder, some kind of air freshener, and urine, and I see my way to her by the glow of a pink rabbit-shaped night-light. The girl stops crying as I lift her out of her crib-bed. Thank goodness she clings to my shoulder like a baby chimpanzee, because I can't muster much strength in the throbbing arm. Gingerly, I shift Pinky to my other hip and carry her into the bathroom, smooth her nightgown under her bottom, and situate her on the sink. When I turn on the light, the fan comes on, and Pinky rubs her eyes. The smallness of her fists makes me feel melancholy. I wonder if Steve will meet another girl or get back together with the Bitch so he can have another baby, give Pinky a brother or sister. He's said that I ought to come through with a cousin for her to play with so she won't have to be alone when she's older. I would have been lost growing up without Steve.

When I touch the red spot on my arm, I expect blood to gush out, but there's only a little puffiness. With one arm balancing Pinky on the vanity sink, I rummage through Steve's medicine cabinet. When I hold a prescription bottle up to the light, I see the two pills inside are Vicodin, though the bottle says prednisone—Steve's probably hiding them from Pinky's ma. When I shake a pill, etched with a *V*, into my hand, Pinky reaches for it, so I hurry and swallow it.

"What the hell's going on?" Steve says from the bathroom doorway, his face shiny with sweat. I didn't hear him coming in. There's a way that meanness and good humor face off in Steve at certain times, especially when he's high, and usually I can nudge him toward good humor. Now, though, as the heat and humidity billow from his body into the little tiled room, I don't feel like I could influence anybody.

"She was crying, so I picked her up."

"You don't have to pick her up every time she cries. Sometimes she cries in her sleep." My brother's movements feel off-kilter, but it seems unlikely he'd be getting high so late at night, so maybe it's just something off-kilter about me. His broad shoulders fill the bathroom doorway, and he looms over me and Pinky. One word from him would have stopped those guys by the peonies, whatever they were doing with me. If they were doing anything.

"I thought she might be afraid," I say.

"She must've sensed I was gone," Steve says, softening his tone. "We've got a strong bond, me and Pinky. Don't we, Bright Eyes? You need a new diaper—your aunt should've changed you." While he gets her changed and back into bed, I return to the couch with another loosely rolled cigarette and study the plastic funhouse. We didn't have anything like this when we were kids, though JC complains my generation is spoiled. I wonder what JC is doing, if he's worried, if he's made a checklist of what he wants to talk to me about. In a million years I couldn't tell him what Steve says happened. He'd just yell at me, and the thought of the photos would make him lose his mind, even if I promised they were erased. When Steve comes out of Pinky's room, I hold up my arm in the dim light.

"So you think this is okay, even with the way it's swelling?"

"It doesn't look that bad to me, Janie. It's just a spot. But it's your arm, you should know." Steve rubs his eyes. Nobody should make decisions late at night, I think, not when everybody's so tired. The Vicodin starts to kick in and the pain lessens.

"Are you making that up, about the pictures?" I ask.

"Why would I make something like that up?" he says. "I don't want to see that shit. A couple of guys giving it to you."

"I think I must've been asleep."

"Come on, Janie, a person doesn't sleep through something like that."

"Was it really sex, like sex?" I ask and close my eyes. "With both of them?"

He shrugs. "Roger said you were into it."

"Damn, Steve. You should've stopped them." I put my fingers into my hair, which feels frizzy, like somebody else's hair, and yank. "You shouldn't have told them to harass me."

"Don't put it on me, sister," Steve says, and something about the way he says it makes me think he's thought about it plenty and has made up his mind. "You should've told them no if you didn't want it. You should've pinched their balls. You said you were fighting with JC. I figured you wanted to teach him a lesson."

"But you should've protected me." My voice goes squeaky.

"Protected you? Hell, if you ever come trying to protect me when I'm in the bushes with two hot babes working on me, I'll kick your ass." Now he sounds like his normal self. "You know, I had to take Pinky into her room and read her a story to make sure she didn't see you down there."

"I think maybe they raped me, Steve." The word *raped* feels all wrong, and my heart pounds in a sickening way.

"Roger? Get real. I work with the guy every day. He's a decent guy, maybe not the brightest bulb, but he's not a rapist, Janie." He says *rapist* as though he might be saying *Martian*.

"Or something like rape," I suggest. The second time I say the word, it feels even more off-kilter, like I really am a drama queen, creating from thin air a victim and perpetrators and accessories.

"That's not how it looked to me, that's all I'm saying." Steve takes a draw on his cigarette, exhales deliberately, and then crushes it out. "I guess you're the one who should know, though."

I sigh. Steve goes off to bed, and I lie down on the couch. Everything is muddled right now, but I can sense the wilting peonies close to my face—or is it skin pressed against my mouth?—and I can smell the cool grass. Remembering these things is like remembering something ancient from before I could talk, like my dead grandfather's great height—he died when I was Pinky's age, but I used to hide behind the couch from him, afraid he might step on me and crush me. I have a clear sense of my pants being tugged off in that cool grass, of being dragged by my feet. The weight of a body on my body. I try the word *rape* once more, and it still doesn't fit with stupid Roger or anybody at one of Steve's parties, doesn't fit with the peonies or picnic table. If only I could see those photos, then I could know what happened. Were my eyes open?

Steve has music on in his bedroom, so he doesn't hear me leave. The side door shuts with a sucking sound, and I gently close the storm door. The pink fobs and daylilies nose me, and I get the feeling that if I stand still, the vines are going to slither down the fence and grab me. In my car, I'm having trouble holding my arm up to steer, and I reach across to shift into drive with my left hand.

After sitting in the hospital parking lot for a long time, I get out and walk past the big-shouldered guard, who turns out to be a hulking woman, who probably knows exactly what happens to her every minute of every day, no matter what. I check in at the ER desk and then take a seat in a chair near the door and watch a dark-skinned woman with gray hair vacuuming. She seems like someone who tolerates no nonsense, so I move to an area she's already cleaned. Remembering the peonies in my face and the grass and my jeans being tugged off doesn't prove anything, but now I can't imagine not knowing those things. After a half hour, a tired-looking triage nurse directs me into a little room with a desk and takes my blood pressure and pulse, listens to my no-insurance lament. Afterward she lifts the arm gently, studies it, and nods. Having someone acknowledge that something is wrong feels like the wind abruptly changing direction.

"We get a lot of power tool mishaps," the nurse says after I explain about the drill and the deck screws. "A lot of guys fall off ladders with saws—chain saws, circular saws. Table saws are big trouble, too. Why did you wait to come in?"

"It's just hard to know if something's really wrong," I say and wonder if I really know any more now than I knew before. "I don't like to be a drama queen," I say. "It just looked like a red dot."

"Well, good thing you didn't wait any longer," she says.

The nurse's words give me the relief I feel when I take that first sip of tequila after work, but then I vomit into my lap even before I can ask her for a towel.

"Sorry," I say. "I keep doing that lately. Don't take it personally."

"How long have you been vomiting?"

"For three weeks. Just now and then. It's worse tonight, though. "

She blinks at me, and I feel an opening, a place where she might want to hear how I feel, might want to hear what I think happened, what I fear happened, but I don't know how to start. And anyhow she'll probably think I'm a slut and tell me to join AA.

"Is there any chance you're pregnant? We'll do a test," the nurse says before I can answer, no, I'm on the pill, which I take at exactly the same time each morning. I had a period two weeks ago, but the world has become a place where anything is possible.

She walks me farther into the hospital, into a windowless room, and pulls a curtain across the entrance so I feel shrouded and alone, frozen in a moment in time. When the doctor arrives, a small, chubby man with a tag that reads *Dr. Sethi*, he studies my arm without even introducing himself, asks questions in accented English, adjusts his gold-rimmed glasses, and explains soberly how he will open the wound and release whatever blood and serum is building up inside it. "You have noticed the swelling," he says.

"Yes," I say and feel proud of myself for having noticed. After the X-ray shows no damage to the bone and the pregnancy test comes back negative, Dr. Sethi injects me with a numbing agent. His assistant swabs the area with antiseptic and tapes sterile gauze over my arm to create a window for the procedure, so a rectangle of skin is all the doctor sees when he returns. His voice is soothing as he cuts into my anesthetized arm. When pink fluid is released onto the gauze, my relief is instantaneous. He takes up the hemostats—like the ones Steve and I used to use as roach clips—and slowly removes something from my arm and holds it up. I have to squint to make out a little magenta spiral, more than a quarter-inch long. As I watch, a tiny drop of watery blood slides off the plastic onto the gauze.

"It's a party favorite?" Dr. Sethi asks, and we all three study the little corkscrew.

The assistant's eyes smile behind her mask. She's about my age, twenty-three, with hair the honey color I tried to get out of a box. A job like hers helping people would be nice, though my tendency to make light of a situation might not go over well here. I'd like to work in a clean place like this instead of behind the cluttered, greasy counter at Smart Mart. Since the party, whenever I see kids grabbing at candy and gum, I'm thinking of Pinky's chubby hands on the wine glasses and beer cups.

"It's part of a funhouse," I say.

"Funhouse?" the assistant asks.

"It's a little girl's playhouse, but she calls it her *funhouse*. It's what my brother and I were working on." I suddenly fear the doctor might blame Steve. I want to say, *Whatever happened is my own fault. He didn't know I had my arm right over where the screw was.*

"Funhouse," the doctor says, still holding the plastic corkscrew, and the way he says it makes me laugh. Who wouldn't laugh when a man has pulled a tiny bloody party favor out of her arm?

"You think there's anything else in there?" he asks. At first he is serious, but then he laughs in response to my continuing laughter.

"It's hard to know," I say. I admire how all the cabinets and drawers in this room are labeled by their contents: *Sponges and Bandages, Face Masks, Swab Sticks, Specimen Jars, Drapes and Covers.* I like being in a place where a person can always know what's inside from the outside.

"This could have caused infection," the doctor announces, "but we have nipped its bud."

I wipe tears out of my eyes. I thought I was laughing, but now I'm crying and choking. I'm imagining Pinky as a teenager. She'll have long legs like her ma and wild curly hair like her dad. She'll sneak out her bedroom window on summer nights the way any girl would, but she won't have a brother to look after her—she'll be all alone. I don't know how anyone can stop a girl from drinking so much she doesn't know what she's doing, what's happening to her. All the precautions in the world might not be enough for a girl who loves fun. For starters, I should've rinsed out my wine glass and put it in the sink before I left Steve's.

"Jodie will clean you up," the doctor says and disappears through the curtain. The assistant unwraps and exposes the rest of my arm. She tears open a paper wrapper and is about to apply a special bandage to close the wound, but she pauses.

"Is this hurting you?" she asks. "You're holding your breath."

What's done is done, I think, but she's asking as though she really wants to know. I feel myself about to spill over, but telling won't make it better, and it will open up a whole can of worms, so I take a deep breath and concentrate on not vomiting. When I think of Pinky safe in her bed in her room with the pink rabbit night-light, smelling of baby powder, surrounded by stuffed animals, I can finally exhale. She's okay for now.

"Miss?" the assistant says. I realize that I've pulled my bleeding arm away from her, that I'm hugging myself.

"Uh-huh," I say, squeezing myself harder, despite the way blood is dripping onto my jeans. "I guess it really does hurt. Now that you mention it."

Tell Yourself

"I'm not going to be here for dinner, Mom," your daughter says. You look up from sorting the day's junk mail to see Mary has emerged from her room wearing jeans that ride so low her pubic hair would be showing, if she had pubic hair. She swears all the middle school girls shave down there, though surely your daughter could've had only a few baby-fine wisps to razor away. Under your gaze she tugs her jeans up and makes an effort to pull down her shirt, but the whole production leaves six inches of bare belly and hips. "I have to go to Amber's. Her dad's making us lasagna for dinner."

"You want a ride?" you offer. You wouldn't mind Amber's dad seeing you in your steel-toed boots and work uniform. You wouldn't mind reminding him that you are a formidable woman.

"It's only a half a mile, Mom."

"What on Earth do you do there all the time?"

You shouldn't question Mary this way about what goes on over there. If something unsavory happens between your

37

daughter and Amber's young and curiously attentive father, Mary is probably not going to confide in you if you seem out of your mind. She would not tell you, for example, if Amber's father were wrestling with the girls on the braided rug and suddenly it was just he and Mary, if she relaxed beneath him and let her head fall back, if she let her narrow shoulders sink to the floor and looked up at him and parted her glossed lips, and he lowered himself onto her.

"We're doing a biology project. It's a poster about cells, and it's due tomorrow, but we haven't started it yet," your daughter says. She likes science, and she didn't used to be a procrastinator. "Amber's dad is going to help us. Did you know there are thirty-seven trillion cells in the human body?"

Amber's father has never been convicted of diddling with minors or of any other sex crime (you've looked him up on the Internet), and there is no reason for you to entertain the image of your daughter slipping down her low-rise stretch-denim jeans, or of Amber's father situating your daughter on his lap, under a blanket. There is no reason to associate Amber's father with your own pot-smoking neighbor whom you, as a fourteen-year-old, screwed while his wife was at work and while his young son napped in the adjacent bedroom. Both men have cowboy mustaches, but that's all.

"There's no reason to put off a project until the last minute," you tell her. And there is no reason for someone to design a midriff-revealing shirt like the one your daughter is wearing, with a pair of bigger-than-life-size cupcakes on the chest. You toss the whole pile of mail into the recycling. Calm yourself down, woman. Not all men will try to screw your daughter, however she dresses. There are men who will not even fantasize about touching her darling new breasts. Some men are distracted, for instance, or gay, while a few may actually prefer mature women.

You sit down in the wooden rocking chair you inherited last year from your grandmother, your mother's mother, may she rest in peace. At first you hadn't wanted the chair—what are you, an old lady?—but it's handmade, and you've found that rocking in it can take the edge off at the end of the day.

"Did you know that the mitochondria are the powerhouse of the cell?" Mary offers. She moves behind you and takes hold of the back of your chair and sends it rocking in her own annoying rhythm. Don't complain—at least if her hands are on your chair, they're off her cell phone for a change.

"You're working on a poster? Maybe I can help."

"So how come you broke up with Stanley Steemer?" Mary asks. "He's the only decent boyfriend you ever had."

"It's my own business," you say to your child, "who I date. Or don't date." This is the first time Mary has mentioned Stan.

"Then maybe what I do is my own business," Mary says and cracks her gum for an invisible audience. Then she stops the chair from rocking so you are thrown forward a little. You get the idea she imagines her girlfriends are always with her, admiring her antics.

"It's not exactly your own business when I get called by the school principal about you flashing boys in the stairwell."

You stand up, cross your arms, and study the girl for whom you suffered thirteen hours of labor, the girl you've fed and clothed for thirteen years—though you don't recall buying any of the revealing items she currently wears.

"I told you, Mom. Amber dared me. We both did it. And there was another girl, too. But I was the one who got caught." She talks casually, but she's gripping the chair pretty hard.

"If Amber dared you to jump over a cliff, would you do it?"

"Yes," she says and lets go of the chair. She tries pulling up her pants again, though she's already working a camel toe.

"Amber is stupid in science, but she's smart about other things. She's street-smart."

There has to be a calm, reasonable way to express to your daughter why she should resist showing her body the way she has been doing, without seeming overprotective or crazy or even jealous. You can't deny how thrilled you were at the way your body got attention when you were her age. You would have bared your breasts for cute boys on a dare, no doubt.

"You know, I had to walk home from cheerleading practice today, three miles. Stanley Steemer drove right past me. He didn't even wave back."

"Stop calling him that," you say. "Anyway, you could've called me to pick you up."

The first time Stan gave your daughter a ride home, you thanked him, but you also recalled how your mother's boyfriend Teddy used to drive alongside you sometimes when you were walking on the old road by the power company. He'd be hotboxing a Marlboro in the driver's seat, and he'd roll down the window and release a big cloud of smoke and tell you that you were looking fine. You thought it was flattering and funny, and you never told your mother. Not even when he molested you—at the time, it wasn't clear what happened in the back seat, but in retrospect it is painfully clear.

"That truck is embarrassing," your daughter says, referring to the Al's Appliances truck you drive for work. "You know, Nicole's mom got a stove from Al's, and it had a dead cockroach in it. And that guy you work with stinks like pee."

"Jimmy."

"He doesn't have any neck. And he's hairy like a Neanderthal." She laughs at this inside joke as though her friends are here with her. "Mr. Glover says we're all part Neanderthal, but some people are more than others."

When Stan showed up for dinner with your daughter for the fourth time, two days after the flashing incident in the stairwell, you couldn't get it out of your head that something was wrong. And then when you kissed Stan, his jacket smelled like Mary's fruity-candy perfume. You've known Stan for three years as your boys' Little League and Rocket Football coach, and you'd been dating him for three months, and he'd been coming to dinner a couple times a week, and you told yourself there was no reason to think he did anything other than pick Mary up and bring her straight home. It wasn't as though he'd had time to pull off into the old power company property—or that he would've even thought of such a thing. And after all, Stan really seemed to like you, admired your jaded view of the world, even laughed when you slipped into cursing. He'd had a rough go in his marriage, same as you, and you'd figured the two of you were kindred spirits.

That last time he brought Mary home, when Mary was doing her in-school suspension, all through dinner you kept telling yourself to calm down and not overreact. Afterward, Stan smiled at your expectant, anxious look as he sank back into the reclining chair to watch *Antiques Roadshow* with you.

"Is something the matter?" he asked. "You seem on edge."

"Is something going on with you and Mary?" you asked.

Even now you can't believe it came out of your mouth, but once it did come out you didn't regret it. You hoped Stan would tell you, *Absolutely not, never in a million years*, or laugh it off and say, *You've got to be kidding.*

"What do you mean?" He tilted his head, squinted one eye. You'd seen him adopt this posture when a little knucklehead kid was explaining why he ran to home from first base.

"Nothing. Not really. I was just asking." You told yourself he was nothing like your mother's old boyfriend or your pothead neighbor, and he'd never shown any interest in Mary beyond joking around and asking her about homework and cheerleading, but you just wanted to be absolutely one hundred percent sure your daughter was safe with him.

"Asking what? What are you asking?"

"I smell her perfume on you."

"She squirted me with that crap when I told her not to use it in my car," he said, and his speech slowed as he realized what you were suggesting. "You know what she's like."

"I know, but I wondered . . ."

You knew she'd sprayed perfume on her little brothers, too, even though it made them shriek. And of course she'd sprayed you.

"You wondered what? If I . . . if I had, what? . . . with Mary?" He seemed to wake up then. He looked hurt, then shocked. He fumbled at his pocket for a cigarette, got it into his fingers, and then forced it back into the pack, pushed the pack into his shirt pocket again. "You've known me a long time. Your kids have played with my kid for years."

"It just seems strange you're always giving her a ride without discussing it with me." Your calm voice defied the turmoil you were feeling.

"Did you see it was raining today? Should I have driven past her on the road? That would be something for a mother to complain about." He was getting mad.

"It's just that . . . And I know she can be a flirt." You hated the word as soon as you said it, though Mary *was* a flirt, same as you were at her age.

"Do you hear yourself?" He sat forward on the chair and looked hard at you. His eyes narrowed, and his lips, too. "Mary's a kid. I'm a coach. And an accusation like that could hurt me in so many ways, even beyond the personal, I can't even begin to . . . If you really believe I'm a predator—"

"I don't. I just need you to tell me."

"For Chrissakes, you act like you don't know me at all. And maybe I don't know you, either." When Stan saw your three kids appear in the hallway, his face went slack, and he got up, put on his jacket, and stormed out. The screen door slammed shut as he muttered a final word about trust.

You weren't really accusing him, you told yourself. You hadn't meant to say anything, but you'd just asked.

"I GUESS YOU can give me a ride if you really want to," Mary says. "Oh, Mom, you should've seen what happened today in science. Nicole spit her gum into this girl's hair, and the girl didn't see it, and she kept touching her hair, and it got really stuck."

But really, what interest could a grown man have in a girl who chews gum the way your daughter chews her gum, noisily and with her mouth open? How could any man be interested in a girl who, whenever she isn't texting on her phone, prattles mindlessly about the other middle-school cheerleaders, tells what happened, play-by-play, in the last movie or TV show she watched? I mean, your daughter drives you and the rest of your family crazy with that mindless prattling, and you want to slap her at least once a day for the way she rolls her eyes at something you've said, even as you want to wrap your arms around her and hide her and protect her. Your shoulders are hunched up around your ears. Take a deep breath, woman!

"So the girl was going to cut the gum out of her hair, but then Mr. Glover asked if anybody had a peanut butter sandwich in their lunch bag. He said gum is *hydrophobic* so it doesn't dissolve in water, so we had to take the gum out with another hydrophobic material. He wiped the peanut butter off the girl's bread and put it on the gum and worked it out. And then he let the girl go rinse her hair in the bathroom."

You hope her love of science will teach her cause and effect as it pertains to her body as well as to what goes on in a science lab. You hope it will allow her to succeed in ways you never dreamed of succeeding, but you don't know how she's going to make it safely through the next few years. You wish she could be a nerd girl in high-waisted pants. You wish she needed glasses, at least.

"Amber and Nicole didn't even know what *hydrophobic* meant," she says. "Can you believe it?"

"God damn it!" you shout at last. "Can't you see? I'm worried sick about you. I'm worried that all the motherfuckers in the world want to mess with you and get their lousy hands on your body. Yes, I'm out of my mind with worry about what you do with boys at school in the stairwell. And worse, I'm afraid some man is going to sweet-talk you and lure you into his car and molest you, Mary. And I'm worried that you might like it. Or you might go along with it even if you don't."

Once you've said this, you can't believe you've said it. But you're not sorry you've said it. You don't know how you've gone so long without saying it. Mary looks stunned, but less so than you'd expect. Her arms hang limply at her sides, and her bare belly seems more pooched and unprotected than ever. Maybe she's been waiting for your outburst since the incident in the stairwell. You fall back into your chair in exhaustion.

"God, Mom. That's just gross," she says finally. "You know I don't like men that way. They're too hairy." She is trying to lighten the conversation, bless her. She tries again to pull up her pants, but even she realizes it is hopeless this time. "You know,

I didn't tell you, Mom, but me and Amber were in Cooper Park after school on Friday, and this guy was staring at my boobs, and me and Amber threw our apples at him from lunch. We pretended we were calling the cops, and he took off on his bike."

"But what if he wasn't gross?" you ask. You wonder why she didn't tell you about this on Friday. "What if he was a good-looking high school boy? A handsome football player? What if he wasn't hairy at all? What if he shaved his whole perfect body and smelled like a flower?"

"Oh, Mom. The guy was gross. And you can trust me. I'm not stupid. And I'm not going to get pregnant, if that's what you're worried about."

"Did Stan ever try anything with you?" you ask and hold your breath. "Or say anything . . . sexy?"

"Stanley Steemer?" Mary kicks at the rails of your chair and shakes her head. "You're crazy, Mom. You worry about the weirdest things."

Your daughter changes her shirt at your insistence, and as soon as her phone is charged, she heads out to Amber's house on foot, cracking her gum, shaking her head, rolling her eyes, and texting in a cloud of candy-flower perfume. You ask her to let you know when she gets there and then to be sure to call for a ride home. She mumbles an okay as the wooden screen door slaps against the frame.

You're busted up over Stan, more than you thought you would be, but with him gone from the house, you can be a little more certain Mary is safe. Of course, he is just one man among millions out there in the world, one of dozens of men who might take an interest in your daughter between this house and Amber's house. You close your eyes and tell yourself that not all men are like that neighbor who allowed you to skip school at his house and smoke bowl after bowl until you couldn't form a complete sentence. Not all teachers—even those who take a girl's hair in their hands—are like your tall, brown-eyed social-science teacher, whose attentions flattered you so much that you would never have said no. And girls are different now, too—look how your daughter says no to you all the time, as you would never have said no to your mother for fear of being slapped. Your daughter knows so much more than you did at her age, and she might even come to you with any problems she *does* have, if you don't work yourself into a state.

Stan hasn't contacted you since that night two weeks ago, and you haven't called him. You think about what it might take for you to be reassured that your daughter is safe. A definitive *No* every day, from Stan and from every man within driving distance. A definitive *Yes, I understand* from Mary every day to let you know she sees there is danger, that you're not crazy. That would be a start.

You heat the oven for fish sticks for the boys, something you give them when their sister isn't here, and you slice potatoes to bake alongside. You liked cooking for Stan, who was appreciative of a homemade meal of any kind, even fish sticks once when that was all you had. Sometimes when you were watching TV after dinner, Stan patted his thighs and invited you to sit on his big lap and relax. Sitting that way with his strong arms around you, with his belly pressing into the small of your back like a support cushion, made you forget about the day's appalling customers, the aches from negotiating washing machines into place, made you forget even about the way the passing years have thickened your body and lined your face. When you allowed your head to fall back against Stan's shoulder, the warmth and size of him made you feel small and pretty, like a girl again.

The Greatest Show
on Earth, 1982:
What There Was

There was the long silver whip of the circus train stretched out on a side rail, heating up in the Arizona sun, and inside train car number seventy-eight, behind the closed pocket door of a steel cabinet, two people inhaled each other's breath and sweat. There was Buckeye, a hundred-pound ditchwater blonde, according to her ma back in Akron, and Mike Field, six feet tall and then some, skin as black as coffee, both sitting in Mike's blue-painted steel coffin of a bedroom with no AC. Coming down the hallway was Red, short, solid, with homemade tattoos on his freckled arms and knuckles (*L-O-V-E*, *H-A-T-E*, eagle, naked lady, et cetera), stomping closer in work boots, banging on the metal door of this corner room, saying, "Buckeye, girl, get out here, now!" Pausing to light a cigarette, then saying, "I'm coming back in five minutes and you'd better be ready to go."

There was Buckeye's bare thigh pressing against Mike's

thigh in black chinos, her hip in short shorts touching his hip, her body filled with desire, filled with more than desire, her body and heart and mind all full up with Mike from loving him on his bunk last night, ready to love him again despite the heat, despite Red showing up. A week ago Red had explained why they had to do what they had to do this morning, Wednesday morning, first morning in Phoenix, how she was going to have to recover in one day, how they wouldn't have any other time because there were three shows on Thursday through Sunday, and the candy boss wasn't going to be happy with his number three candy butcher laid out in her room instead of hawking her racks of pink and blue cotton-candy clouds. This was Phoenix, a big sales town, where everybody was supposed to make enough money to get by and even save some for busted towns like Fresno, though nobody really saved.

"You going with him?" Mike asked.

"I got to."

"You sleep with him ever?" Mike was four years younger than her, had just turned twenty-four.

"I told you, it's not like that. Red's like a big brother."

"Yo! I hear you guys," Red said. "I know you're in there." Red was talking through the door in a mad voice, though Buckeye didn't think he was really mad yet. Buckeye was getting caught up in the way Mike's big hand spanned his own thigh, how his spread-out fingers could as easily be curling around her shoulder or holding the back of her head. Like always, he wore his blue uniform shirt buttoned down over his wrists, and the veins across the tops of his hands were almost clean, just a few needle marks. Buckeye had never shot up anything, didn't even have a tattoo. Her ma had always said tattoos on girls showed the world what whores they were. Only her ears were pierced, one hole each side.

There was Buckeye putting her finger to her lips as Red hollered, Buckeye studying the side of Mike's face, which was sweating. She reached up and touched a V-shaped scar under his eye, healed since two months ago, when a couple of Bulgarians beat him up for not paying their money back fast enough. They bloodied his cheek and his mouth, and he just stood there and took it. While they were punching him, she was imagining herself kissing his swelled-up face, telling him she loved him and saying how he shouldn't leave the circus, how they could get through this together. During the show, those Bulgarians helped make a tower five people high with a little girl in pigtails on top, but at other times, the men could be brutes.

Buckeye put her hand on Mike's head. She liked the way his hair felt strong, the way it pushed back against the pressure of her hand. He made her think about a tomcat she used to have, brave and fast and scrappy, killing mice and birds with a swipe of his paw, bringing those busted little bodies to her and then brushing her leg gently with his tail. She'd loved stroking that tiger cat's rough head, torn up from old fights, but one morning he didn't come back, and after that he was gone for good.

"I know you're in there." Red rattled the door latch.

Mike pushed her hand away from his head.

"Open the door, Black Mike, you black son of a bitch."

She'd tried to explain to Mike when he first arrived how there was already a Mike in the show. Really there were already two Mikes. Regular Mike from Sells Floto, second in charge of concessions, and Spaghetti Mike, who had black hair and looked like he could've been Italian and ordered spaghetti in the pie car on the first day and leftover spaghetti on the second day, and asked for it again on the third day when there wasn't any, so the name got stuck on him. Buckeye had been the first white person to befriend Mike when he joined six months ago—first, the King Charles Unicycle Troupe had to figure out what they thought of him, and right away King Charles didn't like Mike; they complained that he acted ignorant by wearing long sleeves in the summer, that his hair was nappy, and that he listened to death metal. The Mexican and Bulgarian troupes got around to noticing new people about the time the new people wanted to borrow money or buy meth.

"Damn it, Buckeye," Red shouted through the door. "Black Mike, you let her go."

Buckeye whispered, "I don't like the way everybody's got to call you black all day long."

"I am black, if you didn't notice."

"You should've told them your name was Mick or Mitch. If I could start over, I'd come into the circus with a beautiful name." Buckeye sighed. "I'd say my name was Rosella. Or Annabella. Or Margerina." Though it made no kind of sense, all week she couldn't help but think of beautiful girl names. "Marmalada," she added.

"Why do you want to be called something you put on toast?" Mike asked, as though he meant to laugh but couldn't manage it. "My mom made marmalade by cooking orange peels instead of throwing them away. She didn't believe in throwing things away," Mike said.

Buckeye thought the sound of some names could carry a person away. Marmalada. Rubelina or Rosemaria. When she heard the snow boss's wife was named Becky, she should have said she was Rebecca or used her middle name, Jo, or Josephina, maybe. And she should never have told them she was from Ohio.

"If you had some fancy name, you wouldn't want to be with me," Mike said.

"That's not true," Buckeye said. She took his big hand in

both of her smaller hands. He'd had a couple of his fingers broken, and they'd healed crooked, and she had the idea she could straighten them if she kept caressing them day after day. She squeezed the hand until she felt his electricity running through her. He was just waking up, getting his blood flowing through his big heart. He'd told her that when he was in high school the wrestling team doctor wouldn't let him compete, said he had an oversize heart, and Buckeye thought that sounded just right. Mike hadn't shot any speed yet this morning, so he was talking slow and relaxed. The snow boss knew about the speed, but liked the way it made Mike run up and down the stadium stairs selling snow cones faster than anybody else. A lot of times it was the new butchers like him who sold the most, and he was famous for sales in the six months since he'd been here. If he hadn't spent all his money on drugs, he'd've been half rich by now.

"I'd be with you no matter, even if you were in the animal car and I was a showgirl," she said. Saying the truth like this felt nice. She was glad he wasn't in the animal car, number seventy-six, where the men who took care of the ring stock lived. They slept in bunks stacked against the wall, with no privacy except a taped-up sheet, if they had a spare. Some of the men smelled like the animals they cleaned up after. Buckeye was number three in candy sales because she kept herself showered and smelling nice, because she scrubbed the stains off her uniform shirt right away. Nobody would say she was pretty, but she wore her hair pulled into a neat, short ponytail, and there were some white people who would only buy candy from a girl like her, from somebody who looked like she could be a girl who lived next door to them.

She'd never known a man so broad in the shoulders and slim in the hips as Black Mike. He was built like an oversize trapeze artist. As soon as she met him, she wanted to swing all over him, and pretty soon she told him so. The quiet way he talked made her know he wouldn't hit her, and that was something she'd never been wrong about. Her ma, back in Akron, got bruised and beat up by every man she ever went with, and some of those men had knocked Buckeye around, too. Her friend Red wouldn't hit a person, either, but one time he'd shaken her shoulders so hard it made her neck hurt, the way you're not supposed to shake a baby. Red did that to her the day after she'd made love with a man in the animal car with the other men listening from their bunks. Red didn't believe in putting love over everything else the way she did. Red got his name because he used to have red hair, but that was mostly gone now, and he always wore a hat or bandanna. Buckeye used to know his real name, but she couldn't remember it now. Jim something, or maybe Alan. The heat was messing with her brain. She blew her ditchwater bangs out of her eyes.

"It's too hot sitting in here with the door closed," Mike said.

She pulled his hand to her lips and kissed his crooked fingers and needle marks, kissed his fingernails, which she had filed smooth for him yesterday during the slow ride from Oklahoma City.

"Just one more minute before we open the door. Please," Buckeye said.

He squeezed her hand, pulled the back of her hand to his cheek, which was beaded with sweat. His sweat soaked into her skin like it belonged to her as much as to him.

"How come you don't ever sweat?" Mike asked.

"I don't know."

"You're probably sweating on the inside."

This single room was only a little bigger than the bunk, so Mike's kneecaps about hit the metal door. Buckeye rested her bare heels on the army canvas duffel bag containing all Mike's worldlies, which he kept packed at all times, as though he might just grab the bag and run. He had nothing else but a stack of empty cassette-tape cases on a ledge and a Metallica poster. He'd duct-taped black plastic over the Plexiglas window. The canvas bag had the name *McIntyre* stenciled on it, though that wasn't Mike's name. If Buckeye married him, she'd be Mrs. Field. Her soft cloth purse was nestled on top of the duffel. She'd put her ChapStick, army knife, wallet, everything she would need at the clinic, in her pockets. If Mike noticed the purse there, he'd tell her to go put it in her own room, he didn't want to be responsible if she left it here.

Buckeye wondered what if she didn't go with Red, but stayed here. This afternoon she and Mike would go to the stadium together like they did in every other town to help set up concessions. They'd step inside the stadium doors together and get blasted by the air-conditioning, a cool comfort after two hot days riding from Oklahoma City.

"I'm going to open the door," Mike said.

As his fingertips touched the handle, there was a *bang*. A fist smashed against the metal door from the outside and sent a shock through the space. They both sat up straight. Buckeye lifted her feet onto the bed and wrapped her arms around her bare legs.

"I'm taking you now, Buckeye, or I'm not taking you at all," Red said through the sheet metal door. "You got two minutes and I'm saying forget it."

"Don't pay any attention to him," Buckeye whispered, even though she herself was scared of Red, not for fear of him hitting her, but something like how you'd fear your father, if you had one. Red had lasted in this circus for twenty-some years, longer than anybody. In the seven years since she'd joined the Greatest Show on Earth, Buckeye had found Red lying drunk on the railroad stones all across America, a few times beat up, a few times with a new scabbed-over tattoo, and she'd cleaned him up and gotten him into his bunk on the train. Mostly, though, Red got by without making trouble for anybody else.

"I don't know if I can live on this train anymore," Mike said. "This room's making me crazy. It's so small."

"It's just the heat that's making you say that. And you ought to be wearing a short-sleeved shirt, not long sleeves."

"What if you have the baby?" he asked. "Like my ma did. She said people thought she was crazy to have me all by herself."

"You and me, we aren't settled down like your ma. And like my ma. We have to take care of each other, not a baby."

"But if you did have a baby," Mike said, "what would you want to call him?"

"Well, okay. If it was a boy, I'd name him Mitch or Mick, something simple, but something nobody would take away from him." Funny, but she hadn't even been thinking of boy names.

"Mitch. That's a name for a white kid. My baby's going to be black."

That was true, Buckeye knew. Black Mike was blacker than anybody in the King Charles Troupe, way blacker than the two black showgirls, who wouldn't talk to him and wouldn't talk to Buckeye, either, or anybody living below the pie car, which was car number eighty-two.

"Maybe that's why you don't want to have him," Mike said. "Maybe you don't want a black baby."

"That's not why." Buckeye imagined holding a baby the color of Mike's face against her pale breast. She'd thought of it about every hour of every day these last few weeks, and the thought still took her breath away. Holding that baby so nobody could hurt it.

"How about Mary for a girl?" Mike asked. His voice was no longer a whisper. "My mom's name was Mary. Mary Sarah Field."

"You don't hear what I'm saying," Buckeye said. "A name like Mary, somebody else'll have it first, and you don't want your daughter to always be Black Mary, do you? How about name her after a flower, like Marigold? We'll call her Mary for short, you and me, but she would tell other people she was Marigold, and they'd call her Goldie, maybe."

Mike pulled down his sleeves so they covered his wrists, something he did when agitated. Buckeye felt sad and sometimes a little crazy at how Mike always kept himself covered except in the dark. He wouldn't let her turn the light on until he was dressed. He begged her not to steal a look, not yet, he always said, not if you love me, and she hadn't gone against him.

"We could have an apartment," Mike said, looking down at Buckeye's legs, "you and me and the baby."

Red was lying low outside, but Buckeye could hear the floor creaking, so she put her finger to her lips. Mike ignored her.

"I'd like to have a baby sitting on my knee, bouncing, knowing I was his daddy." He patted his own knee through the chino fabric. "He'd know I loved him."

Buckeye dressed the opposite of Mike, because she wanted Mike to see her body all the time so he would want her more. From climbing stairs with cotton candy every afternoon and evening, her legs were as shapely as a showgirl's, and when she wasn't wearing her work uniform, she wore the shortest skirts and shorts, kept her legs shaved smooth.

"You couldn't do meth no more, then," Buckeye said. "Or coke. You'd have to give me all your money."

"All of it? Why?"

"So I could feed the baby and buy diapers and pay the rent. And you can't stay covered up all the time. You'd have to get undressed like other people."

"Why?"

"So I can see you. So the baby can see you."

Whomp! There was banging on the door again and Red's voice. "Get out here, Buckeye. Open that door, Black Mike. It's been five minutes."

Her circus ID card still read *Becky*, but she'd more or less gotten used to "Buckeye." Sometimes she used an ink pen to decorate the palm of one hand, drawing a deer with horns, a buck. On the other she drew a big watchful eye with an eyebrow and eyelashes. She always scrubbed the ink off at night.

"It's just weird that I've never seen you naked," Buckeye said. "You've got to see how it's weird, don't you?"

Mike had a tattoo like a collar on the back of his neck that read *FIELD* in big Gothic letters; Buckeye tried to make out other tattoos in the night, tried to feel them on his skin like Braille, but she found only welts and gouged places, lines of needle scars, and a swath on his arm that was a grid of tiny bumps. She sometimes imagined swirls of ink covering his body, beautiful cursive words circling his scars, telling his true story that would end happily ever after with her. She imagined that if she could keep taking care of him, someday his skin would heal and be smooth.

Black Mike slid open the pocket door, and there was Red standing right there with his two lower front teeth missing, his hands on his hips, his T-shirt with armpit stains that hadn't come out in the wash, the worn fabric of his jeans straining against his thighs. The hallway air blasted them like air-conditioning, five degrees cooler than the shut-up room, and Buckeye could smell last night's whiskey on Red's breath. Today he wore a red bandanna over his head like a pirate.

"Hi, Red," Buckeye said. She always felt happy to see her friend.

"Let's go," he said. Since he'd fallen on a steel rail last year and broken off those teeth, he hissed when he talked.

"I don't know," she said. "I'm not sure."

"Don't go thinking you're going to change your mind, Buckeye. As soon as the candy boss notices you getting a belly, you get dumped, whatever town you're in."

"Mike says maybe we should leave the show anyhow." She'd been like this twice before in the seven years she'd been in the circus, and both times it was Red who helped her out of her situation. Those other times she waited until it showed, but this time she told Red after she missed her first period.

"I could get a job in a warehouse," Mike said, addressing neither Red nor Buckeye. "I used to work in a warehouse when I first got out of jail."

"I could work in a Laundromat or a nursing home like my ma," Buckeye said. "Or I could be a waitress and make tips."

"Shit," Red said. He paused to light a cigarette. "You two think you're going to be able to raise a kid? Where you going to live?"

"This town, maybe," Buckeye said. "Phoenix. It's warm in the winter."

"You know what an apartment costs? You got a security deposit? Black Mike, you got anything left after buying speed and coke?"

"I had an apartment once, back home in Akron," Buckeye said. "With a girlfriend."

"Shit," Red said again, as though he were spitting. "You're not leaving the show, Buckeye, and you know it."

She shrugged.

Black Mike looked deliberately away from her, away from

Red, toward the stack of cassette cases in the corner, but he was holding Buckeye's hand now, letting the back of his big hand press against her bare thigh. The other times before this, once in Ohio, once in Los Angeles, she'd felt sick and ready to get rid of what plagued her, but this time wasn't like that. She wasn't even sure how it would work, her going to the doctor all filled with love and desire the way she was—her body might not let the thing go. A clinic was a place for regret and mistakes, and her body wasn't feeling like there was any mistake. This time she felt strong and perfect. She knew it didn't make sense to anybody else to think about Mike as a father, with all his troubles, but when she was close with him, her body told her something different, that maybe this was the time to have a baby, that maybe the baby was the fix for all their troubles.

Red said, "Put your damn flip-flops on and get out here. I ain't the bad guy. Tell him what a condom is and you won't be in this trouble. Yo, Black Mike, you go around with your goddamned arms and legs covered like you got skin cancer. Why don't you keep your dick covered instead?"

It was true, Red was not the bad guy. He was the only one who'd looked out for her, the only person who'd stuck with her when other guys moved on to other girls or got thrown in jail or just disappeared one day, staying in some town instead of getting back on the train.

"Maybe some time later we can have a baby," she whispered to Mike, but he wouldn't look at her.

She knew he would stay here in this room, stay on this circus train, as long as she was sitting with him, but if she went with Red, he might not be here when she got back. Mike didn't understand how Red was right, how she couldn't just park herself in a town and have a baby like some other people did, sit in an apartment and wait for a man to come home and hope he brought some money. Buckeye's ma had had a baby when Buckeye was fifteen, and her ma used to send her out to steal baby food, until she got kicked out of every store in her neighborhood. And Mike wouldn't just give up drugs like snapping his fingers—nobody did that. If he was high, she wouldn't know if she should leave the baby with him while she went to work. When she'd had an apartment with her friend in Akron, they couldn't afford air-conditioning. Being in heat like this all the time would make anybody crazy.

There was Red standing before her, his freckled arms thick from twenty-some years of holding snow-cone trays over his head, his thighs ropy from climbing stadium stairs eight hours a day. In a voice like gravel from shouting, *Snow cones! Get your snow cones!* and *There's no balls like snowballs!* Red was telling her she needed to come with him. Now. She stood up, and Mike let her hand slip away, but then grabbed her wrist and held it. Pretty soon even Buckeye wanted him to let go. She tugged, and his face remained expressionless like when those Bulgarians had been hitting him. Red grabbed hold of Mike's hand and tried to peel off the fingers, but he was clamped tight. With the Bulgarians, Mike had just stood there with blood running down his face. Now he kept hold of Buckeye while Red pounded his arm with a fist. Mike didn't even use his free hand to stop Red from hitting him.

"Don't, Red," Buckeye said. "He's not hurting me."

"Let go of her," Red said. "We got an appointment."

"You got to let go of me, Mike," she said.

After the Bulgarians had punched him a dozen times in the face and a few times in the gut, Buckeye had begged them to stop, said she'd pay the money back. Mike had wanted to leave the circus that day, to just give up, but she begged him to stay. Today Buckeye was borrowing money for the clinic from Red.

"Me going with Red is for both of us. It's helping you, too, Mike. You just don't see it right now."

Red stopped hitting Mike. Red pinched his cigarette between his lips, squinted against the smoke, and reached down to Mike's wrist, the wrist of the hand that was holding her, and worked at a button on Mike's shirt cuff. As soon as Red got it undone, Mike pulled away to rebutton it, and Red yanked Buckeye's arm free. And there was Buckeye walking out with Red, leaving Mike sitting on his bunk with the sheet sprung off the dirty mattress.

"I'll be back in a couple hours," Buckeye said from the hallway. "Stay here and wait for me. Please, Mike." The other two times she'd gone to a clinic, there had been nobody waiting on her, no man other than Red who even cared about what she was doing.

"We got to walk a half mile to the bus stop," Red said as they passed through the vestibule. "Bus comes every fifteen minutes, a guy told me."

She followed Red outside and across the railroad stones, some of them sharp enough they cut into her feet through the soles of her sandals. When she had picked her way over the second set of tracks, she turned and looked back at Mike's window. He had taken down the black plastic and was watching her through the scratched Plexiglas. No man had ever wanted her to stay with him the way Mike was wanting her to stay now.

"Wait," she said to Red.

"Where you going?"

"I forgot my purse."

"Hurry up," Red said. "I'm not coming after you again."

She climbed into the vestibule, left Red standing on the stones with his arms crossed. She found Mike still sitting on his bunk with the door slid open, his forehead beaded with sweat, headphones on, music turned up so loud Buckeye could hear the rage of a guitar solo from the hall. She saw her purse on his duffel bag, but instead of picking it up, she smoothed the sheet over the bare mattress and brushed away a little sand. She stood close to Mike, close enough that he could have reached out and taken hold of her and begged her not to go one more time, could have told her again how they'd leave this show and make a life in Phoenix, or someplace. He took off the headphones, and death music screamed out of the tiny speakers beside him.

"I might not go through with it," Buckeye said. She knew that before she saw the doctor she would have to fill out forms and somebody would talk to her about having the baby or not.

Mike laid his wrist on his knee, palm up. With his other hand he unbuttoned the cuff of his shirt. He started rolling up the sleeve as she'd never seen him do in the months she'd been with him, revealing blue-black jagged marks that became two lightning bolt tattoos charging down his arm. He revealed a dozen scarified reddish lines stretching over his wrist like a man would make himself with a razor blade. As he continued to roll up his sleeve, she saw a series of crude, swollen crosses the size of dimes or pennies. He folded the sleeve at his elbow, exposed the length of the lightning bolts and a scar that looked like a centipede as long and thick as a pinky finger, with ragged stitch marks across its body. There were three scabs on his vein. When he turned his arm around, she saw blackish welts like stab wounds on his muscle, and shadow bruises that seemed to have come from deep under his skin. There were places where his flesh rose in knots. He tugged the sleeve up still farther to reveal gray-pink burns, most as small as the ends of cigarettes, one as big as a mouth screaming, and more blue-black smears. A swollen vein at the inside of his elbow had bumps so close together they formed a dark ridge. Above that was a teardrop-shaped patch of raised irregular dots. The wounds she'd felt in the dark had always seemed sad to her fingertips, but in the blue-steel light of this room, the wounds were ferocious, hungry.

She grabbed her purse, pressed it to her belly, and backed away, moved slowly into the hallway until her shoulder hit the steel wall as hard as if she'd been thrown against it. When Mike looked up at her with angry bloodshot eyes, she stopped breathing. She'd never seen him angry, not at the Bulgarians, not at Red, and certainly not at her, but his look was as hot as blood.

She turned away and walked, still without breathing, toward the vestibule, supporting herself with one hand on the wall. She descended the stairs and leaned against the outside of car seventy-eight. When she dropped to her knees under Mike's window, she almost fell into the train's steel wheel. She had studied Mike's wounds with her fingers in the dark, had dreamed the marks were telling a story about the two of them, but she saw now that they were his own terrible story.

She cupped her hands over her knees. She'd scraped them on the stones, and one was bleeding.

Red was standing where she'd left him with his arms crossed, tapping his foot against a rail that was shining white as a bone in the Arizona sun. Buckeye picked up a railroad stone, so hot it burned her hand. She'd thought Mike's wounds were something she might soothe or even heal. She pressed the jagged gray stone into the softest, whitest part of her thigh and squeezed her eyes shut against the pain. Mike wouldn't be able to see her below his window, but he was so close that she felt his oversize heart swelling. Buckeye heard Red shout, but couldn't make out his words. This town was no place to raise a child. No town was. She couldn't do it, couldn't bring forth another body that was just going to feel confusion and humiliation and pain. She looked out over the tracks, saw people walking away with bags of laundry, returning with groceries and six-packs of soda and beer. Two showgirls laughed as they bumped shoulders. Without wigs and makeup, dressed in their jogging shorts and tanks, they seemed like carefree teenage boys. Beyond them, a few beat-up palm trees wavered, distorted by the heat. She ground the stone deep into the wound as Red approached. She remembered Red's name: James Allen. He crouched beside her and said, "What the fuck are you doing?" He pulled his bandanna off and pressed the red cloth against her knee. He took the bloody stone out of her hand and tossed it onto the other stones. She heard moaning from somewhere, or maybe it was the hum of the train's generator. As Red bent over her, she touched his bald head with both hands, found baby-fine hairs, pressed her cheek there.

My Dog Roscoe

As my big sister predicted from her cell in the county jail, I became pregnant early into my marriage to Pete the electrician. That tarot reading Lydia did for me was the last before one of her cellmates reported her so-called satanic activities to the authorities and got her cards taken away.

Just when I was starting to show, a stray dog—bigger than a cocker spaniel, smaller than a retriever, white with black pepper spots and a black circle around one eye—appeared at the back door of the house that Pete and I were renting with an option to buy. The dog's faded red collar had no identification tags, but *Roscoe* was written on the fabric in alcohol marker. At first I tried to shoo him away, told him to go on home, but he stuck around, and I became fond of his lopsided face—one ear hung down lower than the other. Pete suggested we might wait and get a puppy after the baby was born. Until recently, I'd always appreciated Pete's long-term view, but here was a living, breathing creature who needed me now, and in my fifth month, maybe my hormones were talking, too. For a week, I reminded Pete of how lonesome I was when he worked out of town, and all the while I fed the dog breakfast cereal and left-over meatloaf and pizza under the back porch stairs where I had built him a nest of blankets. When Pete agreed to our adopting Roscoe, I bathed his coat with coal tar shampoo, took him to the veterinarian for shots, and, on Dr. Wellborn's advice, made an appointment for the surgical neutering a few weeks down the road.

Soon after he moved in with us, I began noticing a worldly light shining in Roscoe's dark eyes. His soulful expression revealed that he had known pain—if not in this life, then in a previous one. Perhaps we had suffered together in times past. Maybe we'd been on a Roman slave ship, chained side by side to our oars. Or if I had been Cleopatra, then he might've been some hardworking stevedore on the Nile, or a deckhand, a handsome swarthy man I'd hardly noticed until he threw his body between me and an assassin's blade.

Roscoe was wary around Pete, perhaps because Pete was so tall, but when the dog and I were alone, he had a habit of rolling onto his back and opening his legs in a way that reminded me not of a fellow slave or an Egyptian, but of my old fiancé Oscar, may he rest in peace. Two years ago, the dashing and philandering Oscar fell headfirst from a hayloft, where he was nakedly comingling with a Galesburg girl, who at the funeral claimed Oscar had been *her* fiancé. My sister Lydia, who as a practicing wiccan should have been respectful of the dead, never even let me speak Oscar's name wistfully without reminding me of the ways I'd been betrayed. In the eight years Oscar and I were together, he had twice given me chlamydia (swearing both times it came from an exercise bicycle) and in the last few years of our time together had taken to disappearing for hours or days without explanation. Life with Oscar had

had a lot of ups and downs, but I had fallen for him in tenth grade and had loved him with a blindness and durable intensity that I wasn't sure I could muster for my husband Pete, better man though he might be.

One morning, a week into the adoption, as I scratched Roscoe's chest, which was surprisingly muscular for a twenty-pound mongrel, his tongue snaked out and he began to lick the underside of my wrist. It gave me a shiver. Only two people in this life had ever known that my wrists were my most romantically sensitive body part. Perhaps Roscoe had been studying Pete and me in our intimate moments through the crack in the door. Or perhaps this dog and I had been very close in our previous life together. Maybe those slave ship captains had severely whipped him when he voiced his opinions about human rights, and maybe I revived him with fresh water from my own meager rations before we found ourselves in a passionate embrace.

Roscoe turned from me to minister to his own privates. When he tired of that, he headed toward the kitchen, but he paused in the doorway to look over at me and puff up his chest and, if I wasn't mistaken, to suck in his little belly, exactly the way my sexy boyfriend Oscar used to. I followed him into the kitchen and kneeled to look into his face. Couldn't be. Ridiculous. Plenty of dogs had soulful brown eyes. Plenty of dogs licked people's wrists and inflated their chests. How could I even think such a thing? Roscoe took a nugget of dry food in his mouth and crunched it distractedly, pretending not to notice I was looking at him—but hadn't such pretending been another of Oscar's postures?

When I stepped out of the shower a few hours later, I looked down and saw Roscoe gazing up at my breasts with his tongue hanging out. I'd felt proud of the slight swell of my belly, but something about the the dog's expression embarrassed me. I wrapped my bathrobe around myself and stepped over him. "Stop it," I scolded. The dog whined and lowered his eyes with a look of guilt I knew all too well.

While Pete was outside changing the oil in his truck, I reclined on the couch and opened a bag of Be-Mo sour-cream-and-onion potato chips. Although Pete preferred plain salted chips, he found no fault with my eating these or any other snacks—recently he had allowed me to spell out the letters of baby names on his bare stomach in cheese doodles while he read a biography of Abraham Lincoln.

Roscoe's eyes followed my hand as I lifted each chip from the bag to my mouth. When I finally offered him one, Roscoe stretched up and took it in his teeth. I breathed a sigh of relief. Oscar had always hated chips, and he had especially hated the sour-cream-and-onion kind and complained when I ate them. But this dog liked them, and that was that, and all the rest had been my imagination. Roscoe sauntered into the kitchen, and I leaned off the couch and caught sight of him spitting out the chip. He proceeded to lap water from his dish, as if to wash the taste away. Then he puffed up his chest and sat ignoring me.

"Oscar?" I said.

The dog turned my way and sucked in his stomach.

"Is that really you?" I asked.

He trotted back to me and tilted his head sideways—it was a darling gesture. Dr. Wellborn had said the droopy ear indicated frostbite damage, but now I knew better. Oscar had departed this world as a result of falling from that barn's loft onto a threshing spike, which had entered his brain through his right ear.

Roscoe opened his mouth and let his tongue hang out over his small bottom teeth.

My first feeling was of joyful recognition, but I quickly

reminded myself of all that had passed between us. I took a deep calming breath and snorted. "So you're back, are you? I should've known you weren't done taking advantage of my forgiving nature."

The dog approached and pushed his nose under my hand.

"Don't try to play nice with me after everything you've done."

I got up and put his dog dish up on the counter where he couldn't reach it, and, after some thought, took away his water dish, too. He could drink out of the toilet if he was thirsty. "Did you really think I'd take you back? Forgive you for all your crimes?"

He leapt up toward where I'd put his food. When he realized he wouldn't be able to reach it, he did a kind of foolish little turning-around dance that ended in him falling on his butt on the floor, but I refused to laugh.

"You're not as cute as you think you are, mister," I said. "You could always sweet-talk your way out of trouble before, but not this time."

At length I reminded him of some of his worst behavior, starting with the venereal diseases and working up to his frolic with that mean librarian. Oscar always denied the encounter, but after the evening in question, the woman continually renewed his books so he never had to pay late fees, while she required of me the strictest compliance. She even let him check out reference books, for crying out loud. "And you thought I wouldn't notice you had a second fiancé? You've been very, very bad," I concluded.

Roscoe didn't respond, but finally closed his mouth and whined.

"Ha!" I said. "At last you admit your guilt!"

He could no longer explain away all those hours he'd claimed to be at the nursing home with his grandmother, and he certainly couldn't deny dirty-dancing in that hayloft. And because he couldn't reach the doorknob, he couldn't storm out in an indignant huff as he might have done in the past. He gazed at my finger with regret, until suddenly his head whipped around and he gnawed at his back leg, pretending to bite a flea.

"Look at me when I talk to you," I said, grabbing his nose. "You can't avoid me, Oscar, Roscoe, whatever you call yourself. Now that I'm loved by a man who is true, I know how badly you treated me."

After some consideration, I tied the little mongrel outside on a piece of clothesline and informed him about the surgical castration in store for him in about a week.

When Pete asked later why I put the dog outside, I told him it was because Roscoe still had fleas and needed another treatment. Pete gave a few worried glances into the yard during the evening, and before going to bed he carried the dog's food and water dishes to him.

"Maybe you should put some flyers up to see if you can find his owner," Pete suggested the next morning. Though it was Sunday, he was heading out for a three-day job in Ann Arbor, with overtime. But I had worked the business over like a chew toy all through the sleepless night and decided the solution was not to get rid of him—after all, he'd always been happy to abandon me to my anger. My plan was to finally make him pay for what he had done to me.

As I was heading out to work on the first full day of Roscoe's banishment, he watched me with those passionate eyes I knew so well. As I walked to my car, he sighed and rested his speckled nose between his speckled paws in the dry leaves. When I came home, he jumped up with joy, leapt right up into the air in his excitement to see me. And soon enough my heart began to soften. Sure, Oscar had betrayed me plenty, but he had taught me plenty as well, and his bad behavior didn't negate the depth of his love for me. He and I had grown up together, after all, and if Oscar had lived, he probably would have turned his life around and behaved better eventually. I pulled the bag of treats out of the kitchen garbage can and gave him a few. When I poured some water into his dish, he lapped up a pint. But to give in now, when I finally had the upper hand in our relationship, seemed foolish.

That evening I fed and watered him and tried not to reveal my weakening resolve as I tucked a blanket around him, and then I couldn't sleep for thinking of him out there. In the morning I discovered he'd pushed off the blanket and was shivering—obviously he wanted to suffer to prove his love. The way he looked at me, I could tell he'd never felt so much regret for his actions as he did now. I didn't know what he'd been through since he died, but he was paying a steep price for his crimes by having to come back to me as a helpless animal.

That evening it was raining when I returned from work. Roscoe was shivering under the porch, but he came out to greet me and stood there, soaking wet, until I untied him and invited him inside. After eating and drinking a good amount, he gazed at me with eyes full of pure gratitude.

"I guess I can give you one more chance," I said. "But this is going to be your last chance forever. If you blow it, it's over between us. Do you understand?" I was pretty sure I'd never before given him an ultimatum with such force, or at least I'd never meant it the way I meant it now.

As I was getting ready for bed, I heard a ruckus in the utility room, and then Roscoe appeared with a dead mouse in his teeth. He laid it at my feet.

"Well, you are proving yourself useful, Roscoe." I relieved him of the mouse and tossed it out in the yard for the crows. When I returned I said, "Now tell me how sorry you are for everything you did wrong over the years."

He whimpered.

"I mean really sorry, not like before when you just wanted to shut me up or go to bed with me."

He whined and then punctuated his whining with a couple of yelps. When he saw me start to smile, he began wagging his tail. The frantic wagging told me he was sorry more than words could have.

"I always told you that you couldn't live without me. I guess you couldn't stand to be dead without me, either, could you?" I smoothed the fur on his head and felt him shiver with sincerity and gratitude. I patted the couch cushion beside me. "Come up here, big fella." The dog jumped onto the couch and laid his head on my stomach. He watched my face for a while and then focused his attention on the television. I pushed him away only when his drool soaked through my nightie.

I'd never liked sleeping alone in the king-size bed, so that night I called the dog up beside me and reminded him of our first sweet trysts in my brother's tree fort and in the shed behind the bus barn. I recalled the prom, where he danced with a cheerleader most of the night. After rehashing the good and the bad, I couldn't deny the passion I still felt for my own first love. For months I had been dreaming of Pete and our new baby, but now I wanted a break from those thoughts.

I needed advice, but I couldn't confide in my husband. Pete knew I'd been betrayed by Oscar, but he didn't know the depth of my love for the man or how intensely I'd grieved Oscar's passing. And especially Pete didn't know that, as he and I sank into the routine of our marriage, I was beginning to long for some of the old excitement and uncertainty of my youthful romance.

THE NEXT MORNING at work the clock on my desk seemed to slow as it approached ten-thirty. My sister Lydia was allowed to make one call at this time every Wednesday. After a quick hello I told her that Oscar had come back to find me.

"To haunt you, you mean, like a ghost?" she said. The prison phone line always sounded staticky, as if my sister herself might be a ghost. "I wish I could come to your house and do a banishing spell while your Pete's out of town. Otherwise you'll have to dig up Oscar's dead body and sprinkle salt on it and burn it. But I guess that's not practical, is it?"

"No, I don't want a banishing spell, Lydia. It's more complicated than that. He's not exactly dead," I said.

"He died in the farming accident. I went to the funeral. I held you sobbing in my arms."

"He fell out of a hayloft, but he's reborn in a new form. He's a dog now."

"He was always a dog."

"A real dog this time. Woof-woof. And he caught a mouse last night and brought it to me to prove he's changed his ways and wants to be helpful."

"Sarah, this isn't good," Lydia said. "I've been worried sick about you since yesterday. I did the tarot for you and got a disturbing reading."

"I thought they took your cards away," I said.

"I made a new deck, out of toilet paper. It's only temporary. Listen, the Lovers appeared prominently, upside down. I drew it last night, too, with the Fool." The Lovers card was not necessarily bad, of course, but it suggested temptation, choice, the struggle between sacred and profane love, and upside down it warned of the wrong choice. "Don't you worry, though," she said. "I'll put a curse on Oscar to get him out of your life for good."

"You don't understand," I protested. "As a dog, he might be much better than he was as a boyfriend. And I think he's really sorry for how he treated me. You should see the look on his face. He's so contrite. And cute." And I told her about the potato chips.

"What about Pete?" she asked with alarm in her voice.

"He doesn't need to know anything. He doesn't believe in this stuff."

"It sounds to me, little sister, like you're about to betray your husband. You'd better get a grip!" she shouted into the phone loudly enough that I had to hold it away from my ear. My sister was usually an open-minded person, so I was surprised by her harsh tone. "Your Pete is a light shining above the rabble. You have found true love with a good man, and now you're going to have a baby, so shut up about Oscar and shut up about that damned dog. In fact, get rid of the dog. It's too dangerous to have him around."

I clutched the phone in silence, wondering if maybe they'd slipped lard into the crust of her vegetarian potpies again.

"Are you saying you don't think it's Oscar?"

"What has the dog done? Whined at you and looked up with sad eyes in order to get food? He's a dog, for crying out loud. That's what dogs do."

"Are you saying you don't believe in reincarnation?"

"I'm saying you ruined your life for eight years with that guy. And your potato chip test is stupid," she said. "If I could bust out of here, I'd steal a car and drive over there and kick your ass."

"Well, I'm not sending him out to live in the street," I said. "He needs me and loves me. You never understood what Oscar and I meant to each other."

"And if it really is Oscar, that's more reason to send him to the pound."

"Thanks for being so supportive. Next time I'll call the Psychic Friends Network." I hung up before telling her I would deposit money in her jail account and that I'd bought her a book about improving the feng shui of very small spaces.

"I SHOULD'VE FIGURED she wouldn't understand," I told Roscoe when I snuck home at lunchtime to bring him a treat and take him for a walk. "It's always just been me and you. Nobody else can see what keeps us coming back to each other. Nobody else understands our animal magnetism."

That evening, I stopped at the butcher's and bought a pig's ear—Oscar had always liked pork rinds, so not surprisingly the ear was a hit. As we lay on the couch together afterward, I marveled at how much my old boyfriend had changed, mostly for the better. Oscar had always been a prime-rib and filet-mignon man, yet Roscoe dutifully ate his Waggy Meals and Chew Bites in both beef and poultry flavors. To my relief, he had also mellowed in his television habits—Oscar used to roll his eyes whenever I turned on my ten o'clock police and lawyer dramas, but Roscoe seemed content to watch with me now, never suggesting that he'd prefer news or wrestling. On the negative side, while Oscar had been fastidious about his personal cleanliness, Roscoe didn't miss an opportunity to rummage through neighbors' recycling or to roll on the carcasses of squirrels hit along our road. Roscoe had also pulled one of Pete's dirty work socks out of the hamper and chewed it to pieces. I stuffed the evidence in the kitchen garbage, and then, upon consideration, carried the garbage bag outside to the dumpster.

That night I began to wonder what deal Oscar had made with the universe to return to this world as my dog. Was there a set of circumstances under which a kiss or incantation would turn Roscoe back into Oscar? My husband worked a dangerous job. What if something happened to him while he was installing electrical cable on the twelfth floor of a new office building? What if he were shocked with twenty thousand volts in a freak power surge? Would Oscar be able to transform to console me?

PETE RETURNED home on Tuesday night. When he climbed into his side of the bed, Pete saw Roscoe was lying on the rug by my side, looking more melancholy than usual, and I was leaning down to pet him.

"Fleas all gone?" Pete asked.

"Every flea. Roscoe was a great comfort to me while you were gone."

"I guess he'd make a ruckus if anybody came to the house, wouldn't he? I hate leaving you alone when I work out of town."

"He'd defend me to the death," I said, though I wondered if he might be distracted from that duty by a squirrel, either a live one that needed chasing or a dead one that needed rolling in.

Pete's work clothes were laid out on the chair on his side of the bed. The timer on the coffeemaker was set, the doors and windows were all checked and locked. The bills were all paid. Living with Pete had seemed safe and sensible all these months, but lately the security was making me feel a little restless.

"Maybe we shouldn't get him neutered," I said.

"What?" Pete looked away from his paperback of Stephen Hawking, *A Brief History of Time*.

"Is it really fair? What if he wants to have a family? What gives human beings the right to impose their wills on other species?" I was thinking that castration might be one of those things that would stick with Roscoe even after his transmogrification back into a human, should that take place. And our future life together would be tainted by his knowledge that I had done that terrible thing to him.

"Sarah, you're not imposing your will on him. You're rescuing him. If not for you, he'd probably have gotten hit on the road or gassed at the pound already."

When Pete fell asleep, I invited Roscoe onto the bed, and the following morning, early, I left a message for Dr. Wellborn canceling the Friday surgical appointment.

THURSDAY MORNING, ROSCOE whined to go outside earlier than usual, while Pete was showering. I dragged myself out of bed and fiddled to straighten the leash and noticed that Roscoe had thoroughly chewed up one of Pete's brand-new Red Wing work boots. Pete had just paid hundreds of dollars for a new pair to replace his five-year-old pair. I thought about the dozen pairs of leather shoes that used to perch in Oscar's closet, shined and stylish, ready for dancing or going to any sort of restaurant. I hadn't thought I wanted to go to restaurants back then, but dating Oscar had kept me on my toes—a gal had to look smart to feel worthy of walking beside a well-dressed man like Oscar—and now I missed my old stylish self a little. Thinking about those shoes reminded me of how much Roscoe had lost in this new life, reminded me that I was all he had now.

I held up the work boot, stuck my finger through one of the holes in the leather, and imagined Pete telling me the dog would have to go as punishment. I would have to choose between the two of them. I took a big breath and sighed, imagined holding my head high as I headed out into the morning with my old love on a leash, leaving my husband in the doorway, shaking his ruined boot at us. And Roscoe would know I had chosen him over Pete, and he would finally love me the way he should've loved me before, absolutely and without deviation. For the moment, though, the main thing was to make sure Roscoe didn't piddle on the carpet. I snapped the leash onto his collar.

As I opened the front door, a leg cramp took hold of me. In my moment of inattention, the dog banged against the screen door, which was not latched, and he was off. He pumped his legs faster and faster across our yard, dragging his leash around the basswood tree, over our neighbor's pumpkins and through his Brussels sprouts, dragging down several stalks in the process. There was no doubt about where Roscoe was headed. Last night he'd nearly broken my arm when we were at the old highway, tugging me toward the kennel where a female black chow was coming into heat, as evidenced by a half dozen other male dogs jumping up on the chain-link. I'd told him he should be ashamed, but he'd been too carried away to hear me.

My slippers slowed my pursuit until I kicked them away and continued barefoot through the frost-tinged grass. I'd had a sweet vision of Roscoe and me trekking side by side, covering countryside, having adventures and cooking meals over campfires, communing with each other and nature, feeling sad about all we'd left behind. (Though Oscar hadn't cared much for nature or camping, surely Roscoe would.) But this morning's chase was no doubt a harbinger of things to come if I chose a life with Roscoe.

"Come back here," I shouted, panting as I ran. "This is your last chance to be faithful, dog. I swear, the very last chance. If you don't stop, I'll never forgive you." Even moving at this brisk pace, I was reflecting on how I'd said this sort of thing dozens of times before, and how I'd always gone on to give him another chance.

Roscoe took the road at a shallow angle. If he'd been paying attention to anything other than his desire for the bitch in the kennel, he'd have noticed the approaching menace of the blue car, which braked and swerved, but couldn't avoid slamming— whomp—into him. His body flew through the air and landed on the dirt shoulder. In pursuit, I didn't hesitate to run right in front of the car, which halted a foot from me. My heart stopped, and the world took on a greenish tinge as I realized I had just risked extinguishing not only my own light, but also the five-month-old flame inside me.

Roscoe's lifeless body lay like a twenty-pound sack of flour in the gravel, and a stain of blood was blossoming across his spotted haunch. I kneeled beside him and laid my hands on his body. Though my vision blurred with tears, I could see, through the opening in the fence, the kennel attached to the garage end of a ranch-style house, and I knew that inside it perched the object of Roscoe's desire—that black female chow with lush fur and a ridiculously curly tail. She was now rubbing her rear end against the side of the pen. Three other male dogs scratched and whimpered at the chain-link.

The woman who'd hit Roscoe got out of the car and stood beside me in the kind of ugly, padded shoes librarians wear. Her dark hair was tinged with gray beneath a crocheted cap. "He just ran out in front of me," she said. "I'm so sorry. I have two dogs of my own. Golden retrievers. Mixes, I mean, not purebreds. I love dogs."

I put my face into the lifeless fur and began to weep. I wept until a rough tongue unrolled itself onto my cheek.

"You're alive!" I shouted.

Just as I was about to profess my love to Roscoe and forgive him yet again, yelping erupted around us. A big loopy-gaited Irish setter ran past, followed by a yellow hound, who came within six inches of stepping on Roscoe's head on his way to the opening in the fence. This flurry of activity inspired Roscoe to maneuver himself into a sitting position. With great difficulty, he pulled his body up and stood shaking on three legs. I noticed blood pooling, and for a moment I thought it was my blood. I grabbed at myself, but found my body dry inside the bathrobe, which I tucked more securely around me. My belly still heaved with my breath, and I nearly choked on my own realization. What on earth had I been thinking these last few days? That I really wanted to be back with Oscar?

"Maybe he's going to be okay," the woman in the padded shoes said.

"Go get my husband," I yelled. "Down that little road, the yellow house, third on the left."

Roscoe heaved a sigh and sank to the ground again. The woman seemed glad to have been given a mission, and she screeched her tires on the pavement as she departed. Librarians were probably never as mild as they pretended to be.

The male dogs were snarling at one another as the female paced in her cage, desperate to meet them, but probably scared, too.

"You just can't be true, even as a dog," I said and shook my head.

Roscoe's ears both drooped, but when he sniffed in the direction of the cage, the one good ear lifted.

"They shouldn't let females out when they smell that way," I said to Roscoe. "They're just death traps." But in my heart I knew it wasn't the bitch's fault.

Roscoe continued to watch the cage even after somebody called the chow inside. As the other males dispersed to sniff stupidly around the yard, Roscoe turned and looked at me through the most regretful, guileless eyes in the world.

"I guess it would always be like this for us, wouldn't it? You being terrible and me forgiving you because you can't help it. For that I was going to walk away from my husband?"

Roscoe whimpered and looked from the empty cage to me.

"If you live, I'm going to have to assert a little control in this relationship," I said. "You can't be trusted with your own welfare, let alone mine."

"Sarah, honey, we'd better get him into the truck," said Pete from behind me. "I called Dr. Wellborn's office, and she's coming in early for us. Looks like the little fellow's lost some blood."

I hadn't heard Pete's truck pull up, and I somehow hadn't even registered the amount of blood soaking into the dirt shoulder, but at the sound of his voice my heart buoyed—here was a man who would be there to handle any situation calmly. Together Pete and I lifted Roscoe into the truck as the lady who had hit him watched patiently—she could probably stand there all day in those comfortable shoes. Though Pete argued it was unsafe, I insisted on riding in the truck bed with my dog. Pete drove slowly, and I stroked Roscoe's head.

As we slowed to a stop outside the clinic, I opened the tailgate and lugged myself out, feeling the heaviness of pregnancy in a way that seemed new and profound. I pulled Roscoe toward me, and then Pete took the creature in his arms and carried him. The veterinarian's blond assistant held the door for us. She didn't even see me, but kept her eyes on Pete the whole time in a way that made me want to slap her. He was a good-looking man, but I thought the girl should show a little restraint.

"Is he going to die?" I asked.

"He's bruised and traumatized," said Dr. Wellborn after the examination. She was a serious dark-eyed woman with her thick hair pulled back into a stout braid. "But nothing seems to be broken. He's almost stopped bleeding, but I'd like to stitch that gash."

"Thank you, Doctor," I said uncertainly, and I looked at Pete's tall figure. Ever since he'd picked up the dog, his aura was brightly glowing. Lydia had said he was the King of Cups, and now I realized what she meant. It was as though my vision had been clouded for weeks, since Roscoe came into our lives, and now it was clear again.

"He'll do the same thing again, though, unless he's neutered," Wellborn said. As she studied a yellow chart, I decided that she was a Queen of Pentacles, rich with practical talents. "It says here you canceled tomorrow's appointment."

"You canceled the appointment?" Pete turned to me.

"I just couldn't bring him," I said. "Or I thought I couldn't."

Pete stared at me, genuinely puzzled. While I may have misled him slightly on occasion, and while I had failed to mention the Oscar-Roscoe affair, I'd never told Pete an outright lie before.

"Your horoscope or something?" Pete suggested. He wanted to believe me as much as I'd ever wanted to believe Oscar.

"We've still got the surgical opening for tomorrow morning," said Wellborn. "You can leave him here overnight. That way we'll keep an eye on his wounds, and we'll do the castration if he's up to it. It's a simple surgery. Snip. Snip."

Until death do us part, I'd told Pete. I thought I'd committed to him, but there I had been these last few weeks, contemplating betrayal.

"It's up to you," Dr. Wellborn said.

"Are you sure you still want a dog?" Pete asked. "He chewed up my new boot last night. I'll show you when we get home. I'm not very happy with this little fellow right now."

For a few moments, I'd given Roscoe up for dead, but I wouldn't let him go again if I could help it. Things were not finished between us. If I kept him in his place, as a dog, he could be a comforting presence, a living reminder of the troubles I'd left behind and the good life I had chosen instead. As a dog, he could be devoted and companionable. He listened when I talked to him, and he'd always been good with children. There was nothing wrong with a woman having it all, was there?

"Of course we'll take the appointment," I said. And to Pete, I added, "If you want, we can have him sleep in a crate so he doesn't chew anything else up."

Roscoe gazed miserably at me from the exam table, but I smiled at Pete. The dog's welfare was in my hands now. I put one arm around my shining husband, and I placed my other hand on my belly, where I sensed a sweet sigh of relief.

Mothers, Tell Your Daughters

Used to be a doctor would wrap a woman up tight to hold body and soul together, but when I fell last week trying to get to the kitchen to pour myself a drink, they just untangled my tubes, picked me up like I was a child, and put me back in this awful bed. Told me I'd had a stroke. Now I'm lying here with a broken rib that aches.

Stop going through my cupboards and drawers and envelopes that are none of your damned business and sit down and hear me out, Sis. Being unable to say a word means my mind is about to burst. And since I can't even hold a goddamned pen, I'm counting on you, my flesh and blood, to somehow read my thoughts. They say if they wrap my broken ribs I'll get pneumonia, but I never got pneumonia before they stuck me in this hospice bed. In the old days, they fussed about a punctured lung, but maybe a busted rib hasn't punctured a lung in this county since 1932, when old Mr. Wickman's dapple-gray pony trampled him and sent him to an early grave.

As soon as I was big enough to climb onto my daddy's bay

mare, I used to pull blue jeans on under my skirts and ride all over the township. One day at a crossroads that mare took a sharp turn, and I continued straight on. That was all it took to break a rib in them days. A jackass kicked me when I was pregnant with you, Sis, cracked another couple of ribs. Maybe that's why you were born distrusting and watchful, always waiting on things to fall apart. At nine pounds fourteen ounces, just the size of you could've busted me up from the inside.

After your daddy left, after he wrenched my arms from around his waist and tossed me aside like garbage, a Hereford bull crushed me against the barn wall, cracked three more, took my breath away. Funny, your daddy used to take my breath away just by walking into the room—I loved the way that man was always laughing. Look at my breath now, oxygen piped into me! If you want to make a fool of somebody with your smart remarks, tell everybody about how your daddy traveled all the way to Texas just to get shot and killed by somebody else's husband.

You ought to get us some elderberry wine from the root cellar so we can sit together, you lifting the jelly jar to my lips. You remember the good old days, when I could drink and smoke all night, when I could feed more kids than any woman alive and love a man better. Now I'm dying in this house I was born in, dying with no wine, no cigarettes, no laughing or singing. The snow's falling outside today, but with this oxygen running, they won't even let me light my woodstove, much as I love the smell of burning oak and cherry. Last week, even with the lung cancer and morphine, I was speaking my mind, talking circles around every man and woman to prove I was not a fool, and I was still arguing with you, but now I'm lucky if I can spit out a word an hour. I've got a head full of

stories you still need to hear, starting with my ribs, ending
with my whole life.

———————

REMEMBER WHEN MY milk cow Daisy went down in the
barnyard? I did the skinning myself, though I loved that cow.
Remember when every man I loved left me? When your daddy
drove out the driveway with me chasing the truck, while you
held onto your little brothers? When Arnie Carmichael joined
the army and shipped out? Or Bill Theroux? You were glad
Theroux went back to his wife, and I kept my crying to myself
until I smashed into that bridge railing on the way home from
the Lamplighter. It wasn't any six ribs I broke on that steering
wheel, like you told your brother the other day, not one for each
of my children I would have sacrificed for that man, but just five
ribs. Maybe I can't talk anymore, but I'm not deaf.

You knew me when I was something, when I had what it took
to hold a man, to find a man who wanted to hold me. Nobody
needs to tell me I'm nothing now but a snag of gray hair, a sack
of bones that I tossed toward the fire when it was cold, bones
that I used to leave lying in the kitchen sometimes when I finished washing dishes: leg bone, arm bone, jawbone rattling
around in drawers with the emergency candles and batteries and
napkins with sayings on them and a little plastic box somebody
gave me that presses hard-boiled eggs into cubes. Eighty-nine
pounds last time they weighed me. You must weigh twice that,
enough to think you can bully me. You've made your complaints
clear over the years, and now I'm ready to answer, but I close my
eyes and mouth to your oatmeal and scrambled eggs.

I *didn't* worry about you kids growing up. You're right. So what? I was too busy to fuss, was always at the end of my rope, and I've come to think that not worrying was my greatest triumph. I never denied you kids the experience of pulling yourselves up with your own strength and holding tight to this life with your own claws. I had faith in you, because I knew you could be strong and would thrive against the odds. And look at you now, winning that big college teaching award, traveling to places like New Orleans and California that I only read about in murder mysteries from the library. You've got more than anybody else has got around here, but you still worry an old thing that got done to you worse than a dog worries a bone. A couple of nights of trouble makes your whole life bitter.

If only you'd seen what I've seen! A man drinking a pint of ginger brandy and then refusing to get out of the way of a train, holding out his arms like greeting an old friend. I've seen a little bitty man tell his little bitty wife she could go to hell and take her there himself. I saw my own mama die in the Kalamazoo Asylum for the Insane. One night a stranger put a knife to my throat and cursed me while he took me from behind like a bitch in the gravel lot behind the Lamplighter. I've seen fool men risk their lives to rescue mewling kittens just like the kittens I've drowned in gunnysacks, and I've seen all six of my kids grow up strong and get fat in middle age. What I've never seen is a man who loved me enough. A man who loved me enough would have taken me with him.

When I was a blond-headed, blue-eyed girl, before your grandpa drowned himself under a mountain of corn in his own grain bin, he taught me about the worn soil, the way this stretch of the clay earth breaks into hard clumps to allow entry of seed, and the way rain can soften soil or wash it away. He shot coyotes, raccoons, left me with a shovel to bury them. I fattened his veal calves for slaughter. My mama couldn't stand the work of the farm, especially not the slaughter. After a while she couldn't stand anything, and then your grandpa sent her away. I used to be afraid I'd end up in the nuthouse too, was afraid your grandpa would send me there if I didn't work hard. Later I was afraid your daddy would commit me, because I never knew the end of the powers a man had over his woman.

You can always find pain and suffering in this life, but why look for it? Before you went to college and got them degrees I had no idea there was something called women's studies that would teach you to poke around under the skin of women. Don't you know we need our skin to cover what's underneath, to protect us from the burn of air and sunlight? Women get themselves hurt every day—men mess with girls in this life, they always have, always will—but there's no sense making hard luck and misery your life's work.

YOU SITTING BESIDE me, holding my hand and showing me old black-and-white photos of the farm, that's nice, and I don't know if we ever held hands even when you were little. The spring after you were born, when I had no choice but to go out and plow, that's when I tied you in your crib by a wrist and an ankle—it was to keep you safe, not to make you a prisoner like your daddy told you. Since you were my first, I didn't know yet how children could take care of themselves. My own ma didn't teach me what to do with something so helpless as you seemed. She fed me from a bottle, so I figured out breast-feeding from our milk cow, and each time I turned the tractor so this old two-story house came into view, my breasts ached. One time when I was out there, a tornado turned our big wooden barn into a dance of planks and loose hay. As I watched and prayed, strands of my own hair whipped my face. Now I'd give anything to be in that field, the wind in my face, looking at this house from the outside again.

The doctor said for me to let you cry when I first brought you home from the hospital, but I couldn't stand knowing I was the only answer to all your troubles. When you gazed up at me in them days, I never had the luxury of looking back at you—I had to keep my eyes on the horizon, to watch out for what was coming next. When you were three days old, I warmed up rice cereal and cow's milk, and you swallowed a whole damned bowl. At four days you ate half a mashed banana—nobody believed me how hungry you were.

You like that photo of them spotted horses? You must've been what, five years old when your daddy brought them home? They showed up snorting smoke and fire, wrapped in strands of barbed wire to keep them contained in that tin-can trailer, and we rode them nearly to death to break them. And still your daddy came to bed drunk, stinking of the young Mrs. Wickman. I never thought your daddy and I would tame them spotted horses. Some nights while you children slept, I slipped into the frozen pasture and whispered to the horses to forget their lessons, to fight their bits and bridles, so we'd have to keep on.

Your daddy gave you babies liquor, not me. He poured it, burning, into your tender mouths when you cried and kept him awake—men did what they did back then, and there was no stopping him. You complain about the way I raised you children, but I only wanted to survive another day. You see me as powerful in my crimes, but I was bone tired. Yes, I raised my babies, but today I'd crawl on hands and knees away from the responsibility of them needful creatures. Your brothers bring my great-grandkids to my bedside, and I close my eyes.

I heard you whispering with the redhead nurse: *This is the first time in her life she's had nothing to say.* Fine. If you want to spoil what's left of my life, why don't you just go ahead and yank out my oxygen tubes? Or better yet, let's set this place on fire and get it over with. I've always loved a flame burning wild, and if I went out in a blaze, you'd have a story to tell. If I could lift that hatchet, I'd help you chop kindling for the job. I wouldn't flinch, not even if the hatchet wobbled and came down on my hand.

YOU COMPLAIN THAT I let men around here beat my children. *With sticks and belts*, you said, but mostly the men just smacked you kids when you said something smart or did something stupid. As I saw it, those men were just picking up where your daddy left off. He would have kicked your asses plenty if he'd been around. How was I supposed to figure out by myself when you children needed beating? How was I supposed to have the energy to beat you? And when you ran away from home—from Bill Theroux, like you said—I guess you left the whippings to your little brothers. And when you went away to college, you abandoned all of us. Of course I was proud of you going to college. Any mother would be. I didn't think it needed saying.

All the men added together made the solid world—they were the marbles in the jar, and women were whatever sand or water or air claimed the space left between them. That's how I saw things as a young woman, that was my *women's studies*. Now

I've come to know that women are like vodka poured over men, who melt away like ice cubes.

It was a man who broke my nose, bent it like it is now. I let you kids think that big paint gelding had kicked me again. Patchy Pete was that horse's name, black-and-white like a Holstein cow. I bought him for two hundred dollars and ended up selling him for two hundred after a year of getting kicked and bitten and thrown. I would've dressed him out for dog food or fed him to you kids if he hadn't been so gorgeous, but a good-looking horse like a good-looking man can always find a place in somebody's stable, however bad his behavior. Men climbed into my bed after they fenced my pasture, after they messed with the furnace and changed the oil in my Chevy truck and Ford tractor. They climbed into my bed after their wives threw them out. We needed their help—there was so much work to do around here—and mostly they were nice. I'm still alive, if barely, and a lot of angry wives are long dead, including Bill Theroux's wife, who wore herself out bitching about me, if you want the truth of it.

When I was a teenager, my friend Julia said one day, *We got to look pretty.* I shaved my legs for the first time, and it took a long while to stop the bleeding. Us and two other friends got hold of a six-pack, though we didn't like the taste of beer. We carried the bottles to where some men lived and reclined on their couch, ankles crossed. We didn't know how to talk to men, so we just smiled, and silence hung above the bag of pretzels they brought out until the men started to laugh, until we laughed with them. They were older and muscular and smelled of smoke and solvents from the repair shops where they worked. One man had a glass eye, said he'd been shot. When he popped it out, we were all possessed by a powerful desire to hold the blind thing in our hands. Julia touched it first and passed it around. She got pregnant right away, and the rest of us followed, and for a lot of years we raised our children, fed our husbands, worked hard at low-paying jobs or at jobs that didn't pay at all, and learned just how tired a body could be. Those men took me by surprise, but I never looked back, never stopped singing love songs, never longed for a time before men.

Men's machines still sing to me: revving chain saw, motorboat, log splitter, rototiller, leaf blower, generator humming, cordless drill, rattletrap tractor, power washer, hedge trimmer, biting grinder. Motorcycles with mufflers torn off, diesel trucks chugging in the driveway. You remember those men who came to me after a fishing trip up north and filled my wringer washer with smelt? *Come out with us and play*, men used to call, like tomcats, and out I went. That old wringer washer was never the same after all them fish. The men who came around never passed up an easy target, so they killed all the rabbits. I meant to sew a blanket from the soft skins to replace my own skin, which I imagined wadded up under the bed in my room, smeared with menstrual blood, stiff with sperm, stretched by pregnancy. For years, I'd warmed myself in the borrowed skins of men. I was good at cutting pelts from flesh, muscle from bone.

After partying all night, a passed-out man might resemble a great cut of meat in my bed, or on the couch or floor, leathery bronze shoulders and a fish-white behind. Men inhaled great swaths of oxygen, exhaled smoke and sweat, so sometimes I could scarcely catch my breath. I remember finding you and your brothers fishing through a man's wallet like grubby elves. *Shoo, shoo*, I said, and the men slept on. After your daddy left, I tried to raise you to know men and to not fear them, so you wouldn't be taken by surprise. I figured that if any of them bothered you, you would make a fuss, the way you made a fuss when I wanted you to get out of bed early and haul buckets of water from the creek when the pipes froze. Of course you were scared of your daddy—he was a fearsome man, and he scared me, too—but you could've whined and glared at them other men the way you did at your poor worn-out ma who tried to feed and clothe you with no money. How was I supposed to know there was trouble with the way they pulled you onto their laps if you never told me you didn't like it? It seemed like you were having fun when they said how pretty you were. You never were the kind of kid who smiled, so I couldn't tell.

STRANGE TO THINK, watching you wash my dishes, I'll never stand there at that sink again, never put my old hands in warm soapy water. I always sang old songs as I looked out the window over the septic tank, over the clotheslines and creek. I used to try to get you to sing along about dying for love or waiting for a soldier to return from the war, but you shook your curly head—I guess you never believed in them folk songs, how a man's love was going to be the reward for the hardships of a woman's life. After the autumn leaves fell, I saw all the way to the pond, and sometimes when I washed dishes late into the night, I could see past the edge of this property to the rest of the galaxy. I've washed thousands of cast-iron pans, a million quart-size canning jars, some of them made of pretty blue-green glass that glowed like moonlight. My back ached sometimes from lugging hay bales and bags of grain, but once I got started, I never rested until I finished, until every dish was washed.

Haven't had a clothes dryer since mine broke in 1972, so I've hung my clothes on the line in all seasons. In winter they freeze-dried, in spring they smelled of pond thaw, and sometimes in summer I'd find them streaked with bird shit. When this farm was thriving, when I was thriving, I used to dress out chickens, used to wire their feet to the clothesline and slit their throats. You thought me hardhearted, but you ate the meat, same as your brothers. Where the blood drained, wildflowers grew, red trillium, ghostly Indian pipes.

Old Mama Cat and I lost our teeth about the same time. She was a purring pile of bones, and soon she'd have found a secret place to die, some bed of moss or pine needles along the creek, but the Mattimores' pit bull broke her neck. We buried her out there as deep as the frozen ground allowed, and that night your brothers shot the dog and dragged his carcass, half as heavy as a grown man's, out into the field for the coyotes. Your brothers dug me a new well the next year, on the quiet so I didn't have to get a permit. Some women might be happy with daughters, but there's a reason every place in the world the folks cry out for sons.

No reason I should be thinking about that old Mama Cat now, but I remember how she suffered with a new litter every spring, and another in summer before the swelling was even off her teats, something like me having six kids in six years. And I understood why she wanted to go back outside when them tomcats yowled for her. You think I ought to regret drowning all them kittens, but I'd made no promises to the damned kittens.

My pillows are fine, so stop messing. You're so keen to wash my dishes and fuss with my pillows and morphine pump now, but where were you this summer when the vegetables in my garden shriveled? I haven't been able to drag a hose or lift a bucket since July. In good years I hooked up the old beer fridge for the overflow of zucchini and cucumbers. Bad years, like this one, I could only watch every damned thing fail to thrive. Where were you this spring when rain was falling through the roof of the chicken coop? Your brother Jack said I should take down the whole building before it collapsed, build a new one. I told him to patch the roof, *it only has to outlast me*. He poked his knuckle through the soft bluish wood of the ceiling to prove me a fool. Balanced on my walking stick, I told him I was leaving the farm to you so you'd sell it. He slammed his truck door and spun his tires in the driveway.

OF COURSE I fed you kids PBB, but it wasn't on purpose. It wasn't me who mixed that fireproof powder into the cattle feed at the Farm Bureau and poisoned half the county. Nobody knew why cows were dying, and I couldn't throw away fresh milk from my beautiful Daisy when I had kids to feed. Poison filtered through four stomachs could hardly be poison anymore, could it? Daisy stopped eating just before cancer sprang her eyeball from its socket, before cancer filled her like pink foam. Do you remember that loyal cow, waiting for me in the paddock, plodding to her stall to be milked? Years later, when I had cancer the first time, I plodded to my surgery, my radiation, swallowed my chemotherapy.

Women like me couldn't afford to keep themselves pure like you girls do now. We inhaled gunpowder, spray paint, aerosol wasp killer, smoke from everything that burned. We transported fireworks from Indiana that blew off fingers and stood barefoot in puddles of used motor oil dumped in our driveways. And to clean and soothe our aches and wounds, we went down to the swamp to lie with fish and snakes and bloodsuckers, every slithery thing. The waters barely flowed, silt became slime because of the waste from upstream, and we sank deep into the muck beside the snapping turtles. We didn't complain about our discomforts because we saw men head down into the man-killing mines, into flammable, smothering grain bins, up onto scaffolding without any safety harness. We saw men crushed under tipped tractors, their arms and legs amputated by augers and cardboard-cutting machines. Men fought over them jobs, so how could we begrudge the men our bodies? Or whatever they asked for?

Men put asbestos insulation in the attic to keep us warm, they drove trucks that sprayed a fog of DDT to kill mosquitoes before they could infect us with the ague—as kids we chased them trucks through the mist, shrieking with joy. Lead paint's against the law now, but it used to stay on walls forever before latex came along to fade and peel. And for crying out loud, nobody told your little brothers to chew the old paint off the windowsills. You say my house is like the house finch nest, a tangle of plastic bits and cigarette butts, Styrofoam and fiberglass, and old green Easter grass. You say an albatross soars like an angel a thousand miles to retrieve bottle caps and syringes and fishing line to feed her young, but I wandered only a few hundred yards to the henhouse for eggs, to the barn for fresh milk, to the garden for vine-ripe tomatoes grown in manure.

I fed all you kids on the tomatoes and string beans I grew and canned and on the meat men gave me: venison, elk, moose that got hit by a truck, even bear they'd shot in garbage dumps up north. They say bear is gamy, but I figured bear tastes how a man would taste. Bears, like pigs, like men, carry disease, so I ground up the meat and yellow fat and cooked the hell out of it, added my high-acid tomatoes and garden potatoes and onions to make goulash and spaghetti sauce and Spanish rice. That's what I fed my children, and you always held out your plate for another helping.

THE SURGERY TO remove my first cancer was nothing. Such a fuss they made over a tumor the size of a pinto bean! *I didn't see your face behind the mask*, I told the doctor as I came out from under the drugs. *I wouldn't recognize you in a lineup of men wielding knives*. With morphine, it's sometimes hard to untangle what's happened. *I hope I didn't contract a virus while I was lying there open*, I told one of the men, my husband or the cancer surgeon or my rapist. My insides exposed like that, I might have caught something that turned into the cancer that's killing me now. *Do not move during radiation treatment*, men in masks told me. *Lie still with your eyes closed*. You say that when Bill Theroux stood in the doorway to your room, you closed your eyes and lay still, and you never opened them until he left. But you say he didn't have sex with you, so what's the big deal? I was raped behind the Lamplighter, but I had better things to do than get bent out of shape about ten minutes of my life. I didn't want to testify in court about my private business, and I didn't want my name in the *Gazette*. Your daddy got all pumped up, promised me, *I'll find the guy myself and kill him*, but, far as I know, he didn't even look.

Did I ever tell you the trouble they had finding my appendix? During my first surgery, the doctors, dogged in their masks, kept chasing that traveling organ, dragged my body like a river, and finally hauled it out of me. They made a mess of my belly and then stapled me back together—they might as well have wrapped me in barbed wire like them old spotted horses. I'll show you the scars. None of my busted ribs left scars. Neither did my rape. No scars from bringing six children into the world, and if there was great pain in giving birth, I don't remember it, and you can tell people that. I've got a tattoo above where my cervix used to be—that's how the cancer doctors mark you. Don't feel sorry for me, Sis. My rapist's surely dead and gone by now, and that old surgeon, too. The radiation treatments for the cancer warmed me up inside, gave me a new lease on life. That's what I said back then, and that's the story I'm sticking to.

PEOPLE SAW YOUR picture in the *Gazette* after you got that big award for teaching at your college, for going above and beyond, it said. The lady from the newspaper called the house, and I was tempted to tell her about the night you were born, how I poured myself a pint jar of homemade wine to calm my nerves and then headed up to the hospital where they shot my spine full of dope, how I then spit you out like a watermelon seed, no trouble at all. Of course, I told the newspaper lady I was proud. What mother wouldn't be proud? You win awards and make a career, but you can't let it go after fifty years that Bill Theroux went into your bedroom and I didn't stop him. You admit he just kissed you and put his hands on you, okay, *all over you*, nothing more. The man is dead and gone, for crying out loud, and pretty soon I'll be dead, and you'll wake up and realize you've got your fist clenched around nothing.

You're a middle-aged woman, too old to hold onto a child-hood grudge. I always told you I didn't remember him going in your room, but I did know, and I've been lying here for a long time deciding there's no sense my taking the truth to the grave. And if we've all got to spill our ugly feelings in this life, you ought to know I was mad as hell about it. What did you, a kid, have to offer that man? I had a steak to cook for him. I could lis-

ten to his stories, tell him my own. When he played the guitar,
I sang along. He played beautifully, and singing along with him
was like floating on a cool lake in hot summer after a long day's
work. *I think I'll go teach your daughter how to French kiss*, Bill
Theroux said to me one time, the first time, I guess. *Is that okay?*
he said. *Ask her*, I said, and under my breath, *you son of a bitch*.
I kept my back turned, but I heard the stairs creak under him.
I washed dishes waiting for him to return, playing records and
singing along about women drowned by their lovers and snow-
white doves nesting on girls' graves. I thought his wanting to
kiss you was one more test, one more hardship I had to endure.
Maybe I lied to you all these years because the thing was a confusion to me. But you got it wrong, Sis, when you said I didn't
care what a man did to you. I didn't like it, and I've been lying
here racking my brain about it. Maybe it was the way he asked,
so casual, like it was an ordinary thing, like, can I borrow your
truck? Maybe that was why I couldn't say no. Maybe I thought
it would've been selfish to say, *Hell, no, you can't kiss my eleven-
year-old daughter*. So I left it to you. At eleven you knew how to
chop wood, start a fire in the stove, milk the cow, and strain
the milk into bottles and make butter out of the extra cream.
You could get your little brothers dressed for school. Surely you
could tell a man to leave you alone if that's what you wanted. I
waited in the kitchen, hungry, with the raw steaks, a cribbage
board, singing out my sadness—you say you heard my voice
upstairs while he did what he did. I waited for you to send him
away, to send him back to me.

He was the handsomest man I ever knew, looked like Robert Redford, and with such beautiful hands. And you were so
pretty then, with your curly blond hair like mine used to be.
When he told me he thought you were beautiful, I thought how
that used to be my hair, my freckled face. A girl has to learn

a little about men somehow, better just a kiss from a man you knew than all at once with a near stranger like it went with me. You didn't run away from home after the first time. I figured you must've wanted him in there. And when you finally did run away, did that solve your troubles?

You can't possibly understand, Sis, can you, with your women's power and women's rights, how I couldn't say, *Hell, no, you can't kiss my daughter*? It's strange to imagine them words coming out of my mouth, even now. Theroux was the most elegant man I knew—made your daddy seem like a farmhand—and I loved him as much as I'd ever loved your daddy, and he worked hard tending bar, sometimes sixty hours a week, and he could have gone back to his wife anytime—and when you ran off, he did go back to her.

You should've had a daughter of your own. That would've been a bone for you to chew on all your life. I guarantee, though, you wouldn't win any award for raising a daughter. Hell, if you had a daughter, she'd probably admire me more than you ever could, for my toughness and the way I like to laugh and party, for the way I've never given up, for my knowing how to break horses and grow vegetables and bale hay, and the way I overlook nonsense and small troubles. If you'd had a daughter, you'd be more forgiving of what people do. You think I've failed you, Sis? Well, my ma failed me, too. She let herself get locked in the nuthouse. And you would've failed your own daughter if you had one. That's women's studies.

AFTER YOU RAN away, I told Bill Theroux how you weren't really gone, how you must be sleeping in the barn or the tree house, how you came in for food and to use the shower. He searched for you in all the soft secret places, but you were too clever to choose comfort. You didn't help us with the hay or the garden that summer. Bill came to see me over the years, brought his guitar, but he would never again leave his wife. He always asked how you were doing, was glad to hear you graduated, glad when you got to be a professor, and the way he cared about you hurt me a little every time—he should've regretted what he'd done, driving you away. Twenty-some years later, after his wife died, he came to me with his raw loneliness, and I took him in. I thought I'd already paid the price for his company, so I was damn well going to have it.

After we buried Bill next to his wife four years ago, I went down by the Kalamazoo River, watched the fishermen troll for suckers and carp and drink from paper bags. I carried my own paper bag and sat watching the moon, its reflection in the water as blue as one of my old canning jars. Beneath the willows and white pines, the moss and needles made a soft mattress. I thought I might curl up and die, figuring he was the last man who would love me, but mosquitoes bit me, crayfish pinched me. Men baited hooks with crickets and listened to my singing. Over and over, I sang that song that used to make you cover your ears, where the woman visits her lover's grave wearing a long black veil. We all spent the night together, and in the morning when I was still alive, I realized my life was exactly what it had been, nothing more, nothing less.

That redhead nurse reminds me of one of them angry wives from my younger days. The way she turns me over and jerks the sheet out from under, she's going to break another rib. When I could speak, I charmed the hospice folks, told them I've always lived in this house my daddy built, told them about my garden brimming with tomatoes, my beautiful chickens laying blue-green eggs. I didn't say how I killed raccoons who came after my laying hens, how I drowned the kittens that would suck my Mama Cat dry, how I chose my allies as best I could. I wasted so much time talking to all them. When I had a voice, I didn't know how much I wanted to say to you, Sis, to explain that I lived my life the way I could, and that I couldn't say no to some things.

AND NOW YOU'RE here, going through my personal things, the gifts men gave me, the photos of my favorite horses, walking past me like I'm a wadded-up blanket. I wasn't an affectionate mother, that much is true, but now I like it when you hold my hand—though each time you touch me I'm a little afraid you're going to hit me. Maybe when I die you'll toss me out for the crows. A casket seems like a waste. Better you and your brothers dig a hole, wrap me in a sheet, and bury me under my trees, trees I raised by letting them alone. Bury me beside the graves of my horses and old Daisy, the parts of her we couldn't eat because of the cancer. Bury me with one of Mama Cat's teeth and a write-up of the last Pap smear before my cervix dissolved in the radiation. Bury me at the crossroads so my spirit can travel, so even in death I won't be forced to rest or grow mossy. Every one of you children was born at the crossroads, because every woman giving birth becomes a crossroads. Like they say in the song, a crossroads is a place that's *neither here nor there*. With your critical comments, you're hanging my corpse out on the hanging tree for folks to despise, but no daughter wants to leave her ma that way. I hated my poor mama's weakness and foolishness, but now I long for her, to hear her out just one time.

Someday, I hope, you'll want to cut me down and gather me up in your arms, forgive me even if I can't say I'm sorry.

The most important thing is that you make my funeral a real bash. Promise you won't spoil the fun. Let my own stories get told one more time before telling your stories, before letting your river of criticism flow around my corpse. Protect me, Sis, hide the photos of me as an old woman. We'll need a dozen strong men there in attendance to roar with laughter. All the men who've loved me are gone, but maybe you can pay for some extra men, big strong ones, the way some folks in the old days paid for women to wail and moan and grieve. While they carry away this body that I have used all up, play the old song I used to sing while I washed dishes and made wine, the one about the golden bird who loves the sun so much that she forgets to eat or drink, forgets to protect her eggs or her nest. I have always loved that song about the bird, how she looks up to the sky from her thorny tree and sings her heart out every day, all day, that bird who sings herself to death.

My Sister Is in Pain

Unbearable pain when she gets up in the morning to go to work, pain when she goes to bed at night; when she sleeps, she sleeps in pain and wakes up again in pain and dresses in her stretch-waist pants and bright, complicated sweaters, heats up meals from packages, substitutes low-fat margarine for butter, sucralose for sugar, and smokes cigarettes in pain on her porch, while squirrels scramble like idiots up trees, and cars without mufflers vomit smoke and clatter through this neighborhood of potholes and broken windows, where kids steal anything to sell for money to buy meth. Her doctors shrug in their lab coats, send her to specialists who throw up their arms. Pain like airplanes with their airplane engine noise, flying over and messing up the sky. Pain like dishes in the sink—not just her own dishes, but dishes of strangers who've left them there for days, in cold, gray water. She is our mother's daughter, but we don't know who she is or what her pain could mean, her cicadas of pain on summer nights, the jolts in her spine like flashes of red-hot fireflies, pain that radiates from her intestines like the shocks of electric eels. Stabbing pain sixty hours a week as she bathes and medicates and feeds and tends to the needs and the pain of others for minimum wage, throbbing pain when she has a day off. She was born more beautiful than the rest of us and called out more loudly from her crib, cried in her bed, and outside in the woods she wailed—she never said what those boys did to her beside the creek. Imagine a long corridor with hundreds of rooms all closed against pain; she walks down the corridor and her pain does not diminish. Whether or not she stops and knocks on any door, whether or not anyone invites her in for a cool drink, whether or not one of the people who invites her in for a cool drink is myself, still her pain does not diminish. We rarely call her, are polite at Christmas, give tentative embraces, compliment her sweaters, her beads, her hair bows. We nod when she explains about her special shoes, her Copper Wear as seen on TV. The gifts she brings us are elaborately wrapped. We untie the ribbons in terror.

A Multitude of Sins

According to the abdominal CT scans, the tumor was the size and shape of a beef tongue, but perhaps the edges would be discrete, perhaps the surgeons could yank the cancer from Carl Betcher's gut the way a cook pulled meat from a broiler. The surgical team opened him up, raised their eyebrows at the thousands of filaments spun around his organs, and then closed him quickly. In lighter moments, the doctors refer to this process as a *cut and shut*. They sent him home to die, not even bothering to remove his belly fat the way they sometimes did for a man.

"Keep him comfortable," the hospice nurse told the wife, who stationed her husband's hospital bed in the living room in front of the TV and bought a case of Ensure high-calorie nutritional drink. She'd never lived alone, not for a single day. She'd married Carl at age sixteen, moved away from home, and had gradually lost touch with her family, had not even seen her sister Joan in decades, until Joan moved back from California four years ago; even then they'd mostly spoken on the phone because Carl didn't like her coming to the house. They'd had a son, Carl Jr., but Carl Sr. had fought with the boy from the get-go and kicked him out for good when he was still a teenager. That was twenty years ago, and since then Mary Betcher called her son secretly every month. He was living in Florida now, staying in a big house with some people, and he swore never to come back to Michigan while his father was alive.

"Give him something to drink if he wants it," said the nurse, a tall, reassuring black man, after installing the morphine drip. "Don't force him to eat, though. He'll spend his last few days here with you, in the comfort of his own home."

Carl's wife had been losing weight herself, and she figured she could take the rest of the Ensure if Carl died before it was gone.

She would continue operating her husband's upholstery and fabric repair business that they ran out of their attached garage and pole building. She learned through Carl's caseworker that she and Carl had not paid into Social Security, so she would get no benefits after his death. She'd have to work harder than ever to make it alone. It felt strange at first to go out to the shop without her husband, beside whom she had worked, eaten, and slept for more than forty years, but it felt more natural with every day, and she enjoyed deciding for herself which project to work on from among the jobs she'd listed on the chalkboard. Each time she came back into the house, she opened a can of Ensure, put the straw to Carl's lips, and watched him drink down the whole thing. Six cans a day he drank. Each of the half dozen visiting hospice nurses was surprised in turn. She didn't tell the nurses what Carl said, how he cursed her from his bed, called her names, struck her sometimes when the can was empty, or while she changed his diaper or the sheets. He'd cursed her occasionally before the surgery, but since he'd been home, whenever they were alone, it was a constant stream. Not only did he not die like they said he would, but he didn't seem to be grow-ing weaker.

"You dumb cunt," he said one morning in his delirium. He never looked right at her—she wasn't even sure he could actu-ally see her—but spoke into the air, as though his words were for a larger audience. She was bending close to him when his hand whipped out and stung her lips. He had hit her every day since he came home from the hospital, but this was the first time it hurt. She was tired from working from morning until night, and maybe that was why she smacked him hard without thinking. She'd never hit her husband, or anyone, and her heart rushed as her arm arced out in a motion like beginning to swim or fly, and it felt so good that she smacked him again, harder, and a third time. Carl's eyes opened wide and he grasped at air with his open hand before slipping back into his morphine daze. That night when she bathed him, she noticed a bruise had formed above his wrist, and in the morning she tugged her hus-band's pajama sleeve down over it, covering it as she had cov-ered her own bruises over the years.

"You're doing a beautiful job of caring for your husband," said a big white lady nurse a few days later. "He seems a little stronger than the last time I was here."

On Monday of the third week, Mrs. Betcher was adminis-tering the first Ensure of the day, still in her nightgown, and Carl grabbed her breast and squeezed. She begged him to let go and tried to pull away, but he held on. Finally she was able to grab a spoon, and she stabbed him in the leg with the han-dle, stabbed him again and again until he let loose. Then she stabbed him a final time, hard enough that she knew a welt would form on his thigh.

"How does that feel?" she asked. Her voice quavered. "You should know how it feels, Carl."

"Whore. Bitch whore," Carl Betcher said in a voice deeper than his voice had been in life.

"You are going to hell," she whispered, and her heart thrummed. She'd never dreamed she'd say this aloud to him, though she'd thought it plenty.

"Nigger bitch," Carl Betcher said to the air around him. He'd started calling her the *n*-word about ten years ago, when her sister sent a copy of an old portrait she found of their paternal grandfather and dark-skinned grandmother.

"I'm not a whore, Carl. And your son, he's not a bastard and he's not stupid. You're the one who's stupid. And mean." There, she'd said it, and her heart soared a little.

The shaking in her hands went away after an hour or so, but it came back when she called her son that evening.

"I miss you, Junior."

"I miss you, too, Ma."

"I should have helped you more when you were little," she said. "I shouldn't have let him do those things to you." Mrs. Betcher wondered if her son still had marks to remind him of his father.

"It's okay, Ma. But I won't come home until he's dead."

"The nurses keep saying he won't last much longer."

"Call me for the funeral, Ma, so I can come home and spit on his grave."

She felt a warmth in her chest as she hung up the phone, the warmth she'd always felt at hearing him criticize his father when she hadn't been able to do it herself.

Their lives had not been all bad, but Carl Jr. seemed not to remember his dad ever being funny or loving as he had sometimes been. Didn't remember the pleasant dinners at the round kitchen table, or how fond his dad had been of him sometimes, when they'd played quietly together with a train set or with

Legos. She didn't blame Carl Jr. Nowadays the ugly things were what Mrs. Betcher remembered, too, and maybe that was why she didn't regret hitting her husband.

She microwaved a Salisbury steak from the freezer, forced herself to eat half of it, though it tasted like mud, and put the rest in the refrigerator in a little plastic container.

She expected to feel bad for saying Carl was going to hell. She even sensed that her husband was waiting for an apology. But the most she could bring herself to do was try to warm his feet, which were cold because she had to turn down the furnace at night to save propane. She situated the electric space heater on a chair near the end of the hospital bed.

In the morning, Carl Betcher said, "I'm hot." His feet were uncovered, and he was rubbing them against each other. When she didn't speak, he said, "Am I going to hell? My mama and the minister warned me. Woman? Who's there?"

She didn't turn off the space heater right away, but stood a few yards away and watched his agitated rubbing. She felt invisible, like an old fairy-tale witch hidden inside a dark cloak. When she finally came close and felt the hot bottoms of his feet, he kicked at her. He hadn't mentioned his mother in years, and he'd never mentioned a minister.

"Where's my nigger wife?" he asked, and still she said nothing.

When a car pulled into the driveway, she finally turned the heater off. It was the big white lady nurse, and this time she had an assistant with her, a skinny child of a woman who nodded sympathetically at everything everybody said. Before leaving, the child-woman said in a squeaky voice, "You're an incredible person, Mrs. Betcher, to care for your husband this way."

Though the girl sounded as phony as a greeting card, Mrs. Betcher let the words thrill her. Nobody had ever told her she was an incredible person. As a girl she'd tried to be a good per-

112   BONNIE JO CAMPBELL

son and a good Christian. After she got married, she'd tried to honor her vows to be a good wife and a hard worker in the business that sustained them, and she'd prayed for strength and wisdom, but she'd often felt slow and dumb, and she'd learned the best response to any of Carl's fits of meanness had been to ride it out, to get through it in one piece and then hope it would be a while before the next one. She knew the importance of forgiveness, how it was as much for the giver as for the receiver, so even when he didn't ask for forgiveness, she'd always said, "Carl, I forgive you." That had made her feel better, and sometimes it had even silenced him. Mrs. Betcher had coped with life's difficulties, had sometimes thought she was good enough, but she had never considered she might be *incredible*.

That afternoon, she turned the space heater back on, put it a little closer to her husband's bed, and uncovered his feet to give him another taste of fire. She returned to work in the shop with an alertness she hadn't felt for a long time, maybe not since she'd swum in the gravel pit with her sister Joan as a kid, when she slipped into that clear, cool water on a burning-hot day. She opened the window curtains in the back to allow sunlight onto the sewing machines. Carl's idea that opening the curtains would encourage break-ins never had made sense; more likely, when thieves saw how little of value there was inside, they wouldn't bother.

A Volvo station wagon pulled up in front of the shop door, and a slender man with pale skin and black hair got out. Mrs. Betcher greeted the new customer with a smile, as she had always done. She held open the door for the man and two teenage boys, the three of whom struggled to hold up a great swath of fabric.

"This is a theater curtain," said the man, who lugged one

end of the thing onto the counter and explained he was from a community playhouse downtown. "It's irreplaceable, but some actors were practicing with swords for a Shakespeare play and sliced it." She saw the old thing had long been coming unstitched at the seams and that there were two gashes in the crimson fabric.

"This isn't the kind of thing we do here," Mrs. Betcher said. She and Carl had always turned away such projects, which were guaranteed to require more hours of work than a customer would want to pay for.

"You're our only hope, Mrs. Betcher," he said and grinned. All his body movements were fluid, and she wondered what kinds of things he did on the stage, what kinds of people he pretended to be. She stroked the velvet fabric on the counter, and she found she didn't want to take her hand off it. She'd felt velvet before, but never anything like this, so heavy and plush. If she were ever onstage, she'd want to be behind such a curtain as this. Of course, her being on stage was a crazy thought.

"If you can't fix it, I don't know what we'll do." The man grinned again, in a way that seemed at odds with his supposed helplessness.

"Let me give it a try, then," she said. She wanted to have this material in the shop. She didn't even want to bargain for a reasonable price—bargaining would feel too much like arguing. "It's going to be a couple of weeks. My husband is sick, and the work has piled up." She directed the three to carry the heap, which must've weighed a hundred pounds, onto a low table in the back of the big garage.

"Thanks, Mrs. Betcher. If you can do this, you'll be our savior. Our show opens in six weeks," the man said before he left with the boys.

Before they got in the station wagon, the man cuffed the head of one of the boys in a friendly way. *Our savior*, she thought. *Incredible.*

"My feet are burning," Betcher said at dinnertime. He sounded more delirious than before, but he drank an entire strawberry Ensure. She'd bought it because it was her own favorite flavor of ice cream, and she hadn't had it for years.

"Am I walking the devil's path into hell fires?"

"Take some water, Carl," she said. The heater on low wasn't going to hurt him.

"Whore of Babylon," he said.

She gave him more water right before she went to bed. Then she stood back and studied her husband's body, stretched out, looking smaller than before, almost harmless.

She turned the heater to high.

"I'm walking in Satan's fires," he said the next day at noon, between gulps of his drink. "Listen to me, whore!"

"Am I a whore?" she asked. She pulled the straw away and let him suck at the air.

"God shall permit Satan to fall upon the wicked and seize them as his own," he said in a slow, thin voice. "A whore is a deep ditch."

"I want you to take it back once and for all, for all the times you've called me that." She had never before argued with the word, figuring that any arguing would just draw out the ugliness.

"God loves me," he said, "despite my multitude of sins."

"Multitude of sins is right. Say I'm not a whore. Say it!" Her voice raised this way sounded shrill, unfamiliar.

"Not a whore," he said and sighed.

Mrs. Betcher had never heard him sound regretful or resigned before this, and she liked it. She turned on the television to a rebroadcast of *Oprah*, a show she'd never watched before Carl was dying. She let the confident, positive voices fill the living room while she picked at her lunch, a piece of sandwich bread with margarine, a scoop of tuna salad with relish and mayonnaise her sister had made for her, and a peach half from a can. She glanced over at her husband, who was moving his head side to side as though in pain or ecstasy. Seeing her husband weak should have made her want to forgive him— she had always wished she could protect weak people and animals—but instead she was feeling renewed anger, a delicious angry heat that flowed all through her and gave her strength. She should've been ashamed that she was causing her husband pain, but instead she just felt mad at him, and a little mad at herself for never speaking out against him. When her husband whipped their son hard enough to raise welts for wetting his bed, she should have marched into the street and shouted to the neighbors what he'd done. Instead she had only worked to calm Carl down by cooking him bacon and eggs and going out to the shop to work as usual, leaving Carl Jr. crying in his room. If Carl Sr. was in the shop with her, she'd figured, he wouldn't be able to punish Carl Jr. for whimpering.

At the memory of her son crying, she now threw her fork at Carl Betcher. When it bounced off the bed rail onto the carpet, she threw the plate of tuna salad and the bowl with a peach, too, but they hit the mattress and bounced gently to the carpet. Because throwing felt so good, she tossed the salt and pepper and sugar and a saucepan that was on the stove, and those landed on his torso and stayed there on the bed. She picked up the scoop of tuna salad off the floor and smashed it with her open hand on his chest, and then washed her hands and went out into the shop; she had plenty of good-paying work, but instead she put down some craft paper and unfurled the deep red velvet curtain across the floor. She tuned the radio away from AM talk, where it had always been, to FM classical from the university and studied the old seams.

That Sunday, she went to her sister Joan's church, shook the minister's cool hand, and prayed and listened alongside the others. Joan claimed to be praying for Carl's *poor withered soul*, but Mrs. Betcher prayed mostly for her son to come back. She wanted to see his face, hold his thin body in her arms. Her son was a gentle person, though often rash and not terribly smart. He was not the sort of person who should be removing asbestos from buildings, but that was what he was doing. She let Joan and the minister assume she was praying for her husband to be free from pain, but really she wished for her husband's suffering to increase until he confessed to his crimes, until he begged her for forgiveness.

In the fifth week, the skin on Carl's feet tightened and reddened and turned shiny. When she called her son that night, she started crying as soon as he answered, and he tried to comfort her. "Ma, don't worry. I won't spit on his grave like I said. I wouldn't hurt you like that."

Why not *spit on his grave?* she wanted to ask, but she said, "I'm sorry, Junior. I'm just feeling the strain."

"Maybe Dad just got screwed up in Vietnam," he said later in the conversation. "Maybe that's why he was how he was. I work with a guy whose dad killed himself after coming home. Do you know where Dad was stationed?"

She said she had to go out to the shop and hung up the phone. She was not looking for excuses for the man.

In the sixth week, five weeks after Carl was supposed to die, the hospice nurse who had come the first day, the tall black man, seemed surprised. He checked Carl's pulse and blood pressure and smiled. "The man's staying steady. Maybe God's keeping your husband alive for some reason," he said. "A higher purpose."

Mrs. Betcher noticed the nurse had a gold cross with a flame pinned to his jacket, the same church logo Joan wore on her blazer. It gave Mrs. Betcher a sense that these people all belonged to a cult.

"Nigger," whispered Betcher as though contemplating something awesome. "Satan is a nigger."

The wife looked up at the nurse apologetically.

"I've heard worse," he said. He sounded tired. "God works in mysterious ways."

"How painful is this for him?" Mrs. Betcher asked, as she'd asked the other nurses.

"The morphine drip helps," he said, "but there's no denying he's in pain. He may not be released from pain in this life."

"Once he stapled his foot to the floor in the shop and it took the paramedics a half hour to get here. He didn't complain about the pain. He just kept telling me how to sew a pair of fancy boat cushions we had to finish." She stopped herself from saying what came next into her head, the complaint that Carl had not paid into Social Security. She had never been one to complain, but she was feeling like a bottle that was uncorked.

The wife and the nurse stared at the gray old man on the bed. Mrs. Betcher hadn't dared try to trim his beard or hair, so he looked like he was from biblical times. His stomach had shrunk appreciably since he'd come home to die.

"God forgive me, please," Carl Betcher whispered in a way that made his wife think a fever had broken. "I am your servant."

"Well, it's nice to hear a man say that," the nurse said. "He's a religious man?"

"No, never," she said. "But now he says he wants forgiveness for a multitude of sins."

"*Multitude of sins* is from Peter. It's about loving your fellow man."

After the nurse left, Mrs. Betcher lifted the straw to Carl's lips, and he drank a whole glass of water. She was grateful that he never said anything that made the nurses suspect she was less than kind to him.

"Carl," she said, "what do you want God to forgive you for? What sins?"

"Forgive me, my Lord, I have forsaken Jesus," he announced to the air.

"What other wrong have you done in this life that needs forgiveness?" she asked. "Who else have you forsaken?"

"My mother warned me to keep Jesus in my heart, but I didn't listen."

"Isn't there anything else?" she said and whispered, "I can stop the hell fires."

Carl Betcher fell asleep.

CARL'S BELLY FAT continued to diminish, and in the eighth week the tumor stood out under his skin like a pot-roast-size tongue pressing to break through and speak, and the surgical staples holding his belly together kept that flaccid mouth shut. Mrs. Betcher dabbed ointment on those wounds as his skin grew slack. The doctors had assured her the cancer would continue to spread, but the tumor itself remained the same size. The hospice folks advised her to apply lotion to his feet.

"Sometimes they get dry and crack. Not usually this bad," the big white lady nurse said when she came again. She shook her head. "The air must be very dry in here."

When a storm knocked out the power one night in the ninth week, darkness fell upon them, and the heat stopped blowing on Carl Betcher's feet. When the sun rose, Mrs. Betcher awakened and found the house cool. She put extra blankets on Carl and fed him a can of nutritional drink, which he didn't finish. Bundled in sweaters, she lit a hurricane lamp and carried it through the breezeway out to the shop, which was heated with propane. She started work on a canvas boat cover, but lost interest and spent all morning with the curtain, re-sewing the old seams that had come undone over the years, studying and then copying the beautiful stitches. She wanted to get a sense of the fabric before she tackled the big rips in the middle. In the lamplight, the crimson color took on greater depth. When she took a break for lunch a few hours later, the house was cold, and Carl was motionless.

"Wake up," she said. She opened a new case of Ensure and took out a can of strawberry, which was all she bought now. She wished she'd saved one can of chocolate or vanilla, flavors he preferred, as an incentive for him to stay alive a little while longer. "Wake up, Carl."

Carl Betcher mumbled, and for the first time, he refused the straw she offered. His voice was so quiet she had to put her ear nearly to his mouth to hear him.

"I'm not going to hell," he whispered. "God is leading me home. He has shone his light on the path to Him. God has forgiven me."

"For what, Carl? What has God forgiven you for?"

"Forsaking Jesus." He sounded exhausted, his voice a hiss.

"What else?"

There was a long pause before he whispered, "Jesus is my Lord and Savior, my light in the darkness."

"How about forgiveness for hitting your wife? And your son? Is God forgiving you for that?"

She felt that weird swimming energy enter her arm, and she struck his chest hard with the back of her hand, but his body was so relaxed, she might have been hitting a pile of canvas. Had he felt so remorseless when hurting her over the years?

"What about the things you've said to me, Carl? Did God forgive you for calling me a whore? For telling me to shut up like I was a dog? What about all those times you forced me, made me sick from it? Well, I don't forgive you, and God shouldn't forgive you, either."

Her husband didn't seem to hear her. She shook his shoulders. Carl Betcher appeared to be trying to open his eyes, but in spite of the effort, he was falling away from her.

"No, Carl, you can't leave it like this. No!" She brought over the photograph of Carl Jr. and held it to his face; Carl Jr. sported a scraggly beard and a big sweet smile. "Look. He survived, even with what you did to him. Say you're sorry to him and me."

She thought that she had forgiven him during their marriage, each time he had hurt her—she'd said it aloud—but if she had truly forgiven him, then her anger would not be overwhelming her right now. She knew the importance of forgiveness, understood the grace of the gesture that she among mortal creatures could make for this dying man for his *multitude of sins*. And for herself. But he needed to ask for *her* forgiveness. For who was God to forgive what Carl Betcher had done to her?

Strange that in life she'd never thought of hurting him, not for revenge or punishment, but had only wanted to free herself and Carl Jr. from his hurtfulness. Now she wanted to keep hurting him, more than she wanted food or drink or warmth.

She went back into the dark shop that afternoon to work, but fell to her knees on the cold concrete. She didn't know if she even believed in God anymore, but she prayed for the electricity to return so she could fire up the space heater. When

Joan arrived an hour later, she found Mary Betcher kneeling on a cushion, fighting to tear out a seam on the heavy velvet curtain—she'd never known such strong thread, as strong as fishing line, but silky. She'd found some good new thread and dyed it the exact color she needed, but wasn't certain she could make the repair invisible.

"Oh, sweetie, get up off the floor," Joan said. "You work too hard, and you're going to make yourself sick. You should have called me right away when the power went out. I heard about it on the radio."

"My phone needs electricity to work," she said, knowing she could have plugged in the old phone she kept in the closet.

Her sister had arrived in a white van with a cross and flame on the side, driven by the pastor of her church, a tall, thick man in a puffy yellow parka, and they were accompanied by a small bald hatless man. The pastor loomed over the short guy, who wheeled Carl Betcher's diesel generator outside between the house and the shop and fired it up, restoring enough power for the refrigerator and the microwave and the electric start on the gas furnaces. He warned Mary not to use any unnecessary appliances. She wondered if she might consider the space heater necessary by any stretch of the imagination. Once the kitchen warmed tolerably, Mary and her sister sat at the table, and Mary unwrapped the tuna salad sandwich her sister had brought for her, but the fish tasted metallic, and she spit the first bite into her napkin and couldn't bring herself to take another.

"I thought you liked my tuna salad," her sister said and took a bite of the sandwich herself to taste it. She found it satisfactory and returned it to Mary's plate.

"He told God he was sorry he had sinned," said Mrs. Betcher, wiping her face. "He said Jesus was his Savior."

"He said that? Praise the Lord!" Her sister nodded her head in an exaggerated way, as Mary had seen her do in church.

"Will God really forgive him? I mean, after all he's done?" Mrs. Betcher asked. She had never told Joan any particulars of her life with Carl, so her sister couldn't really know what she was asking. The sky outside the window was bitter gray, hopeless. The trees looked like bundles of giant dead sticks. Mary Betcher couldn't imagine spring would be here in a month.

"Of course he will," Joan said. "If he returned to Jesus, he'll be saved. You kept him alive long enough to save his soul, Mary. You don't even realize how you've done the Lord's work."

For a big man, the pastor moved quietly, so Mary didn't notice him in the kitchen until he leaned over the table and blocked the light from the hall. The yellow of his parka was a kind of artificial sun.

"Soon your husband will be with the Lord," the pastor said. "And you are a part of our community now, Mrs. Betcher, God's community. We understand your grief and will hold you in our embrace." He held out his arms to offer an embrace, but Mary turned from him.

"I'll be fine," she whispered.

"The boy favors his father. He's got a strong face," the pastor said. With a long arm he reached out and picked up the old photo of Carl Jr.

TWO DAYS LATER, Mary slept late and awakened to the sound of the hospice nurse knocking. When she stepped into the living room and saw the lifeless gray body, she felt a surge of anger more overwhelming than anything she could remember. It felt like a bookend to the joy she'd felt forty years ago on her wedding day. She threw a full can of strawberry Ensure at Carl hard enough to break his jawbone, but it only nestled between his neck and shoulder.

"I'm sorry, Mrs. Betcher," said the nurse, when Mary let her into the house. "Are you going to be okay?"

A few hours after that, the power came back on.

Carl Jr. would arrive in Michigan the night before the funeral service at her sister's church, but when Joan called and offered to come over, she lied, said Carl Jr. would be there shortly, and he'd be tired from the road.

"Call me if you need anything," her sister said expansively. "Anything at all. It's no bother. Oh, Mary, we were so close when we were growing up, and I want to be close like that again. And if you ever just don't want to be alone in that house, I'll come over and stay with you."

Mary said goodbye and pressed the disconnect button on the phone. Not want to be alone in her house? What a notion—it was *her* house! Nothing in the refrigerator—*her* refrigerator!—looked palatable, so she opened a can of strawberry drink and took a long sweet swallow. As a teenager, she and her sister had attended an outdoor party where she'd been served a slice of Neapolitan ice cream on a paper plate. Under the ice cream was an elegant sheet of gold-and-white paper. She ate the chocolate and vanilla, and was letting the strawberry melt a little in the sunlight, intending to savor it. She was perched on a plastic stool, looking at a row of giant pink peonies in perfect bloom. And then a naked little boy ran through the party—there might've been a swimming pool of some kind, because she remembered the sound of splashing—and he'd knocked her plate out of her hands, sent her strawberry ice cream into the air. Joan, three years older, was right behind him chasing him—maybe she was supposed to be babysitting—and she stepped on the ice cream, smashed it into the grass, and kept going.

All her life Mary had felt the hurt of the incident, had held onto her anger, but now she saw the plain truth: she should have eaten the pink first.

She finished the can of Ensure, and it felt good to have something in her belly before going out into the shop. She was looking forward to working on the curtain, which lay spread out on the floor, glowing in the diffuse morning light coming in through the windows with open curtains. She was planning her repair for the first sword wound, which was nineteen inches long. She had gone through the old things in her sewing basket and then her closet and decided that she would cut a piece from a lap robe from a Cadillac from the 1920s. She would dye the tan piece red and work it in her hands until it regained its original suppleness, and then use it for backing. She hoped it would not interrupt the flowing of the curtain. She had never been to a play at a theater, but she would go to one just to see this curtain after she repaired it. She took a handful of the curtain and pressed it to her neck.

She hadn't yet turned on the lights when she heard a vehicle pull up outside the shop. She moved along the wall until she could see past the counter and through the front window. It was the white van with a cross and flame on it. She thought how similar the white church van looked to the black van into which they'd slid Carl Betcher's body—few people she knew drove such new, expensive vehicles. A big figure stepped out, and she could see puffy snow boots and the bottom of a sun-yellow parka. When he was halfway to the door, she could see the pastor's whole body. He stopped and gazed around like a landowner, as though he and God had a plan for what Carl

Betcher had left behind. Joan was not with him. Mary locked the door to the shop and moved slowly back into the shadows.

"Mrs. Betcher, are you there?" The big man knocked and tried the door handle so fiercely that Mary's heart began to pound. She sat on the big red curtain and then stretched out flat, and slowly she pulled the velvet all around herself and over her head like a cloak. He shouted, "Mrs. Betcher, are you okay?" and cupped his hands against the window on the door. She hunkered down. The old velvet curtain, so heavy, so hard to handle, so difficult to repair, felt fine against her skin. Heavenly.

To You, as a Woman

When the clinic nurse told me I should wear only cotton underpants, I laughed out loud—a nervous laugh—I couldn't help it. She didn't smile, just shook her head and wrote something down. Maybe my not wearing panties disturbs you, too, as a woman, but surely it doesn't disturb you as much as other things I might have done, things we all might have done. Maybe there is a scale or a number line, and on it are all the things that disturb you, such as having people see your kitchen dirty, gaining twenty pounds, having a menstrual accident in public, or getting raped by gangbangers. Your nightmares probably don't involve anyone who resembles me, with my slender figure or my wide-set brown eyes or my hair curling around my triangular face. You will understand I'm not being vain when I say my face is naturally attractive and does not require cosmetics, which would take time and care to apply and would cost money that I don't have, the way ladies' underwear and children's shoes and chocolate candies cost money.

Maybe in your nightmares you're trying to run away from

someplace where you've been held prisoner, but then you discover your legs don't work. Or maybe you're running away from men like the ones who hang around in the lot beside the Elm Street Convenience Store drinking out of bottles wrapped in brown paper bags. Certainly your worst nightmare does not feature a woman like me who is doing her best to raise two children and who takes time to compare the quality and nutrition, as well as the price, of grocery items before making a purchase. When I shop, I reflect upon how women like our mothers and grandmothers made from scratch many of the foods we now buy ready to eat, especially cookies and snacks. My maternal grandmother grew up on a farm, as your grandmother or great-grandmother probably did, and you, too, may lament not having a connection to the wholesome rural lifestyle of the women who came before us. My mother and grandmother wore skirts rather than pants, and so do I, because skirts make me feel feminine. In the cold weather, I usually wear panty hose, but my last pair got ruined early this morning in the parking lot next to the Elm Street Convenience Store. My skirts are shorter than my mother's or grandmother's ever were, because that is the style now, though in winter it can be cold. In the clinic waiting room, a student-looking woman started clearing her throat loudly, and I realized I was nodding off and had let my legs fall open. She probably thought my female parts were flaming with venereal disease—I've met plenty of stuck-up college girls at the bar and the Laundromat who would assume that. Just when I was going to explain to her that I'd had a rough night and hadn't had a chance to clean up, the nurse called me inside and asked me to undress and lie on the table. After my exam, the nurse gave me some ointment for what she said looked like trauma, and a ten-day dose of tetracycline for the possibility of infection. It takes several days to get lab results, so technically I have not been diagnosed with anything. And because I made no police report, technically there was no crime.

Once I was inside the room with the nurse, I explained that, despite what I first said when I got to the clinic and begged for an emergency appointment, I was not raped by a gang. You would agree, unless you are like Nancy VanderVeen, who owns my building, who thinks that every group of three or more men hanging around an empty lot drinking, smoking, or shooting up constitutes a gang. Those guys across from Elm Street Convenience do not have special jackets or tattoos, and they are not usually as mean as they were this morning. Often after dark one of them will give a girl a beer or else pass her a joint. Those guys all know and protect one another, so you can understand that if I file charges, I'll never get anything from any of them again, not even in an emergency. Sitting in a clinic waiting room for an hour gives a woman the chance to think about the big picture, but not being able to tell anyone what happened last night feels lonely.

Imagine if you had an emergency need for something stronger than what you usually needed, and you had no money, not even food stamps to trade for twenty cents on the dollar, and the shortest and stockiest of the four guys told you they wouldn't be sharing anything special with you unless you shared what you've got with them, and they all looked at your slender figure and triangular face as though you were some kind of creamy homemade treat presented on a platter. If this happened to you, and you'd been drinking already, you might want what they had so badly that you'd say something like *Okay, I'll fuck you* to the guy. You'd figure it'd be over in a few minutes, and you'd be right. Except that there are three more guys.

You would think that a man who probably had a sister like you, a sister who used to bake brownies or yellow cake that filled the kitchen with a warm delicious aroma, would wait for you to get your panty hose all the way off before pushing you against the front quarter panel of his car. It is hard to believe that a guy who remembered his grandmother reverently measuring ingredients such as cocoa powder and vanilla with cups and spoons would cover your mouth when you started shouting that you had changed your mind, that you had to go home to your kids. The way they each in turn ignored your crying and complaining, you'd think these guys had never loved anything their mothers cooked for them, though it is obvious their mothers fed them plenty, and that is why they've grown big and strong enough to hold you down. You'd think that if their mothers had cooked special dishes that were their favorites, then they would not laugh at you afterwards as you tried to straighten your skirt and get your curly hair back into barrettes without a mirror, when you shouted that they ruined your last pair of hose from the basket of panty hose that your mother gave you before she left town. Even after they all finished with you and gave you the aluminum foil packet, as agreed, you wanted to shout: *I might not be your mother or your sister, but I am somebody's mother, I am somebody's sister.*

As a mother, as a sister, you know there are things you should not say around children. You have to be a role model in the way you speak. For instance, you should not say that a man called you a *dumb cunt* while he pushed your face down onto the cold car hood. Or that another pushed his dick into your ass with such force that, according to the nurse, he tore the skin, and that was where the blood was coming from. You should not talk about sex or swear around children at all, because children get enough sex and swearing on television. You know you should try to keep your children away from unhealthy food, especially packaged sweets. This is difficult because children desire snack cakes and cookies, and especially they crave candy, probably because images of candy are broadcast nonstop on every TV channel, so that when you call your son from the Ringside at night, to tell him to go to sleep (though you don't work at the bar officially, they let you keep the tips if you help when it's busy), he begs you to bring home a particular sweet snack from the convenience store, and if you have any money, you will do it, because children, especially your own children, for whom you went through twelve and fifteen hours of labor, are hard to resist.

I dream that someday my son and daughter and I will have our own home, a comfortable, well-lit place nobody can take away from us, where each of us has our own room and closet and where our kitchen cupboards are stocked with nutritious goodies. I jangle my keys as I enter this home and hang up my jacket on my own jacket peg or on the back of a chair that matches the other chairs. My kids spread out their homework on the dining room table and ask me questions I know the answers to. For now I live in the one-bedroom apartment above Nancy VanderVeen's son, who calls me ugly names and hosts weekly evening meetings attended by a half dozen white men in heavy boots. If you lived here, you would surely, like me, try to give your children enough candy that they wouldn't beg for it or steal it from Mr. VanderVeen, whose rooms are clean because he pays a neighbor woman to dust, scour, and sweep at least once a week. He did not offer the cleaning job to me, though I learned from my mother—as you probably did from yours—how to dust, and how to scrub walls and floors with rags and brushes, and to make bathroom chrome shine. You might be surprised if Mr. VanderVeen refused to help you up after you fell down the stairs the way I did early this morning. And if he laughed when you said you were going home to cook something for your kids' breakfast, if he said to you, "Get your useless, whoring, stoned ass up by yourself," not taking into account that this morning had been an emergency situation because of the crippling toothache, and that the men in the parking lot had hurt you, and that the stairway was unheated.

But, as much as you would not want your seven-year-old son going downstairs to the apartment of a man who bad-talks you and lets your kid thumb through magazines full of guns, you also wouldn't want your son out in the street, and especially you wouldn't want him going to the Elm Street Convenience by himself. You've taught your son safety, and you've taught him not to steal, but the allure of candy near the cash register, especially chocolate-coated nougat, nuts, or caramel, can overwhelm any child's better judgment.

The man downstairs invites your son to use his computer some evenings to play games on the Internet, so that when you call your apartment to ask your son if he has remembered to feed his little sister, who, according to the social worker, is behind in her speech and motor skills, you get no answer. The man's large first-floor apartment features a gleaming enameled kitchen sink, shower curtains with no mold, and a very large television screen. In front of the plush couch, dishes of candy rest on a low coffee table and are accessible to children of all ages, including your tiny daughter. You have found in your son's pockets fruit-flavored chews and chocolate toffees and creamy butterscotches in foil wrappers, and your son offers candy to you when you get home. You unwrap and eat these pretty candies, because eating them is a sweet simple pleasure, though after you eat them, too quickly, the pleasure is over. And it turns out that eating a lot of these candies rots your teeth, as your mother used to warn you it would. And if you have ever had a toothache like a scream that wakes you from a dead sleep so that you have to go to the lot next to the convenience store at three a.m., and you don't have money for something to kill the pain, and you tell those guys you will do anything for something to kill the pain, then you will know how candy can become your worst nightmare.

The nurse said she would call me with the results of the lab tests. She told me three times that I must finish this entire bottle of antibiotics even if I feel better after a few days, even if the pills upset my stomach. *I understand*, I told her. *I'm not stupid.* I asked her about my tooth abscess, and she told me the county has no adult dental clinic, and that I should take Tylenol, but I know that Tylenol can be dangerous mixed with alcohol, which is also a painkiller. She told me that I should go down the hall and see if my son and daughter qualify for free dental care. It's important that kids learn good dental hygiene early, she said. As a mother, I already know this, and next time I'm there, I will look into it, but at that point I had been at the clinic long enough.

I don't know what you have been through today, but since I woke up in pain at three a.m., my whole day has been a nightmare.

Perhaps, like me, you have found that there are discrete, concrete moments in your life as a woman when you realize what you could do to make your life better, such as walking out of that stifling, medicine-smelling county clinic and into the cold winter sunshine. You decide you will go right home to pick up your daughter at Mr. VanderVeen's apartment where you left her, and your son, too, if he is home from school already. You'll try to explain about the toothache to Mr. VanderVeen when you are as sober as you are now. Maybe it will turn out he had a sister who used to make him crispy cereal bars or peanut butter balls dipped in melted chocolate, and he will apologize for calling you a whore, and he will explain why he always has neighborhood children in his apartment in a way that will make you think your daughter and son are in no danger from guns or molestation, and also that he is not planting in their minds negative ideas about you. You think of calling your own mom, whom you haven't talked to in the year since she moved to Indiana to live with her sister, and you decide to start spending more time with your kids, starting tonight when you will bake something nice for them, a cake or a batch of snickerdoodle cookies that will fill the air with the sweet smell of cinnamon. You can imagine the three of you gathered around the table as the cookies cool. You might even put a few cookies on a plate to deliver to Mr. VanderVeen to say thank you for babysitting. For generations, sweets have been a safe way to thank men for their help. But as you walk home, bare-legged, past the convenience store, the pain in your tooth flares again, and you remember that your phone is blocked for making long-distance calls and that you have sugar, margarine, and baking powder at home, but no flour or eggs.

Surely you would agree that now is not a good time to make big decisions. It will be all you can do to endure the pain when you are lying in bed at three a.m. tonight, though the nurse said the antibiotic will begin to help that infection, too, within a few days.

You would also agree that, despite the danger candy poses, people do not hesitate to use candy against our families—and not just the man downstairs. Somebody puts those rows of candy, hundreds of individually wrapped pieces, next to the cash register at the Elm Street Convenience and then focuses a surveillance camera on our hands. A large quantity of candy could arrive anonymously through the mail with no return address, and it would be difficult for us and our children to just throw it away, in spite of our suspicions.

Our grandmothers and great-grandmothers knew the allure of candy decades ago, before convenience stores and shiny packaging, when they neglected important work in the house and field in order to spend hours in the kitchen combining sugar and butter and chocolate and cream and vanilla. And as women like you and me are aware today, candy, despite the pain and damage it can cause, is nearly impossible to resist.

Daughters of the Animal Kingdom

I.

Say you're the middle-aged only child of an increasingly fragile mother who can no longer chop her own firewood, lug bales of hay, or—though she is loath to admit it—even harvest the honeycomb from her hives. For the past two months, since you decided to take some time away from your entomologist husband, a full professor in the department where you are an underpaid adjunct, you've been living in a camping trailer on the family farm, and now your mother has found a breast lump and says it's nothing, says she wishes she'd never mentioned it. She seemed unmoved when you initially howled at her in exasperation and pantomimed clawing your head with your fingernails, but she is scheduled for surgery this week. Also, let's say the youngest of your own four daughters has become pregnant and every phone call ends with her hanging up on you because you don't understand what she's going through, what she's trying to achieve, *holistically*, by becoming a vegan so as not to poison her baby, physically or psychically. No meat or milk, no eggs, no honey—though you made sure she spent summers on her grandmother's farm, where she learned to process raw honey using the crush-and-strain method as well as to make butter out of the fresh cream from a sweet-natured milk cow named Bambi.

And say, meanwhile, in your mother's henhouse, your respite from the world of humans—you carry a book in there sometimes—there's this screwy little Silkie with white feathers on her five-toed feet and more feathers sticking up showgirl-style on her head, and she's just decided to hunker down in a nest box and peck anybody who touches her. She stays on that nest all night without food. She pulls out her feathers and warms the eggs against her bare flesh.

In this same henhouse there is also one Barred Rock rooster lording it over the dozen hens, squiring them to and fro. Sometimes you toss a handful of straw at him, tell him if he doesn't behave, his sky will fall. In truth, that black-and-white rooster reminds you of your husband, who has young women gathered around him after every class and during office hours. He was your own professor when you were a young single mom, but he has remained a charming, slender man while you have grown fat and grumpy like your mother. He's suggested you skip dessert, and this year gave you a gym membership for your birthday. You used to think it merely absurd, the effect he has on college women, until you spotted his Audi outside a café in Texas Corners, miles from campus. You were headed for the Cheese Lady shop to satisfy a craving for Maytag Blue—something you haven't wanted for years. You were surprised to find him there, and he was every bit as surprised to see you, as was the girl beside him in the booth.

When you try to convince your youngest daughter to supplement her diet with some eggs for the easily digested protein she needs at this time—free-range organic anti-cruelty eggs, you suggest—she informs you that the whole poultry enterprise is immoral for what it does to the males. You are not feeling terribly sympathetic toward the male of any species just now, but you know it would be unconscionable to share with Rosie the particulars of her father's adventure. Your daughter knows you've gone to stay with your mother, and you've suggested it's a sort of spiritual retreat on the farm, a response to the nest emptying, a desire to get your hands dirty. And you would not, especially, share your most shocking personal revelation, that a stout woman in her late forties with arthritic joints and age spots can get pregnant. You reflect that in the animal kingdom, females usually reproduce until they sputter out and die.

The broody Silkie guards her clutch against the other hens, knowing some of them steal eggs—tuck them under their wings the way running backs stash footballs—and start sitting on the stolen property themselves. Though normally a hen's poops are dainty pastel blobs, while she is hunkered down she will be constipated for long periods, after which she will shit stinking manly loads. All broody hens have their hackles up, but some lose their bird brains before the three weeks are over and break their eggs in a fit of madness. An especially crazy one might attack the other thieving hen bitches or even the rooster, disturbing the peace of the henhouse, a kind of peace for which you imagine many women would give their egg money or even ransom a child conceived late in life.

II.

My mother has long assumed she's immune to the ravages of mortality, but an investigation of the recently discovered

lump has meant a whirlwind of tests and doctor visits, a diag-
nosis of breast cancer, and, finally, yesterday, a left-side mas-
tectomy, to be followed by a three-day hospital stay, during
which she is very cranky and during which I have to watch my
two grandchildren, as usual. My oldest daughter, who works
as a physician assistant in an office across town, relies on me for
babysitting Monday, Wednesday, and Friday because I teach
three sections of biology only on Tuesday and Thursday and
so must have loads of free time, and this would be the case
if I didn't assign any homework or write lectures. She smiled
dismissively when I said last week that I would really like to
finally finish my PhD in zoology. While the children and I
are waiting in the lounge for the nurse to finish torturing my
mother, I sort through the Scholastic books on the kid pile to
find *The Encyclopedia of Animals*. Julianna points excitedly at the
tigers, but I flip the pages until I find a brown-and-gold tree
snail with a speckled foot.

"I don't like snails," she says. "I like the tigers. And horses."

"That's because you don't understand snails," I say. "Let me
tell you a story."

"You never tell the story in the book. You make things up."

"Listen, Julie," I say, and I turn the book upside down in
my hands. "Most terrestrial pulmonate gastropods are her-
maphrodites."

Eight-year-old Julianna stares at me dully, as though I am
speaking a foreign language. What kind of science do they teach
kids in school now? For all I know, they've just thrown in the
towel and gone back to the Bible. At this age my youngest
daughter loved science, and it has only been in adulthood that
she has followed every crackpot theory the wind blows her way.
She says she believes that toxins can be drawn from the body

by pure thinking, that quartz creates a healing aura. Or is it a healing force field?

Alex, who is four, has found a toy consisting of spools that slide along curved plastic-coated rods, and he is working at it with an unsmiling intensity. I put my arm around Julianna, though she seems disinclined to snuggle. "Why does the book have to be upside down?" she asks.

"Snail mothers lay eggs containing only daughters," I continue. "And everything is fine until those daughters start thinking for themselves. They get it into their knuckle heads to grow penises. Can you believe that?"

Julianna looks up at me in alarm, as do two graying women sitting nearby, who resemble each other enough they could be sisters. When Alex can't get a spool to slide onto a certain peg, he pounds it with a hardcover volume of *Reader's Digest Condensed Books*.

"Even the freshwater non-hermaphroditic gastropod mollusks change sex now and again," I say, and Julianna sighs. I do miss conversing with my brilliant husband, sharing the language of science, more than I miss living in his high-ceilinged house on the hill, which has never quite felt like home to me. The walls are painted pale green and yellow to harmonize with the Audubon and Ernst Haeckel prints. We both love scientific investigation, but I have always taken pleasure in the messier aspects of the natural world, the anomalies that lie outside the usual patterns.

"Apple snails change from female to male, but you will notice they always come back again," I tell Julianna.

The women look at one another, and I wonder if they might be a couple. In a few years, my hair will be as gray as theirs.

"When snail eggs hatch, the daughters are transparent,

almost invisible, and so you can't blame their mothers for not noticing them sneaking out at night. The daughters whisper to one another, tell a story about a single glass slipper and a handsome snail prince whose shell features all the colors of the rainbow."

"I wish I had my unicorn," Julianna says. "Can we go home and get it?"

"But mother snails move too slowly to prevent their daughters' foolish behavior. Snail mating takes twelve hours, but there's no sense giving a girl a talking-to when she is already in the back seat of somebody else's shell."

The women have come around and are now smiling. I address them when I say, "Snail mating doesn't look erotic unless you speed up the film. And then, *wow!*"

One of the women gets up and stops Alex's pounding by gently removing the hardcover book from his hand. When I see my mother's nurse walk by, I put down *The Encyclopedia of Animals* and take the children's hands and lead them back into my mother's hospital room.

"Did you know that the French keep their snails in cages woven of wine-grape vines?" I ask my mother when we run out of conversation. She is switching television channels as if trying to switch me off. She's got a drain tube full of watered-down blood showing through the armpit of her gown, where they removed her lymph nodes.

"What the hell do people watch on TV?" my mother asks. She doesn't have a television at home. She stops clicking only when the nurse brings her lunch, some kind of whole-wheat pizza, a banana, and two cartons of milk.

"Listen, Mom, true story. Frenchwomen pay big money to lie on the ground inside the snail cages and have the snails crawl over them. *Beauty slime* is the great secret of Frenchwomen. They take their daughters to snail farms on their fifteenth birthdays."

"When you were fifteen, I dragged you out of that van parked in the driveway," my mother says, and I can feel how hard she is working to muster the energy to harass me. Her voice has grown more gravelly over the years from working as a horse show announcer and for a while as an auctioneer. "Remember? I kicked your ass, but it didn't stop you from becoming a teenage mother."

"I remember," I say. When my own youngest daughter was fourteen, I dragged her out of a guy's car and afterward made her sit and talk to me at the kitchen table. I didn't tell her father, but she said she'd never forgive me for embarrassing her in front of the boyfriend, and after four years she still hasn't, though that boyfriend is long gone. If I'd kicked her ass, would I be forgiven by now?

"Did you bring me a shot of brandy?" my mother asks.

"During World War Two," I say expansively, using my teaching voice, "in some of Europe's densest forests, both Allied and Axis women fended off starvation by eating the common garden snail, *cornu aspersum*."

Alex squirms out of my lap and runs into the bathroom and slams the door. I hear him turn on the water in the sink and the shower. Julianna looks up from her crayons and paper to stare out the window into the old Catholic graveyard. She's holding a little stuffed bear close to her chest, but I can feel how she regrets this morning's decision to choose the bear over the unicorn. The rule with this grandma is one stuffed animal per kid per day—it's all I can keep track of.

"They say women who ate snails were able to remain calm during even the worst of the bombing."

"Escargot," my mother says. I have tricked her into showing an interest.

"Some hallucinated about world peace," I say. "Others hallucinated about melted butter."

"Snails probably taste better than the crap they're feeding me here," my mother says. "They call this pizza?"

"You seem to be eating it," I say.

"This milk is skim, tastes like water. Go find me some salt, will you? And a couple shots of brandy."

"You're not supposed to have salt."

"I'm not supposed to have cancer, either. If you don't bring me some brandy, I'm kicking you off my property."

"It's my trailer, Ma. You can't kick me out of my own shell."

I extract a little airplane bottle from my jacket pocket and hand it over—she's been asking for brandy since last night. I give it to her not because of her threats, to which I'm as immune as my four daughters are to mine, but because, as she says, she's not supposed to have cancer. Just as I'm not supposed to have what I have. She secretes the little bottle under her blankets. When she continues to stare at me, I hand her the second bottle, plus a few packets of salt I swiped from the cafeteria. The smell of liquor has made me sick lately, and even the sight of the bottles makes me gag.

"You should go back to your museum and your husband. He called this morning, just to check on me. He's a charming man."

"He's charming, all right."

My mother refers to our house on the hill as *the museum* because of the way the prints are all framed and the way the wood floors shine. Her house is all knotty pine with dusty horse-show posters thumbtacked in place, seven-foot ceilings, and clutter that's lain unmolested for decades.

"What did he do to piss you off so much?" she asks.

I kneel down beside Julianna and borrow her crayons to draw a picture of the brown-and-gold tree snail, and then I draw a slug, pressing hard with brown and then purple to suggest a dense, moist blob of a body. Pity the slug with no house on her back, no camping trailer in which to hide—she is all sex and no safety. And the semi-slug as well, whose ancestors were snails, but whose shell has shrunk over the generations until she sports nothing more substantial than a jaunty calcified cap. Neither slug nor semi-slug has any protection against another slug following her glistening trail, and that is why you will often find a slug with a love dart sticking out of her head.

My students never believe me at first about the love dart, the gypsobelum, that needle-sharp arrow made of calcium or cartilage. A snail or slug will shoot the dart from its body like a hormone-slick porcupine quill to subdue the object of its desire. Sometimes they don't believe me until the quiz, though I've drawn love darts on the board and explained how they can be long enough to pierce a semi-slug's foot, pinning her to the ground. A love dart can take an eye out. In all fifty states, it is against the law for a person to shoot anything resembling a love dart at another person, but there is no such law protecting the daughters of the animal kingdom.

"What's that thing sticking out of the snail's head?" Julianna asks, pointing at my picture.

III.

"Thank you for talking to me," my husband says a few hours later when my mother hands me the phone from her hospital bed. "We really do need to talk. Mailing me a photocopy of your pregnancy test is not the same as talking."

"I'm not ready to talk to you yet. Especially not here. Or on the phone."

"Humph. Your mother sounds relatively upbeat, says her prognosis is good."

"Invasive ductal carcinoma," I say. "They took it out before it was too invasive, before it had arms or legs or a heartbeat."

"Humph," he says again, which is what he says when he is moving past something he doesn't want to hear. "Good thing you got her to the doctor when you did. Turns out we all have a lot to be grateful for this year."

"I suppose you think it's just a myth that black widows kill and eat their mates," I say. I have avoided talking to Gregory in person or on the phone because I'm not ready to be reasonable and positive with him—his reasonableness and positivity can feel like a kind of bullying. Face-to-face the man can cajole me into anything. I have always loved his clear, intelligent voice, but being away from him has given my mind a vacation, a license to roam grumpily from idea to idea all day. I'm not ready to even think about divorce, but lately I wonder if I wouldn't rather be his student than his wife—I'd listen for a few hours, take notes, then be free of him until next week. Or maybe I just need a few more months alone in my trailer. Or I need counseling. Or a punching bag with Gregory's face drawn on it with a crayon. Tomorrow I'll ask Julianna to draw Grandpa for me. She is now drawing a purple unicorn, like the one she left at home.

"Why are you talking about spiders?" Gregory asks.

"I'm teaching spiders. The black widow males are skinnier than the females, and they grin too much. Maybe that's why they get eaten."

"Humph. I've always suspected the phenomenon has something to do with being observed in a terrarium in a science lab."

"The Heisenberg uncertainty principle?"

"The observer effect. My students confuse those all the time."

I flush with embarrassment, because I know the difference. It is a little-known fact that pregnancy lowers your IQ—it is a phenomenon too dangerous to study.

"Gregory, you can't deny the facts. They really do devour their mates. If only by accident," I say, though I seriously doubt it's an accident. Practical-minded spider mothers teach their daughters to spin silky threads as strong as steel wires and sticky enough to capture prey. Surely these mothers tell their daughters that if they do happen to liquefy the internal organs of a mate, they should go ahead and drink up that protein-rich soup, for in this way the male can help create stronger, healthier eggs. What father wouldn't want each of his hundreds of off-spring to have all the advantages?

"Let's stop with the spiders?" Gregory says, in a tone he'd use with a student disrupting his class. But then he softens his voice. "I'll admit I'm feeling giddy at the prospect of being a new father again."

Uncertain what noise a black widow makes, I utter nothing. My mother watches me intently, and I'm pretty sure Gregory hasn't spilled the beans.

"I know you're still mad, Jill, but it's time to come home. We've got to work this out together. I don't know if you can imagine how sorry I am about what I've done."

"I can imagine," I say and sigh. My mother smiles.

"I think," he says. "No, I'm sure this baby will be good for us. I'm ready to spoil you completely, more than ever before. And I'll start by making you those cheese crepes with raspberries."

He did spoil me in the nicest ways whenever I was pregnant. I'm trying to stay angry, but his weeks of apologizing have worn me down. His bubbly nature makes his students love him from the first day of class, and even after all these years, I'm not immune. He's still the delighted boy who's been out trapping green frogs in a wooden box and who calls the whole neighborhood over to marvel at a deformed specimen with an extra set of back legs.

"A baby will be just the thing for us," he says. "A newborn is a new start, another chance at perfection. You always felt great being pregnant, after the morning sickness was over."

It's true. In my twenties, I did feel great, knowing I was built to be a mama. My body surged with hormones so thrilling that I could ignore most of my discomfort and the way I forgot things. His excitement is infectious, and I think this might all be okay after all. Gregory cooked me sumptuous treats all those years ago and never mentioned my weight. My skin and hair glowed, and when I complained of morning sickness, mostly it was to get attention or to make a joke. I wonder if there's a vegan version of those cheese crepes with raspberries we could make for our youngest daughter, who is on the verge of becoming a big sister as well as a mother herself.

"We might have a boy this time," he says. "The chances of having five daughters and no sons is only one in thirty-two."

"Still a fifty-fifty chance for each," I say, glad I can be the reasonable one for a change. I'm feeling butterflies in my stomach, as I did when I glimpsed his handsome face in the hallway at school yesterday. For the record, it's the egg-laying female butterflies who appear to be fluttering aimlessly. I slipped around the corner so he didn't see me.

"And if you have to stop teaching for a while maybe you'll finally have time to finish your PhD."

"You mean while I'm nursing?" I look down at my poor breasts beneath my sweater, which is stuck with bits of hay, and I imagine my breasts swelling with milk again—the swelling had been nice. "While I'm walking the baby around at night trying to get her to sleep?"

"Or *him*," my husband says. "Think positive. Assume this will be an easy baby. We're awfully experienced."

"Yes, *awfully*," I say, but he is right. We could be smarter parents this time.

"It's a big surprise, Jill, but I'm excited. Aren't you?" he asks. "Of course, there are risk factors, just because of your age, but we'll get all the testing. We'll be very careful about this."

My mother is screwing up her face, listening from her bed. She can't see that all around her left shoulder the sheet is now smeared with diluted blood. Only after I get off the phone do I realize how I am smiling. I didn't even think to say to my husband, *You're no spring chicken, either, pal.*

Carrying an infant around at night through a silent dark house is another experience I've secretly enjoyed, so much so that some nights I stared at one or another of my baby girls in her crib, wishing I could pick her up without waking her. But the baby my arms have been longing to hold is my daughter's new child, not my own.

IV.

My mother is just home from the hospital when the veterinarian, Lola Hernandez, shows up to castrate Jack the donkey. My mom remembers the appointment only when the late-model white pickup pulls in the driveway.

"Let's put this off until another time," I suggest.

"If that horny son of a bitch breaks down the fence and breeds Drew Anderson's mares, that man will sue me for the cost of a half-dozen show horses. Not to mention poor Chrysanthemum. Just go give Lola a hand. Or else I will."

Gregory has taken issue with the language my mother and

I use about castration, in saying we are "fixing" the male animal. For eighteen years he has also avoided discussion of having a vasectomy. The talk makes him squeamish, he says, and he smiles a charming smile.

"Grandma, what are you going to do to Jack?" Julianna asks me.

"Your nana will explain it." I can too easily imagine my mother dragging herself up to the barnyard in her nightgown, trailing her drainage tube, so I put on my boots to go outside.

"Don't let him go down," she shouts when my hand is on the doorknob. "Keep him on his feet and make him walk around afterward. It'll be hell getting him back up, and he needs to keep his juices flowing."

Though I have tossed male chicks into the pigpen like popcorn snacks, though I can ignore the squealing as I extricate the little bitty testicles of little bitty piglets, and though I absolutely do not want the one-year-old donkey Jack to mount and breed his old mother, Chrysanthemum, I still feel bad when Lola sets Jack's balls in my open hand. They are as big as my fists, veinous, and coated with white mucus. I forget whether we're supposed to eat these or bury them.

V.

"Daddy told me you're pregnant," my pregnant daughter says on the phone. I'm in my mother's living room, trying to start a woodstove fire with wet logs. This is the first time Rosie has wanted to talk in weeks. "I can't believe we'll be mommies together!"

It is not just black widow spiders that kill their mates. The female praying mantis often bites off the head of the fellow who has just impregnated her, and some snails, too, get so furious they lash out, albeit slowly. In the honeybee population, the male can't even be trusted to be a member of the hive, and if one should survive the breeding season, he is kicked out in autumn to freeze to death.

"I'm forty-seven, honey," I say.

For starters, I could say the occurrence of miscarriage in American women my age is over fifty percent, or that the chance of chromosomal abnormality is one in eight. But it would only get her worrying about her own potential complications, so I keep the stats to myself. Instead I say, "Things might not work out the way you hope."

"I'm sure you'll be fine. Daddy said you never had any problems with the four of us. And you're built sturdy. You're strong, I mean."

A honeybee queen's daughters are worker bees, loyally attending to their mother. Unlike human daughters, I think, as my daughter moves on from calling me *sturdy* to imagining aloud how fun it will be for our children to grow up together. When I was pregnant before, I had a few pregnant friends to go through it with, but my daughter seems to have no such allies. She's felt alone living out of town with her boyfriend, she now admits, and she's been scared. She also admits she is losing rather than gaining weight going into her fifth month—but it's okay, she insists, because she was overweight to begin with. She refuses to go to what she and the boyfriend call a *Western doctor*.

In the honeybee hive, a queen is not inclined to fuss over her daughters. She is drunk on royal jelly, lost in a fog as she pushes out egg after egg, fertilized by the six million sperm she's been storing in her spermatheca since the day she lost her virginity. No honeybee daughter can hope for indulgence. And yet, who makes that mind-numbing jelly? Who feeds it to her from their own mandibles and proboscises? The only goal for those daughters and their mother is reproduction.

At a certain age, the queen bee is past her prime, and there's no denying it. Her wing edges fray, her branched hairs lose their sensitivity, her many leg joints ache, and her pheromones grow faint. She no longer has the strength to push out one more blessed egg. At this time of supersedure a daughter must be groomed for the job, stuffed with royal jelly, and sent out to collect new sperm. If all goes well, her sisters will dance around her and hail the new queen.

And if the old queen doesn't pass the torch graciously, the same daughters who fed her, groomed her antennae, and massaged her sore birthing muscles will cluster around her to radiate an unbearable heat that will kill her. You might find her desiccated body on the ground under the hive. It's a wise queen who retires willingly, who doesn't cling to that old joy and pain.

WHEN I GET home from the women's clinic, I find Julianna on the couch beside Nana, reading a book about horses. Seeing me, Julianna turns the book upside down and smiles, seems to know I'm feeling shattery and a little weak, and I sit beside her to tell her a story. Alex has fallen asleep on the floor of the closet in which he sometimes hides out with a flashlight. My mother said he opened and closed the door for about an hour and demanded to know where I was. "And where were you, by the way?" she asks.

As soon as the kids are packed up and sent home with their mother, I head up to the henhouse with a stack of quizzes I have to grade for tomorrow and find the broody hen no longer sitting on her nest. For days I've suspected she's been up and around way too often to hatch anything. I lay my open hand across the dozen small cream-colored eggs—they're cold.

On this day, nineteen of twenty-one, she's made it clear she's rejoining the flock.

"You poor thing," I tell her. She looks so naked without her breast feathers—I wish I could fashion her a sweater vest. I grab hold of her at the feed dish and then sit cross-legged in the straw, where there's less poop, and hold her on my lap and pet her. "You had it easy, though. You just had to get up and walk away."

The Silkie is not inclined to snuggle. She makes a purring sound and claws at me until I let her go. She picks her way back to the food, her gray head feathers bouncing.

I'm starting to get hungry, but, more than that, I'm feeling hungry to feed my pregnant daughter. She always loved banana bread with walnuts, and I'm wondering if I can change the recipe, substitute vegetable oil for the butter. But how will it taste? And how will the whole thing hang together without eggs?

I take my phone out of my jacket pocket and hug my knees as I text my husband, who is probably just getting ready to leave his office: *I'm in the henhouse if you want to talk. I'll wait for you here.*

I haven't decided yet what I'll tell him. I wish I had it in me to lie and say I miscarried. Maybe that would be easier for all of us to live with. I look up at the cobwebs hanging from the ceiling. They are astounding creations, falling upon themselves like layers of ghostly theater curtains, thick with dust, smoky-looking, almost completely obscuring the roof joists. My husband's so tall he'll get them in his hair. When he shows up, I'll skip the science and move right into telling him a story about the magical powers of cobs, mysterious beings who enter the coop at night and whisper stories to the hens. If he gets the webs tangled in his hair, I'll motion for him to bend down, and if he brings his face close to mine, I'll brush them away.

Somewhere Warm

Sherry started working full time at Meijer when her freckle-faced daughter went into first grade and her son into third. After his shoe repair shop closed, her husband struggled to find regular work that suited him, and though Sherry tried to be unfailingly supportive, he complained, "You make me feel damned inadequate every day of my life, woman." When her daughter, Isabelle, went into fifth grade and her husband was in chemotherapy, Sherry knew that getting fired would mean losing the benefits her family needed, so she only missed a couple of days cashiering, when her husband was too weak to drive himself to appointments. She went back to perfect attendance after her husband left her for a woman he met at his cancer survivor art expressions workshop and moved with her to New Mexico to escape what he called "the cold hell of Michigan winter." Sherry knew he hated winter weather, but she was taken by surprise when he said his life with her in Kalamazoo had been *stifling* and *oppressive,* and she told herself that when the surgeons were hacking out his tumor, they must have nicked his heart. Sherry kept him on her health insurance, telling herself that her unwavering love was like radiation, that it would eventually heal his deranged heart and bring him back to make their family whole.

Her husband had been in New Mexico for three years when Sherry began dating a much younger dark-eyed truck driver who delivered housewares to Meijer. She didn't intend to invite him to live with her in the little two-bedroom house, but when he changed companies and gave up his apartment in Florida and took up sleeping in his truck in her driveway a few nights a week, she consulted seventeen-year-old Josh and fifteen-year-old Isabelle, and they all decided to give the novel arrangement a chance, though Isabelle couldn't resist reminding Sherry that she wasn't actually divorced.

Sherry was surprised at how much she enjoyed having the truck driver around, not just for his helping out with the bills or his slightly raucous lovemaking—good thing her kids were heavy sleepers—but also for his strong physical presence around the house. He opened jars with ease and cheerfully lifted the end of the couch where her son Josh slept so she could sweep beneath it. He didn't drink at all, said he just didn't care for alcohol, which was a relief, since Sherry had grown up in a house with too much drinking, along with too much shouting and fighting. Though he was only twenty-five, he seemed solid at the kitchen table during dinner, solid in the recliner while watching television, solid snoring on the bed when she left to work at six a.m., an all-around reliable person, deserving of her overflowing affections. He lit her cigarettes, and when he pulled her to him and kissed her, she felt like a heroine in a movie romance. She began to think she would be okay even if her husband did not return to the family.

When the lingerie sale came at Meijer, she bought on lay-away several scallop-edged push-up bras that presented her breasts as a gift to the truck driver in the evenings should he care to unwrap them. (She found the money in her budget by cutting way back on cigarettes.) She'd also picked up elegant panties (requiring hand washing) and lace nightgowns that she arranged in ways that minimized her thighs, which had rubbed together since she was a young woman despite her continual dieting. There were candles, perfume for the sheets.

The truck driver seemed to have a calming effect on her son and daughter, both of whom stuck closer to home after he moved in, and Sherry figured it was the effect of the love in the house expanding—her feelings for the children were unwavering, but now there was even more love in the air. When the four of them watched a television show together, joking and passing around bowls of snacks, Sherry thought she would burst with pride. Once she said, "The four of us make a beautiful family, don't we?"

"We're not a family," Isabelle said when the truck driver got up to use the bathroom. "You already drove Dad away with all your creepy cloying talk. You'll drive him away, too."

"Hush, Izzy," said Sherry. The girl was wrong, Sherry knew. Love brought people together—it was a rule of the universe, the guiding rule. God was love, and so people should follow his example and love in imitation of him. The framed needlepoint sampler on the living-room wall, from Corinthians, read, *Love is patient, love is kind. It does not envy, it does not boast, it is not proud. It is not rude, it is not self-seeking, it is not easily angered, it keeps no record of wrongs. Love does not delight in evil but rejoices with the truth. It always protects, always trusts, always hopes, always perseveres. Love never fails.*

Isabelle waited until the truck driver was back in the recliner to say, "I wish I could have my teeth straightened. I look gross, and the other kids make fun of me."

"Nonsense, you look beautiful, Izzy," Sherry said, feeling a little sick, as she did whenever Isabelle raised the topic of the braces they could not afford. "And the dentist said it's not interfering with your bite, honey."

"I guess love can't fix everything," Isabelle said and sighed theatrically.

ONE AFTERNOON AFTER her daughter was caught skipping summer school—which she was enrolled in because of skipping too much school before the truck driver moved in—Sherry hung up the phone and let her arms fall helplessly to her sides.

"I'm so ashamed. I don't know what I did to make you skip school."

"I just hate school, Ma. It's not your fault. The teachers are assholes."

"If I was a better mother, you'd love school. And you wouldn't swear."

Isabelle growled like an animal and shouted, "Skipping school is not about you, Ma. It's about me. You don't see anything before your eyes, do you? Why do you got to be so stupid?"

The truck driver reached out, as naturally as shaking another man's hand, and he slapped the girl's face.

Isabelle's mouth fell open. She put her hand to her cheek and turned and walked into her room and slammed the hollow door so hard it bounced.

"It's true, though!" she screamed through the door. "She thinks everything is about her and her love. Well, it's not!"

Sherry grabbed the truck driver's arm to stop him from following the girl to demand an apology. "Never do that again," she told him.

Sherry couldn't look her daughter in the eye the rest of that day. Like her daughter's harsh language, that slap belonged in another world, a desperate place without restraints, like a battlefield or a barroom, or the bitter place where Sherry grew up, where people humiliated one another, where the power of love did not hold sway. Neither Sherry nor her husband had ever raised a hand to the children—that was something they had agreed on before Josh was born, when they were just kids themselves. Though the girl had become more and more belligerent in the last few years, Sherry had never even raised her voice, but instead worked to lure the girl back to the path of decency by cooking her favorite foods, by letting her stay up late to watch special shows. Sherry sneaked into her daughter's room that night and got down on her knees and said, "Forgive me, Izzy." She offered to send the truck driver away, offered to sacrifice anything, kept offering until her daughter said, in a deflated voice, "It's fine, Ma. Don't worry about me," and Sherry knew she had won. After that day her daughter stopped skipping summer school, and this meant she miraculously passed the ninth grade.

In September, Josh left for basic training. After much crying and hand-wringing, Sherry let herself be reassured that joining the army was a good thing for him, and she let herself feel proud that her flesh and blood was serving the nation. Unlike Isabelle, Josh had always gotten along well with his teachers and coaches—Josh was a peacemaker, had the easy way his father had with people, and Sherry would miss him terribly. He told her he loved her every day until his day of departure, assured her that he felt prepared for the world outside their home.

SOON AFTER JOSH left, one morning while Sherry was at Meijer stocking cosmetics, the truck driver was awakened by Isabelle. The girl, who was supposed to be at school, crept into her mother's room and crawled into the bed in a tank top and underpants. The truck driver wasn't even completely awake as his hands traveled over the lean body and eased off the shirt and panties. His eyes were closed and her smooth coppery hair smelled like her mother's, or so he told himself. After all, they used the same almond-scented shampoo.

Afterward, he sat with his head in his hands on the edge of the bed.

"You can't make me go to school now, you know," the daughter said, surprised at how easy her conquest had been. She turned on her side, reached past him, and slid a Pall Mall out of his pack. "Don't feel bad, though. When I turn sixteen in six months, I'm dropping out, so I wouldn't graduate anyway. Then I'll just get my GED and start my life. I'll go off somewhere warm like my dad and Josh."

The truck driver imagined the girl's ma was suddenly behind him, but it was only the scent of Sherry's perfume on the pillows. He turned to study the daughter lying naked, smoking, beside the tangle of sheets and the flowered comforter. Her body was covered entirely with freckles. He returned his face to his hands and remained in that position for ten minutes before gathering the strength to move. When he finally lit his own cigarette with a shaking hand, he looked again—the girl had turned on the TV with the remote control and was blowing smoke rings that traveled the length of her legs. Her body exuded a sunny warmth.

"Is that why you came in here like this?" he finally asked. "So you could get away with skipping school?"

"Partly. And I think you're cute. And I can tell you're thinking about breaking up with my ma."

"Well, we shouldn't've done this. It's wrong. It's about the wrongest thing I've ever done." The truck driver's gut-

wrenching regret and determination to repent lasted much of
the morning, but by early afternoon he concluded that once
you'd done something as bad as what he'd done, there wasn't
really any going back. As the weeks passed, the truck driver
found that he loved lying in bed with this foulmouthed,
freckle-faced, cigarette-stealing school-skipper more than
anything. She was funny in her belligerence and smart-
aleckiness, so alive and surprising. At fifteen she was a year
closer to him in age than Sherry was at thirty-six. He'd come
to know exactly what to expect from Sherry, what positions,
what gestures and sighs, what bowl of dry-roasted peanuts or
pretzels before dinner, what casseroles and baked meats would
show up on the dinner table.

The truck driver didn't break things off with Sherry as he
had indeed been planning to do, and he continued bringing her
gifts—occasional pieces of jewelry in addition to the paperback
horror novels and videos he had always brought her from the
truck stops—and he started bringing her flowers, though he
knew she might have gotten fresher ones cheaper at Meijer with
her store discount. He hoped it made up for the lack of sex. The
girl's ma thanked him for making the bed each day, not knowing how intently he'd first searched the sheets for long, straight
copper-colored hairs.

One Indian summer Sunday morning in October, the truck
driver pulled into the driveway, got out, and leaned against his
rig. Sherry came out of the house in a yellow tank top, and he
noted the loose flesh on her upper arms as she approached him,
directing the beam of her smile like a sword. Her lipstick looked
absurdly orange in the natural light, and her makeup was too
thick for outdoor wear. As he kissed her hello, he saw freckled
Isabelle over her shoulder, coming out of the house scowling,
wearing stretchy white hot pants so short, he choked a little

and brought the kiss up short. He wanted to push Sherry out of the way, reach out to grab the girl's biceps in one hand and hook the other thumb into a belt loop and give the shorts a yank, up or down, he didn't care. The truck driver winked at the girl, and she stuck out her tongue at him. "Asshole," she said.

"Be nice, child," Sherry said.

"He doesn't deserve me to be nice. He should be glad I'm not kicking him."

The truck driver put his arm around Sherry again, but kept watching Izzy, and was surprised to discover the head-on guilt was not unbearable. Instead, it made him giddy, made objects around him sparkle all the rest of that day. Lunch tasted as good as filet mignon, though it was just fried bologna, the school-skipper's favorite—fried bologna on untoasted white bread, slathered with melting salad dressing. At dinner, he devoured a good amount of Sherry's macaroni-with-ham casserole before it could even cool.

The following day at noon, when Isabelle came into the bedroom wearing those white shorts and carrying a sandwich on a paper plate, he yanked the shorts off her, but she refused to have sex with him. Instead he found himself rubbing himself on the arch of her foot while she lay facedown watching *Jerry Springer* on the bedroom television.

"Your ma hates this show, you know. She says it's low class."

"At least it's something," she said, without taking her eyes off the girl her own age on the screen. "Living here in this house makes me feel like I'm one of my ma's fucking doilies, one that says, *Home is where the heart is. Home is where the sweet daughter is.* Gag me. I have to get away from here, but my dad says I can't come live with him. He's in a little tiny apartment with four people."

"Your ma makes a good home for you. You really shouldn't

keep harassing her about getting braces. You know she can't afford it."

"I have to fight back somehow. Don't you see how she wraps me up in herself, tries to control me?" Finally the girl looked over at him. "That's why my dad left, you know, and Josh, too. My dad said her love was like a sticky spiderweb that she caught everybody up in."

"Your ma's a saint." The truck driver shook his head to dislodge the notion of a spider. He'd been told that spiders tenderized their prey while it was still alive.

"You don't see it," she said and put her sandwich on its paper plate, directed her steady gaze back at him. "That love she talks about isn't about me or you. She doesn't even know me and you, or anybody. Look at us, what we're doing—if she knew us, she'd know about this. She just fills herself up with love and vomits it all over everybody. My grandma used to beat the hell out of her when she was a kid, so she thinks she has to be the opposite. You know she left home and got married when she was sixteen."

"Your ma doesn't deserve this, Izzy. What we're doing."

"So why are you doing it?" Isabelle asked through a mouthful of mashed bologna and translucent salad dressing and spongy white bread. She turned back to the television, but he didn't stop rubbing himself on her, and she didn't pull her foot away.

WHEN ISABELLE ANNOUNCED in February she was three months pregnant, Sherry's heart almost stopped beating. She begged her for the name of the boy, but the girl didn't tell. She did not tell when Sherry cried on the kitchen floor; she continued to not tell later in the week when Sherry made peanut-butter-frosted brownies for her. In the bitterly cold first week of

March, on the day of Isabelle's sixteenth birthday, the daughter and the truck driver took off together. Sherry found the note, written in her daughter's loopy scrawl: *I'm sorry Ma. Don't try and find us. Don't try to break up our new family. We love each other and we're going to go have the baby somewhere warm. Izzy.*

"What have I done?" Sherry howled in a voice that filled the house. "Where did I go wrong?"

When the furnace kicked on, she looked to the front door. She wished the truck driver would pop his handsome head inside and say it wasn't true, that her smart-aleck daughter was just playing a joke. That he, beloved and trusted, had not molested her daughter, was not planning to make a new life of molesting her.

Only she suspected it wasn't as simple as molestation, not exactly. Rather, it was the encroachment of that other world, the world she had tried to escape all her life, where people acted out of the pleasure and convenience of the moment, where they called in sick to work on a summer day to get drunk or go to the beach, leaving other people with extra work to do. The parallel world was the one where husbands left wives for other women, where children sassed, where parents beat them for sassing. It was the world of those television shows where people showed off bad behavior for the cameras, where passion was conceived not in the heart, but in some other organ, and no urge was resisted. And the world where, it now seemed, those closest to you betrayed you in the worst imaginable way and rubbed your face in how you had failed them.

She reread her daughter's note and got caught on the word *love* in *We love each other*. Isabelle had never used that word lightly, and now it seemed she had left home for love, same as Sherry had all those years ago at the same age, the age of consent.

She knew she should call her husband this minute and

tell him, but the thought of her failure filled her with shame. Instead, Sherry would send out love into the universe in hopes of reaching the girl and calling her back.

Sherry slid off the couch onto her knees, folded her arms on the seat cushion, and prayed there for a long time before looking up at the school photos hanging on the wall, the girl with her freckled nose, her big smile revealing the canine that stuck out wrong above her other teeth. Sherry knew she should've found a way to fix the girl's teeth, whatever the cost. She never should have wasted money on her sexy intimate things—just last week she'd even lit a candle in the bathroom at work and dimmed the lights to test the effect before buying a particular dangling pair of earrings. The shame of those expenditures petrified her in this kneeling position. And cigarettes—she should have quit the cigarettes when the children were born. Though they'd seemed like her only comfort much of the time, she should have saved the money for her children.

When she finally stood to get herself ready to go to work, she looked out the window and saw that a great mound of March snow had been pushed behind the rear wheels of her little Chevy. In his hurry to back his big rig out of the driveway this morning, the truck driver had not shoveled, but just plowed through the heavy drift, knocking aside enough loose chunks to block her in. She would have to go out and shovel now if she was going to get to work on time. Sherry put on her work smock and name tag, sprayed some stuff on her hair where it was sticking up, and held it down with her fingers until it dried.

NINE MONTHS LATER, a navy blue car with a flesh-colored passenger side door and a loud exhaust dropped off Sherry's daughter and then sped away, skidding and sliding dangerously on the icy road. Sherry's heart sparked at the sight of her child, at that bare head of smooth copper-colored hair that used to reflect the light when Sherry brushed and braided it. She held the yellow checked kitchen curtain aside and watched Isabelle slog toward her. Isabelle had gained enough weight that her thighs rubbed together like Sherry's, and she walked with a side-to-side rocking motion, as though her knees were stiff from a long drive, as though her duffel bag, which she was dragging across the snow, weighed a hundred pounds. The tiny baby against her hip was not wearing a cap, either. At first she felt a surge of triumph that she had willed the girl to return, but when Isabelle entered through the back door without knocking, wearing her familiar scowl, Sherry felt a little afraid.

"Hi, Ma, I'm home," she said. "I tried to escape this tunnel of love, but I was lured back by your macaroni casserole."

"Welcome home, Izzy." Sherry helped drag the duffel bag inside and closed the door. At the blast of cold the furnace kicked on. Sherry held her arms out. Instead of hugging her mother, Isabelle handed off the pink-eared baby, and Sherry plopped back into her seat at the table with the baby on her lap. As the little one squirmed and shifted, Sherry felt warm wetness seep from the side of the diaper and soak into her black work pants.

"I never thought I'd be a grandmother at thirty-seven."

"I'm a terrible person," Isabelle said. "I know that now. You've shown me that, Ma."

"I never said that, Izzy," Sherry said. "Do you want to tell me where you've been for nine months?"

"It was awful, living in the truck. I had to hide all the time. The company he hauls for has a rule that he can't have nobody riding with him. One time I pretty near smothered Violet because I had to keep her from crying in the back."

"Violet?" Sherry started. The shock of the name was greater than the shock of hearing Isabelle might have asphyxiated her own child. "After my mother?"

"It's a pretty name. A family name."

"But she was a cruel woman, Izzy. She hurt people. I never wanted you to know her."

"Oh, and I think I'm pregnant again." Isabelle frowned and then smiled. "Just kidding. Remember, I'm a joker, Ma."

Sherry remembered the truck driver slapping the girl's face, just as Violet had slapped Sherry's face dozens of times. She wondered how it would feel to raise her hand and swing from her shoulder with enough force that her daughter would drop to the floor. The violent impulse thrilled her for a moment but left her ashamed. Here in her arms was a helpless baby, after all.

She tried holding the baby out away from her, on one knee, but that made little Violet cry, so she pulled the wet bottom onto her lap again, tried to adjust the diaper so it wouldn't leak, while she got her bearings. *Violet.*

"And then, Ma, you won't believe this, but last week I caught him getting a blow job from a truck stop girl. Can you believe it? I told him I wasn't going to stand for that. He said if I'd do it for him, he wouldn't have to pay somebody else to do it. He told me, 'Your ma used to do it for me sometimes.'"

The girl had always said whatever came into her head, speaking without restraint, same as her father, though she didn't have his other easy ways. Instead of looking at the floor in shame at such an utterance, however, the girl's eyes settled on the pack of Kool 100's on the table. She reached around Sherry and the baby, slid a cigarette out of the pack.

"You know, Ma, when he said that, I told him, *Shut up.* I told him he can't talk about you that way, about you sucking his dick."

When the baby squeaked, Sherry loosened her grip—she hadn't realized she was squeezing so hard. Violet began to wail.

Sherry had never been prepared, nor had she prepared her daughter, for the situations she had wanted to wish out of existence. Sherry had failed to acknowledge the whole unsavory world beyond her gingham curtains and peanut-butter-frosted brownies, a whole world of indecent and inconsiderate behavior and pleasure-seeking. She'd thought that by shining her light on what was beautiful and generous and good, her daughter would want that and nothing more. She hadn't seen the need to teach the girl about birth control.

Though half of marriages ended in divorce, Sherry had also not believed, even after four and a half years of separation, that divorce would be her own fate, until last week when her husband's lawyer sent her divorce papers.

The tiny girl in her hands resembled Isabelle as a baby, round-faced, red-haired, with a pinched-up brow.

"You got a dry diaper in that bag, Izzy?"

"Sorry, Ma, I got no diapers. I got nothing," the girl said, raising her voice over the baby's howl, maybe expressing a certain amount of pride in having nothing. She lit her cigarette from Sherry's orange lighter and exhaled a stream of smoke. "It's just like you predicted, Ma. I'm a no-good failure."

"I never said anything like that." Sherry looked around her little house where she'd lived alone for nine months. She'd thought she had been lonely, but really she'd taken comfort in the quiet evenings with only the company of the photo of her son in his army dress uniform and her daughter's school pictures, any of which could make her cry. Her love had not diminished in the absence of the objects of her love—the mere idea of her son and daughter had been sufficient. Every day she'd considered calling the authorities to say a twenty-five-year-old man had taken her sixteen-year-old daughter away, and every day she decided she could not face the shame.

Sherry had gazed at her husband every day of the sixteen years of their marriage, especially when the sun came into their bedroom to light up his face or his freckled, muscular arm lying above the flowered comforter. In the evenings when his curly hair was tousled, when sweat or grease stained his work shirt, she'd thought she wanted to fall at his feet and thank the Lord for him. Apparently that was *stifling* him. And by supporting everything he did, she was, evidently, *oppressing* him. In her two beautiful children, she saw not just her husband's freckles but his free spirit that had kept him restless, moving from job to job, unfinished project to unfinished project. She had thought her own stability was a benefit for him, for all of them, and she had been certain her love was like a comforter in which they could all stay wrapped, warm and cozy, whatever storms raged outside. As he was packing his things, Sherry had told him she would do anything to keep him home with her and the kids, and he'd said, "That's the problem, don't you see?" She didn't see then, and she still didn't.

"I thought about that sampler while I was gone," Isabelle said now, stabbing with her cigarette in that direction to create a little noose of smoke. "Corinthians doesn't exactly say what love is, not really."

"Here, honey." Sherry tried to hand the baby back to her daughter, so she could get up and find safety pins, maybe sacrifice an old towel to use as a diaper. *Love is patient, love is kind,* Corinthians said, but maybe the girl was right that it was vague, that it only held meaning if you already felt love. While the baby hung in the air between them, Isabelle opened the fridge and stuck her head inside. She rummaged around and then shut the door, cradling in her arm a jar of salad dressing and an open bologna package. "Don't you got any pop? Truth is, I could use something stronger than pop today, but I know you don't have that." Isabelle formed words around the cigarette pinched in her lips the way Violet used to.

"You'll have to finish school," Sherry said, pulling the baby close again to quell the crying. School wasn't Sherry's biggest concern, not really. Her concern was that maybe her life had all been a foolish waste, that the trajectory away from her own cruel mother had brought her right back to this howling creature on her lap. Somebody would have to watch the baby while Isabelle went back to school, if there was really any point. The girl would need to get a driver's license and a car if Sherry wasn't going to have to do everything for her, and they charged hundreds of dollars now for driver's training. Was she supposed to quit smoking for that?

"I'm sorry about everything, Ma, but he was a jerk anyhow. I can't believe it how you didn't ever fight with him. You have the patience of a saint. No, you are a saint. He and I agreed on that. We talked about you a lot, actually." Isabelle put the food on the counter and took another lungful of smoke. With her long exhalation, she looked out at the road as though already longing for another big truck to come take her away.

Sherry had longed for her daughter's return. Now she followed her daughter's gaze out into the driveway and wondered how it could look so dirty and beaten down when it was only the second week in December. She pressed the baby to her chest until the little body relaxed, until the choking sobs slowed. Friend, lover, mother was what she wanted to be—not saint.

Plenty of times as a girl, Sherry had dropped to her knees and thrown herself onto the clean-scrubbed kitchen floor and begged for forgiveness from her mother. Sherry had been crippled, but Isabelle, fortified with a lifetime of unconditional love, should have been able to take on the whole world. Isabelle stubbed out her cigarette so that a bit of tobacco kept burning in the ashtray between them. She reached into the bag of bread and pulled out two slices.

Sherry knew love was not something you created for the reward of it. Loving was as natural for a good person as shining was for the sun, and the sun shone whether the plants appreciated it or not. Some people could return your love, and others could only absorb it, the way a black hole took in all the light and gave nothing back, but that didn't diminish the shining.

Sherry brushed the backs of her fingers against the soft pink cheek and pulled the baby out in front of her again, just far enough so that those dark eyes opened wide and met her granny's gaze. Baby Violet's eyes sparked with recognition, and her crying stopped in an instant. Sherry felt electricity move through herself and the baby, an audacious surge of love, like a zipper closing a warm soft jacket around them.

My Bliss

First I married the breakfast cereal in its small cardboard chapel, wax-coated, into which I poured milk. Then I married a cigarette, for the gauzy way the air hung around us when we were together, then a stone, because I thought he was a brick or a block, something I could use to build a home. There was a bird, but flying away repeatedly is grounds for divorce. The shrub was a lost cause from the get-go, and the TV gave me marital-tension headaches. The kidney was dull, the liver was slick, the car was exhausting, the monster in the woodshed scared the children (though I found his stink enticing). The teacup was all filling and emptying, emptying and filling. When I married the squirrel the wedding was woodland, the guests scampered, but all that foraging and rustling of sticks and leaves was too much. And the males sleep balled together in another tree all winter! How foolish, my marrying the truck, the shovel, the hair, the hope, the broom, the mail—oh, waiting and waiting for the mail to come! Marrying the cat was funny at first, and I luxuriated in his fur, until I heard his mating yowl, until the claws and the teeth, the penile spines, dear God. Forget the spider, the mask, the brittle bone. And then a slim-hipped quiet confidence leaned against the wall of the Lamplighter Lounge, chalking a pool cue, and I said, Lordy, this is for real. He ran the table, and I fanned myself with a Bell's Beer coaster—this was going to last! I called home and divorced a plate of meatloaf. Confidence gave me a good couple of months. I learned aloof and not eating in public, but it did not last. He wasn't from the Midwest, and, besides, tied to a barstool across the room, some drunk's seeing-eye dog was already starting to chew the fishnet stockings off a lady's artificial leg.

Blood Work, 1999

When Marika got home from working at the hospital on December 30, she hung up her parka and put the day's mail on the folding table and sat in the creaky wooden rocking chair her granny had given her before dying. In a few minutes she would go downstairs to help serve dinner at the Good Works Kitchen, from which the smell of tonight's entrée, turkey tetrazzini, now wafted. She stood at the window to see the cardboard sign across the street, saw that *2 days to the end* had been changed to *1 day to the end*. She didn't know who lived there, but she'd been counting down with the occupant for months. The smartest people she knew—her mom, her bosses at the hospital, the volunteer coordinator at the Good Works Kitchen—had assured her nothing was going to happen tomorrow at midnight, and she had no reason to doubt them.

The first envelope she opened was from the Africa's Children's Fund, and from the enclosed brochure a malnourished brown toddler beseeched her with his eyes to send money. Ever since Marika had exhausted her granny's inheritance, she'd been unable to send much to the agencies asking for help, but she always unfolded and read carefully the pages containing personalized letters, descriptions of famine victims, postcards of abandoned kittens, complimentary address stickers. Today she received the most horrifying depiction of cruelty she'd ever seen, a picture of a chimpanzee some hunters had illegally caught and were selling in an Asian marketplace. They'd stretched and pinned the body, as if for crucifixion. The accompanying letter explained that its body parts would be cut off and sold, some while the creature was alive, some as delicacies, some as folk remedies. Nobody was protecting the chimpanzees.

After reading the letter and brochure, Marika folded the pages back into the envelope and placed it on her animal pile. She also had a disease pile, a poverty pile, a refugee pile, and a pile for natural disasters. All the piles wiggled as her table rocked on the uneven floor, and though she considered sticking some of the envelopes under the table leg, she thought better of it and went to the kitchenette to find some cardboard from a cereal box to wedge there.

Marika's mother was furious with her for *squandering* her inheritance on *those damned causes*. She said, "You've got nothing to show for that money."

"I don't need anything to show," said Marika. "I just want to help."

"The more you help, the more they're going to want from you. There's no end to need."

Marika's favorite cousin was spending her inheritance on her upcoming wedding, while her brother had bought a used minivan. Her older sister, who put her money into an emergency fund, said, just last weekend, that Marika had better lose some weight before being fitted for her pink bridesmaid's dress. She added, "Or you're going to look like a butter mint."

Marika knew that this sort of meanness was just her sister's habit and her sister loved her plenty. Her sister was going to help her with the makeup to cover up her acne, which had gotten worse recently, maybe because she was eating a lot of cheap sweet snacks.

Marika's interest in worthy causes had begun seven years ago with her fund-raising drive for the Teen Testicular Cancer Foundation, promoting early detection of the disease that had afflicted her high school boyfriend, Anthony. They'd only hung out together a few times before he was diagnosed, but Marika stayed with him the whole two years of his treatment, sitting at his bedside, accompanying him to chemotherapy and radiation appointments, holding his hand whenever he would let her. After he was cured, he broke up with her, and that was when Marika had begun to learn about hundreds of other worthy organizations. With her current salary, she could send forty dollars to some group every week, but that was only if she ate dinners at the Good Works Kitchen and didn't go to movies. (This Sunday she hadn't been able to resist a matinee of *A Begonia for Miss Applebaum,* based on one of her favorite books.) She got her clothes from the mission store and had put nothing aside to buy a new TV—hers had fizzled to a gray blur months ago—and still the envelopes piled up, rustled and squawked around her like starved nestlings. She opened the last letter, from Pan American Disaster Relief, which said, among other things, that Microsoft mogul Bill Gates had earned more money last year than the GNP of a particular Central American country whose infrastructure had been devastated by a hurricane. Before Marika finished reading, a gust of warm air from the heating vent knocked the whole animal pile to the floor. As she sat cross-legged, gathering the envelopes, she lingered again over the chimpanzee picture, wondering what kind of people could

treat a rare and noble creature that way. She resisted an impulse
to ask God. She took the view, generally, that people ought to
try to work out problems as best they could without putting so
many additional demands on God.

The following morning at the hospital, where Marika
worked as a phlebotomist, she couldn't stop thinking about the
animals, wild and domestic, whose hope for salvation had fluttered so easily to her floor. Marika was the only phlebotomist
remaining after the hospital implemented ReDesign™. The
consultants from New Jersey ordered the elimination of all phlebotomist positions, but the hospital kept Marika for the hard
cases, for the old people with ruined veins, for the junkies who
had to be drawn through scar tissue, for whisper-thin prema-
ture newborns who were poked through the bottoms of their
heels and had their legs milked. Marika was steady enough and
fast enough to draw blood from the people who needed to be
restrained, such as Lightning Man and the lady with the red
wig who accused the doctors and nurses of stealing the baby
she always imagined she'd just given birth to. At four-foot-ten,
Marika could sometimes slip in beside a nurse without even
being noticed, but she always tried to make eye contact to reassure the patient she was there to help. She'd touch the inside of
a person's arm with two fingers to find a vein the way men in
the wild countryside used to locate underground streams with
a divining rod, and she often had a lavender vial full of blood,
0.5 ml, before the patient registered her poke.

"Oh, Marika," moaned Mrs. Lockwood, her first draw of
the day. "Thank God you're here, dear. I told that nurse you
were the only one who could take my blood, but she insisted
on butchering me." Marika looked over at Lucy the LPN, who
stood by the sink with her arms crossed, looking both apolo-
getic and annoyed. On Mrs. Lockwood's right arm, there were

three inflamed pokes, and one of Lucy's attempts had gone through the vein and out the other side so that some blood had pooled under the old woman's papery skin. Marika tightened her latex tourniquet as gently as possible on Mrs. Lockwood's left arm before palpating the inside of her elbow and swiping the vein with alcohol. When Marika finished, the woman squeezed her hand and held it.

"You don't think there's anything in all this new year's business, do you? I mean the trouble with the computers acting up?" Mrs. Lockwood whispered. "It's been all over the TV."

"Oh, no. Everything will be fine," Marika said reassuringly. "And you should be able to see the downtown fireworks from your window if you're awake at midnight." All hospital staff had been directed to reassure patients that there was nothing to fear, to prevent any sort of panic. This memo caused some grumbling among certain employees who themselves had bought generators and windmills and were stockpiling rice and beans and gasoline for the coming apocalypse. One man in transport had started raising chickens. "The power could go out at midnight," he'd told Marika, "and never come back on, never in our lives."

"Thank you, dear," said Mrs. Lockwood, finally letting go of her hand. "And Happy New Year."

Marika felt a thrill move through her, as it always did when she was able to help or comfort someone, but it dissipated too quickly.

On the way out, Marika whispered to Lucy the LPN, "Her veins are fragile. It's not your fault."

Lucy absentmindedly rubbed the inside of her own elbow. Marika knew the nurses hadn't wanted to start taking blood on top of their other duties, but they all had to go along with ReDesign™.

Marika wheeled her rattling cart down the hall and into the elevator beside an unfamiliar woman minding a four-tiered tray of breakfast dishes. Her name tag read *Crissy*. The skin of her face was chapped, and her mouth was set in a frown.

"Are you new?" Marika asked. She enjoyed making new staff members feel welcome.

"I been here three days, and I never seen so much food thrown away in my life," the woman said. The way her gray hair was pulled back tightly made her narrow face look fierce. Marika studied the plates, which were nearly full. She'd noticed the waste every day and didn't like it, but she hadn't made a cause out of it.

"It's a shame." Marika shook her head. She wished there was some mitigating factor she could mention that would make the waste seem less awful to Crissy, something about healing being a complicated process, about how maybe turning away food might be part of healing. They didn't have waste like this at the Good Works Kitchen, that was for sure—those people came in hungry and cleaned their plates.

The woman blinked bloodshot eyes and responded angrily. "It's worse than a shame. For years my own children went hungry. We didn't have enough to nourish body or soul. Some bad days I fed my babies nothing but dandelion greens. And we're throwing away all this food, just tossing it in the garbage can."

"I'm so sorry," Marika said. She got off at the first floor, leaving Crissy to continue to the basement alone. The woman's anger left Marika so shaken she forgot to say Happy New Year. She made a beeline to her locker in the lab and ate the two Little Debbie oatmeal cream cakes she'd brought in her lunch bag. If only someone could carry that wasted hospital food to the starving children everywhere, she thought. Next time she saw Crissy, she'd mention the Good Works Kitchen, just in case her family was threatened with hunger ever again. Though most of the patrons were men, a few tables were reserved for families.

Marika's next mission was to gown up to draw blood on a patient who was newly transferred from a hospital a hundred miles away to the new Titus Bronson Burn Center. Beside the burn center's main desk hung a fund-raising poster depicting a dark-eyed girl with fringed bangs whose pretty face was scarred; the line below her read, *Help Us Heal*, and below that, *Into the year 2000*. A drawing of a thermometer showed that the hospital had reached only forty percent of the fund-raising goal. Donations from the Kiwanis, the Shriners, and other organizations were largely responsible for opening this unit, but, according to the thermometer, at the turn of this new century, the need was as great as ever.

According to his chart, Marika's new patient—or *client*, as the ReDesign™ people would call him—was eighteen years old. Though his mouth was exposed, much of his face was wrapped in gauze, and bandage pads had been fixed over his eyes. His neck and shoulders looked slender but strong under the gown and sheets—maybe he was a high school athlete, as Anthony had been before the testicular cancer. The boy's hands were covered with white-gauze mitts, and someone had strapped his wrists to the bed with foam restraints so he could only shift his position slightly; perhaps he'd been tearing at his IV or sterile dressings. She read his bracelet to confirm he was indeed Terence Tuttle, born May 8, 1981. She saw that under his covers, his ankles were also strapped down.

"Good morning. My name's Marika. I'm from the lab." She knew he couldn't see her, but hoped he could hear her. "How are you feeling?"

"They've tied me up, ma'am," he said. "I'm a prisoner."

"You're not a prisoner, I promise, but they must need to restrain you for your own good," she said. "Can I call you Terry?"

"My uncle is Terry. They call me Tiny." He spoke with a southern accent as strong as any she'd heard outside of the movie *Fried Green Tomatoes*. His pronunciation made *Tiny* sound like a real name.

"Well, Tiny, the doctors need a little of your blood. It'll take just a few seconds. You might feel a poke," said Marika, grateful for once that her hands were cool as she massaged the inside of his elbow.

"They already took my blood," he said. "How much blood do they need?"

"You're in good hands at this hospital. The doctors and nurses here are the best." She fixed the tourniquet on his arm.

"Your name is Marika?" he said. He didn't flinch when the needle entered. "That's an awful pretty name."

"Thank you."

"Would you touch me, Marika?" he whispered when she pulled the needle out. "Down there? Please." He was asking politely, as a thirsty person might ask for a drink of water.

"I can call a nurse," she suggested. "Maybe your catheter needs adjustment."

"You sound pretty, Marika," he said, speaking slowly, letting his words unroll. "I'll bet you're beautiful."

"I'm not really," she said, though she knew beauty was not just about looks, and she believed that somebody someday might find her beautiful, no matter how she might look in a pastel bridesmaid's dress with cap sleeves.

"Please, Marika, put your hand on me, down there," he whispered with more urgency, and she noticed the pads over his eyes were tinged yellow and soaked with tears. Maybe he would never see again.

"You know I can't do that," Marika said.

"Why not?" he asked. His mouth, she noticed, seemed crowded with teeth. "Why can't you just touch me?"

"How did you get burned?" she asked.

"We were checking out the fireworks we got for New Year's Eve," he said, making *fireworks* into *farworks*. "My uncle says we're all going to die tonight at midnight, so we spent our money on fireworks and brung them up from Indiana. And now everybody's going to be at the party, and I'm going to die alone."

"The world isn't going to end," she said.

"If you could just touch me, I'd feel better."

She studied his little mound under the otherwise smooth sheet. She'd assisted nurses with catheters, had other times nudged away the dangling male organs the way she might nudge a hand or a fold of cloth that was in the way. She'd even drawn men through their penile veins at times when no other veins were usable. Maybe she would adjust him through the sheet and see if that helped. She reached out, but when a PCA ambled into the room with boxes of latex gloves for the dispensers, Marika pulled away. The boy moaned as her fingers brushed the sheet over his thigh.

"Oh, please, lady," he pleaded. "Touch me."

The PCA, a small gray-haired woman with dark bulging eyes, shook her head and said, "That boy's been trying everybody's patience. We had to tie his hands to keep him from yanking on himself, and all day he's been trying to get somebody to grope his pud."

Marika's hand trembled as she stuck the label onto the boy's vial of warm blood and settled it into her wire cage.

"Has he been tested for testicular cancer?" Marika asked. "It's the most common form of cancer in teenage boys. He's just eighteen, according to his chart."

"Cancer ain't that boy's problem."

As Marika left the room, she felt the PCA shaking her head, but that woman was wrong if she thought a victim of crippling burns couldn't also have a deadly disease—that was like saying Bangladesh or Haiti was too poor to have devastating floods.

If Marika had touched him, she might possibly have found cancer, or she might've been fired.

At her ten o'clock break, Marika ate the sandwich she'd brought for lunch. She couldn't focus on her novel, *Now I Lay Me Down to Sleep*, for thinking of the stretched-out chimpanzee in the brochure and the burned boy strapped to his bed. She could still hear him saying her name over and over, as though her name meant something special to him.

Feeding and soothing and protecting people and animals should be so much simpler than it was, and at the hospital somebody ought to find a way to provide comfort for a person in such pain as Tiny was in. Thinking about the suffering of others usually helped Marika forget her own problems, but lately Marika had been feeling sorry for herself for not having had a boyfriend in six years—longer, if radiation therapy appointments didn't count as dates. Self-pity was the least pardonable of sins, but some days it was hard to remember to be grateful she didn't have Lou Gehrig's disease or leukemia or even an empty belly. Sometimes she tried to go hungry, tried to eat less, but her cravings for sweets could overpower her. She never could say no to a meal at the Good Works Kitchen, and once something was on her plate, she couldn't waste it—especially now she wouldn't be able to waste it after hearing about Crissy's family eating nothing but dandelion greens. Being alone wasn't nearly as bad as being a refugee or a victim of a famine or of debilitating burns, so what was the matter with her?

Though the rest of the morning was busier than usual,

Marika kept hearing Tiny's slow, sweet voice in her head. She weighed the pain of each person whose blood she drew and each time felt pretty sure Tiny's pain was greater. One man, who was laid out flat with a broken back, told her about his underground bunker in Allegan County. On the television in the man's room the sound was off, but Marika saw people unloading long guns from a wooden box the size of a child's casket and hanging them on hooks on the wall of a pole barn, alongside blue-plastic fifty-five-gallon drums labeled *gas*. While she applied the sticker to the vial of blood, the picture changed to a hawk-faced man in a wheelchair with two pistols in his lap. A stout woman stood behind him with her hand on his shoulder as he showed one of the pistols to the camera, but they never showed the woman's face.

"The apocalypse is coming tonight, and I'm stuck here," the man with the broken back said, with tears running down the sides of his face. This could not go on, Marika told herself, all this suffering. But what could a person do?

On her lunch break she walked to the bank to cash her check, and she asked the teller how a person might take out a loan. She was directed to a customer service representative, a woman about the age of Marika's mother. When the woman stood up to shake hands across her desk, Marika saw she was over six feet tall.

"I'd like to take out a loan," Marika said as she lowered herself into the chair. She'd often cashed her hospital checks here, but she'd never noticed how high the ceilings were—this room must be expensive to heat, she thought.

"What sort of loan would you be applying for?" The woman laced her long fingers together atop the desk.

"For the hospital where I work. If I could borrow a few thousand dollars to donate to the hospital's burn center, it would help them so much. I can pay it back in a year, a little bit every week from my paycheck."

"Most of our consumer loans are secured loans, first or second mortgages and car loans," the woman said stiffly, and then she relaxed her tone. "Couldn't you just donate a little at a time instead of taking out a loan?"

"There's so much need there, ma'am. You wouldn't believe. As kids grow, they need more surgeries because their scar tissue doesn't stretch. Even adults can barely stand the pain." Marika wished she'd brought a burn-center brochure with her, because her words didn't feel convincing. She thought of the boy's raw skin pushing against the white gauze, his crowded teeth. "I just want to help," she concluded.

The woman declined Marika's request graciously and rose to her great height to shake Marika's hand again. Marika felt sorry for her, so tall and strong, in charge of a vault full of money but unable to do good with it. She wasn't wearing a wedding ring; perhaps she was widowed or divorced, left behind by someone.

"If you ever need blood drawn at the hospital," Marika said as they clasped hands, "you can ask for me." It was all she had to offer.

THE AIR WAS fresh and wet, just above freezing, so she didn't zip up her parka. As she waited at the corner outside the bank for the walk signal, she saw a familiar figure approach from the other side of Michigan Avenue, cutting through the traffic. He was probably only in his fifties, but his face was weathered and spotted with precancerous skin lesions. His flyaway hair was pure white, and his combed beard was filmy, almost translucent. He was dressed for summer, in a T-shirt, with the blazing sun logo of a local beer called Bell's Oberon. She'd never seen him without a confusion of nurses and other hospital staff surrounding him. When he stepped out into traffic, a small white truck screeched to a halt about a foot away from the man, who then reached out and placed a flat hand deliberately on the hood, as though absorbing energy from the truck's engine or maybe sending energy into it.

"The apocalypse is upon us!" the man shouted at the driver of the white truck.

She knew Lightning Man from his hospital stays for dehydration and exposure, but in the past he'd usually been making pronouncements about the weather or the alignment of the sun and moon and planets. The first time he came in, two men from transport and a nurse held his arms and legs as Marika took his blood. Her presence had calmed him; when she'd touched his arm, he'd sighed and said, "This one understands." His skin had been hot with fever, and because his gown was slipping off, Marika had seen intricate red ferns stretching from his shoulder and over one side of his chest, designs so blood-dark she'd thought they were tattoos. "Lichtenberg flowers," the nurse had called them, caused by capillaries bursting during electrical burns, though the doctor had been unable to confirm he'd actually been struck by lightning as he claimed. On his subsequent visits, the red ferns were gone. His blood, however, was always hot in the vial.

"At midnight lightning will come down from the heavens!" Lightning Man shouted now in the street, his voice an authoritative rumble. When he lifted his hand off the truck, the driver sped around him as though energized. Lightning Man continued toward Marika, halted at the curb before her. He looked down into her face with glowing blue eyes. "You understand.

We must prepare for the cleansing millennial fire! Blood must flow, but don't be afraid."

With his eyes glued to hers, Lightning Man reached out, slipped his bare hand through the collar of her jacket and under her lab coat to grasp her bare shoulder. The contact shocked her, but then was warm and soothing. Through his fingers, electricity trickled into her, traveled under her skin and up to her face, which she could feel was flushing pink. The warm energy snaked down into her belly and nestled between her legs. She couldn't look away from his eyes, where she now saw the blue was rimmed with orange. He continued to hold her shoulder, pressed his fingers into her, infused her with soothing knowledge. The end of the millennium was not about a computer bug, he seemed to be telling her, but about the culmination and resolution of all the pain and suffering in the world.

"When the clock strikes midnight, all will be laid bare," he said in a quieter, more intimate voice. "Each of us must choose to see the light or else be plunged into darkness. Will you choose the light?"

Marika thought of how the boy in his hospital bed ached for a simple gesture of human contact—this man would not have been afraid to give it.

"Yes," Marika whispered. Of course this world could not go on as it had.

"This one understands!" he shouted at the sky, which was overcast. He slid his warm hand out of her parka and moved away from her toward two women in knee-length skirts and snow boots. Marika's body was shaking, and she imagined her shoulder was imprinted with red flowers. The light turned to walk, but she couldn't step off the curb.

One of the skirted women yelled at Lightning Man to leave her "the hell alone," and the force of her voice threw his willowy frame against the glass doors of the First National Bank building as it might have in a cartoon. He turned around and flattened his hands against the glass and repeated to the doors what he'd said earlier to the truck. Marika imagined the doors heating up, maybe the whole building, too. She studied his shoulder blades poking out against the back of his shirt like wings, his arms striped with the kind of veins that were easy to draw blood from. The light said *walk* and then *don't walk*. And *walk* again. She considered following Lightning Man to listen further, to try and understand what exactly was going to happen, but people needed her at the hospital. The hospital was where she could do the most good.

All that afternoon, her heartbeat felt erratic, and she had to focus hard to keep her mind from wandering, even while she was drawing blood. She skipped her break, taking only a few minutes to eat some crumbling Christmas cookies someone had left in the lounge. Some of the work orders seemed apocryphal: conjoined twins had been born this morning, and they needed to be drawn separately. Also, there was a lockdown on One North because a man on crutches was roaming the halls, his tubes dangling, demanding the return of the leg that the doctors had just amputated.

After her hospital shift was over, Marika worked for an extra hour to enter everything into her computer and then headed to the Good Works Kitchen. The sign across the street that had been counting down the days for three months was gone, leaving only an empty place in the dark window.

A New Year's Eve meal at the Good Works Kitchen always involved turning away people who'd been drinking, and tonight the anxiety level would be high among those who thought they might be getting their last-ever supper. The volunteer coordinator put Marika in the kitchen instead of in the dining area, for her safety, he said, and she didn't complain, tried not to show her disappointment. She loved welcoming each down-and-out man and occasional woman with children, loved watching people grow warm after coming in from the cold, seeing their hunger diminish, loved seeing them softened by generosity and gentle treatment. The lines in their faces smoothed out, their shoulders relaxed, their breathing slowed. Tonight, she wished she could touch every person and pass on Lightning Man's soothing energy to help them through whatever was coming.

The kitchen was so hot she had to strip down to her tank top, though her plump upper arms, sprinkled with acne, were not something she wanted to show to people. Her skin grew blotchy and she had to keep wiping sweat from her forehead. She couldn't seem to calm her own breathing, and every time a steel spoon hit the side of the beef stew pot or the rice pudding vat, her heart jumped. When Zach, the college-boy volunteer with the goatee, dropped a steam pan of mashed potatoes, the clatter was terrible, and she imagined sparks flying all around, blue and orange. What color were the burned boy's eyes? she wondered. Would it say on his chart? She studied the side of Zach's face as he cleaned up his mess to the sound of the classical music they always piped in. She imagined Zach was wrapped in flesh-colored gauze that would peel away at midnight to reveal miraculous new skin without the little beard. In the dining room, the men moved through the food line, and Marika searched each face as it passed the kitchen doorway, imagined rough and chilblained skin sloughing off to reveal something pure and new beneath. Her own pocked skin, too, would peel away to reveal a clean slate. She was glad these hungry people didn't have to be alone tonight.

At eleven p.m., after the kitchen was closed down for the night, while Marika was wiping the stainless steel surfaces, she thought of the crucified chimpanzee from the brochure, imagined it had somehow survived, was wrapped in gauze bandages in a hospital bed, suffering but alive. Zach returned to the kitchen with a bouquet of flowers in a juice bottle and put them before her: a pink carnation and some miniature red roses, surrounded by baby's breath.

"Somebody left these on one of the tables. They're for you." Zach towered over her.

Another time she might have first insisted somebody else needed flowers more than she did, but tonight she accepted them. When she finished cleaning up, she put on her parka and headed to the hospital. She pressed the bottle of flowers against her breast to protect them from the freezing air, but she found the cold wind on her face refreshing. There were no clouds to speak of, and the moon was a modest crescent over the hospital's parking structure. Little showers of colored sparks peppered the sky in one direction and then another, and each time they were followed by a *pop-pop*. She heard some shouts from the downtown New Year's event. If everyone in the world had to make a choice tonight, she hoped they would all choose light over dark, kindness over cruelty.

She held up the flowers as she passed the information desk and then put them on a table in the waiting area, out of sight of the receptionist—flowers were never allowed in the burn unit. She found the hospital quiet and dim and the elevator empty. All down the hallways, nurses and aides were bunkered behind glass walls, clustered tightly around desks in offices decorated with silver paper and twinkle lights, sipping from paper cups— she sensed they didn't want to be alone at midnight. Nobody from the burn center staff noticed her as she donned a sterile blue gown, mask, and gloves from the isolation cart, nor when she slipped into the boy's room, where he snored gently in the dark. She knew she should let him sleep, but she wanted to hear his voice again.

"Tiny?" she whispered. It was hard to tell, but she thought he might be only a few inches taller than she was.

"Is somebody there?" he asked and tugged against his wrist restraints. "Are you a lady?"

"It's me, Marika," she whispered, fearing he could hear her heartbeat. "I took your blood before. I knew your family couldn't be here, so I wanted to say Happy New Year." The darkness of the room reminded her that the young man had been living in darkness since he'd been here. He couldn't see her face, or anything.

"Will you touch me? Please." His slow voice clicked inside her.

"Shhh," she whispered, and she could barely hear her own voice over the humming of her body. She gripped the metal rail of the hospital bed, and when it began to vibrate, she let go and reached up and touched the bag of IV fluid, which then glowed slightly. Car lights outside showed blue and orange, and the green lights on the monitor smoldered in the dark. She moved closer, so her thighs and belly were pressed against the bed frame, and let her gaze rest on the boy's soft mound. She reached out and touched the inside of his elbow below the bandage she'd put on him after drawing his blood this morning. His flesh went to goose bumps. Hers did, too.

"Please touch me, Marika."

"I am touching you," she whispered. She heard two shots from a gun in the distance. Or fireworks. Or a car's backfire. Then a third, a fourth, a fifth shot.

"What color is your hair?" he whispered.

"Dark blond."

"Is your hair long? Please. I don't want to die alone here."

He slowed down the word *die* so much it seemed like a real possibility.

"I wear it in a long braid. But I don't think we'll die," she whispered. "If anything happens, I think the world will be remade, better than before."

"If you could just put your hand on me for a second."

She looked out through the open door and saw nobody in the hall. Earlier she'd said she couldn't touch him, but all day long she'd tried to puzzle out why not. Why couldn't a person touch another person to bring him comfort in a difficult time? She'd known about the healing energy in human contact, had always put her hands on her patients, but she was starting to understand how touching might be more important than all the money she didn't have to give. When Lightning Man had reached inside her parka, the universe cracked open to reveal a brightness beyond any description.

"Can you see the fireworks?" he asked. "The nurses said there'd be fireworks."

"Yes," she said, but she was lying. His room was on the wrong side of the hospital to see the downtown display.

First she thought she might lay her hand on top of the sheet, but she knew her touch would be more powerful with nothing between his skin and hers. She slid off her left glove. Her fingers brushed Tiny's thigh, which turned to gooseflesh. When she rested her hand on his soft mound, he sighed deeply and terribly, as though he were being released from a suffering she couldn't fathom. At first what she felt around the catheter was cool and toad-squishy, but under her touch it warmed and became the most delicate thing in this world of vulnerable creatures, more vulnerable and naked than that poor chimpanzee. The boy groaned, and Marika's body flushed and buzzed with the electricity she'd been carrying inside herself all afternoon and evening. Her capillaries swelled against her skin.

"Rub me, please," the boy breathed, more desperate than before.

She squeezed slightly. He was a stranger here, alone in a dark world that might be about to radically transform. She could ease him through to the other side. More gunshots or fireworks sounded in the distance. As if switched on, the thing in her hand came to life, pushed back against her palm, pushed and swelled. Even without money she could alleviate suffering, and maybe she could infuse with life that which seemed lifeless.

Marika knew that at the stroke of midnight, as the fireworks display lit up the sky over Kalamazoo, a hurricane or tornado could hit this hospital just as easily as any other place and send this boy's body and the bed it was strapped to flying through the air, or floating onto the floodwaters. Gale-force winds could then open up a closet containing the healing ointments that would spread themselves across the water, so that the flood itself would become healing medicine. She palpated the flesh in her hand, imagined the sky brilliant with orange, gold, and red light. Flames, perhaps, or the new sunrise.

She almost didn't hear his moans over the sound of her own breathing. Then she was gripping something that was slipping away. She grasped more tightly what she was losing and felt her own body shudder. She slumped over the bed and envisioned the bricks falling away from the walls of the hospital, bricks and blocks falling off all the buildings downtown and becoming rubble. Lightning could split the First National Bank building right down the middle, short-circuiting the electrical system. Once the power was out, the bars guarding the vault at the heart of the bank would slide open. Lightning storms could strike banks around the world. Bill Gates's private vault, too, could crack open like a giant egg hatching, and inside would be plenty for all. Humanity would become like Noah's Ark, navigating the flood of need, with people one by one climbing on board and helping rescue those still floundering. Noah's boat would be built bigger this time, big and solid enough to save the whole world. The loan manager from the bank would pour coins into cupped hands and press fistfuls of cash toward mothers swaddling hungry babies. As the sun rose on the new millennium, there would no longer be rich or poor, weak or strong. Strangers would embrace and heal one another with touch. Marika was more than ready to ladle out nourishment, to accept blood from those who needed to give, to unashamedly comfort the suffering in any way she could.

She heard the popping of the fireworks, the beep of Tiny's heart rate monitor, and knew it was connected to an alarm, but she was taken by surprise when the overhead light came on. She blinked and felt herself bursting open like flowers in sunlight, overflowing into the new millennium.

Children of
Transylvania, 1983

Breakfast this morning in the hotel was mămăligă, a firm cornmeal mush, served not with liquid sheep's cheese as the previous morning, but with a slick of pork fat over the top, as clear as the poured-glass windows of the Moon Church they'd visited. Joannah spooned the grease into an ashtray in the center of the table while their guide, Bogdan, assigned to them by the Romanian national tourist bureau, watched. Then he mixed his own shiny fat right into the corn mush and took a big spoonful, and another. He would go on to devour the bread, which was heavy and dirty tasting, as though baked inside factory smokestacks.

"No, thanks," Joannah said after one bite.

"Cornmeal mush is pretty good biking food," said her sister Clarice, who was sitting between herself and Bogdan at the eight-person table in the town of Dr. Petru Groza, named for the first Communist prime minister of Romania. Margie, her other sister, was whispering in an agitated way with her husband. Joannah's sisters were sixteen and eighteen years older than she was and had always seemed as much like aunts as sisters. Occasional bike rides along Lake Michigan were the only thing they'd had in common, besides their parents, and Joannah had been only five when their dad died.

When Joannah had expressed an interest in the trip her sisters were taking to Transylvania, they had suggested she come with them. When they learned that Joannah was sleeping with sixty-five-year-old David Masters, a friend of their mother's, and had no intention of moving out of their mother's senior housing apartment, they pulled out all the stops, paid her way to come along with them. She'd needed a break, they said, from caring for Mom; they acted as though they were saving her soul. If left to her own devices, Joannah would've stayed in Chicago reading vampire romance stories and sitting in a chair wrapped in blankets beside their ma, who had just been moved to a long-term-care facility, the thing she'd railed against as long as she could remember who she was. Now, after ten years of caring for her mother—full time since graduating from college—Joannah didn't know what to do.

"You should take your roll in case you get hungry on the road," Clarice said.

Joannah picked it up and knocked it against the wooden table to show her sister just what she thought of that roll. As they were leaving, she saw Bogdan pocket the rolls left on the table. He went outside and handed them to some children sitting on the steps, just out of sight of the hotel guard.

A half hour later, Joannah's two sisters were in front of the Hotel Dr. Petru Groza loading their bike saddlebags and pumping up their tires, while Bogdan was staring off southward toward Deva, toward green hills. Joannah was packed and ready, standing beside Bogdan, squinting against the early morning sun.

"They say these hills is only place in our country with rattlesnakes," he said.

Joannah smiled and waited for him to explain how rattlesnakes would have ended up in Europe, but then Bogdan blinked as if coming out of a daydream. Though they were outside, well away from the ubiquitous listening devices or spies, Bogdan glanced around as if he'd let slip a state secret, and then he announced that the group members might find for sale in Deva a three-volume set of the political writings of the Great Leader. "One of few places such volumes are available outside of Bucharest."

"Bogdan, you know we don't care about your so-called Great Leader. And why don't you ever say the guy's name?" Joannah said. "Why don't you just say Ceausescu?" Joannah pronounced the name loudly and distinctly, "Chow-chess-koo." A silence settled on them like dust thrown up by a passing car. Joannah's sisters had told her she must not talk about the government or even say the president's name aloud, but the political nonsense was annoying her.

Clarice broke the silence. "Never mind her, Bogdan. It's going to be a beautiful biking day."

"Also, a remarkable statue of Dr. Petru Groza lives in Deva." Bogdan adjusted his heavy black glasses. Clarice had rigged up an elastic strap for him to keep them tight to his head as he rode.

"Tell about the snakes," Joannah said. "You don't want us to get bit, do you?" Though she'd only known Bogdan a few days, his Boy Scout demeanor wearied her, the way Clarice's Girl Scout goodness always had. Signs of deep poverty were all around them, yet Bogdan kept saying how well Romania and its people were doing. Kids were malnourished—yesterday they'd seen a boy bowlegged with rickets, for chrissakes—typewriters were contraband, their possession punishable by death, if you could believe what Clarice said. Clarice was a social worker and provided no end of facts: the rate of death during childbirth in Romania was the highest in Europe, as was the child mortality rate. Margie and the four men were all medical doctors and part-time advisors to an aid agency, and upon returning they would make a report about the health conditions they had observed, but they were posing as ordinary tourists. On Clarice's visa, her occupation was listed as teacher.

"I am mistake about snakes. It is a not-true story some people tell."

"What about vampires, then?" Joannah asked.

"These are folktales of foolish."

"Dracula is real, though. We're going to his castle."

"Dracula," Bogdan said, pronouncing it Dra-cool-ya, "was this prince who was defeat of Turks."

"You know our great-grandfather was from there. From here, I mean," Joannah said and fingered the little beaten cross she wore on a chain. When she was ten, her mother had given it to her, said it was from a secret gold mine in the Carpathian Mountains, and Joannah had worn it every day for fifteen years.

Margie and Clarice looked at one another and sighed. Her sisters were taller, stronger, and blonder than she was, and they'd always had each other in a way that made her wonder sometimes why they even needed husbands.

"I am surprised," Bogdan said. "Also my grandfather is from such places."

"Is that why you were chosen to be our guide?" Clarice asked gently, trying to defuse the conversation.

"I am chosen because I have bicycle."

"You're all ready?" Clarice said to Joannah. "No lollygagging today?"

"I want to try to catch up with the guys," Joannah said. The four men, her brothers-in-law and two other doctors, had left a few minutes earlier.

"That's a change. Are you sure you know the route?"

"I have a map. And if I don't know the way, I'll wait for you guys." Joannah didn't wait for any more conversation. She wanted to bike behind the rest of the pack, but Bogdan had to make sure the Americans weren't left strung out across the Romanian countryside. There was no hope in making her sisters understand that she wanted to be alone, just to be sad and thoughtful for a while. When she'd last seen her mother, her best friend in the world, the woman hadn't recognized Joannah even after prompting, and most likely wouldn't ever recognize her again.

Joannah stood up on her pedals to sprint away, but, as soon as she was out of sight, she detoured into a park and hid behind a monument of Nikolai Ceausescu orating. She waited about twenty minutes until she saw her sisters and Bogdan bicycle past, and then she followed them at a distance out of town. Once she was on the road to Deva, she slowed and let herself fall farther behind.

The first few hours of biking alone were heavenly, despite the heat, and Joannah found herself sighing a lot, releasing old breath she must've been holding inside for a long time. She found she could enjoy the scenery better without her sisters explaining and translating everything. She stopped and splashed her face, feet, and arms in cool streams. If she hadn't accidentally left her camera behind in the hotel room in Oradea on their first day in the country, she'd have traveled even more slowly, trying to capture on film the melancholy of the mule-drawn carts, hobbled horses grazing, women dragging wooden-tined rakes across the hillsides. Though she couldn't have much in common with them, she felt camaraderie with the raking women and those women minding the shops with empty shelves—she'd always preferred the company of people her mother's age, preferred an evening at home with Mom to going out anywhere. Even though she couldn't speak to the local women beyond the words for hello, water, and America, she liked their company. If the medical care here was as bad as her sisters said, when the women here got dementia, they likely died in the early stages. Maybe the daughters here never saw desperation in their mothers' eyes as their memories and bodies failed them.

She kept passing chickens, poor harassed balls of feathers, pecking along the shoulder of the road for bugs and worms, scattering into ditches as she pedaled over potholes. In the hotel the previous night they had each been served a roasted half-chicken with hardly a mouthful of meat clinging to its bones. Joannah had made fun of the meal, but now it occurred to her that the chickens were offering up all they had.

By lunchtime, Joannah was starving, and she veered off the cracked and crumbling asphalt to stop at an open-air roadside café. To her relief, Margie and Clarice were nowhere to be seen. She could enjoy her sisters for a few hours a day, but over the years she'd grown accustomed to being left alone with her thoughts—for quite a while her mother had not really been present. Her sisters always wanted to talk about what Joannah would do with her life now that she wasn't a caregiver.

The roadside café was set beneath an arbor covered with grapevines that afforded shade to the metal tables, painted, like the house to which the café was attached, a bright, chalky blue. Three skinny men hunched over three separate tables, drinking something brownish out of jelly jars. Joannah took off her helmet and gloves, tugged at her stretchy shorts to cover more of her thighs, and walked to the counter. She pointed at a box of biscuits on a shelf, but the proprietress picked up the box and shook it to show it was empty, for display only.

"*Vin?*" asked the woman. Joannah knew the word for wine.

Joannah shook her head. "*Ceai,*" she said. It rhymed with *sigh*. Tea. She didn't try out any Romanian when she was with her sisters, who had taken a language course before the trip. Until now, she'd let them order for her.

The woman's dark hair was arranged in a striking resemblance to Mrs. Ceausescu's matronly 'do in the portrait hanging behind her, a sort of bouffant. On the other side of the door leading into the house hung a likeness of Mrs. Ceausescu's husband, the dictator. As Joannah stood looking back and forth from one airbrushed rosy-cheeked wrinkle-free face to the other, a passing truck emitted a choking cloud of exhaust that swept through the café. The proprietress smiled apologetically. She attempted to write on a slip of paper the amount Joannah needed to pay, but even after she shook her pen, still there was no ink. Joannah felt the woman's frustration in her bones. She held out a handful of change, steel *lei* coins and aluminum *bani*, and the proprietress selected about four cents' worth.

Joannah indicated her water bottle and asked for *apă* and then followed the proprietress back to the entrance. The woman pointed at an open well with a roof over it. Most Romanian words seemed no more real in her mouth than the tissue-paper currency and worn-down coins for which she'd traded sturdy American dollars. The word for water was an exception— needing to drink eight or ten liters a day made it real. Joannah cranked a wooden handle to bring up a wooden bucket from the well. She filled her bottle and dumped the rest of the water onto the ground as their guide, Bogdan, had taught them—Joannah wondered if the air here was so polluted that it poisoned the water after only a minute of exposure. If so, what did it mean for the lungs of the children she saw along the road? Growing up, Joannah had always assumed she'd have children by the time she was twenty-five; she'd always assumed she'd end up with at least a half dozen kids one way or another, but since the only man she'd ever had sex with was a sixty-five-year-old who'd had a vasectomy, it wasn't looking very promising. With some distance and time between herself and Mr. Masters, she was thinking she might not want to go to bed with him any-more—she wouldn't say so to her sisters, though, didn't want to give them the satisfaction of another goal accomplished.

Turned out that the café had no food, not even cornmeal mush, which she really should've eaten this morning. Joannah sat down and was shaking her water bottle to dissolve the iodine purification tablets when one of the men in the café moved from his table and sat in a chair beside her. From a distance he'd appeared ancient, but by the look of the small, bright eyes set in his ruined face, he probably wasn't much over fifty. The man stank of sour wine and sweat. "Kent?" he asked and crossed his bony legs.

Joannah shook her head, and the man looked into her face as though searching there for a co-conspirator. He smiled to show his few remaining teeth, which were small and dark. "Kent?" he repeated in a raspy voice and raised two mangled fingers to his lips, making a stunted V. Joannah stared at the digits, both severed above the first knuckle, the skin pinched and bluish over the ends. For the first time she wished she'd brought along American cigarettes as her guidebook had suggested. When Joannah said nothing, he leaned back in his chair and shouted to the other men in the café in a tone of world-weary disgust, but neither man even looked over. Joannah waved flies from her face, wondering how the man wasn't bothered that a half dozen or so had gathered near his eyes. He was dressed in a patched suit jacket over a threadbare undershirt and flare-legged pants cinched tight at the waist, the same clothes worn by the men she'd seen in other Transylvanian villages. He leaned toward Joannah and grabbed her upper arm with his bad hand.

The man repeated "Kent" a third time and tightened his grip. His droopy eyes seemed both stupid and intensely focused. He watched Joannah as though testing her. He couldn't have been more than a few inches taller than she was, and she outweighed him, but she froze. She wanted to yell *Stop!* or *Help!* but she didn't know either word in Romanian, and anyway her throat had closed up. She imagined the two fat-bellied police officers who patrolled her Wicker Park neighborhood in Chicago—black Officer Washington, white Officer Kroll— driving up in a gleaming squad car, a three-dimensional vision of ordinary American privilege.

The other men in the café paid no attention. The proprietress remained inside, slow with the tea.

"Let me go," Joannah said finally, through gritted teeth. She tried to peel away his stubbed fingers, but they were fastened machine-like around her arm. If her mother had been this strong, would she have kept herself out of the nursing home a little longer? Kept her marbles? Mr. Masters had kept Joannah in his apartment some evenings by telling her stories that went on and on and by begging her not to leave him.

With her foot, she pushed against the drunken man's chair, tipping it, and then she pushed with a little more force, so his chair went out from under him. The two other men turned as he yelped and then tried but failed to catch himself. His chair clattered to the concrete, and as the man rolled over and moaned, Joannah hurried outside and climbed onto her bike. Never mind the tea. Her heart was beating hard, and she was scared, but she felt alive as she pedaled away, fueled by adrenaline. As the café fell farther behind, she slackened her pace. There was little hope of catching up with her sisters so that she could relate what had just happened. And the farther away she got from the café, the less she wanted to tell her sisters, who would know she'd tricked them.

Up ahead, she saw a cluster of children, some sitting on the curb hugging their knees, others drifting into the road as lookouts. Their deeply tanned skin was dusty from the road and sooty from the grit coming from the low smokestacks. As Joannah approached, the seated children stood, and they all chanted, "*Goo-me! Goo-me!*" Her sisters had warned her about the national gum fetish, so she had brought five hundred pieces of Bazooka. In such situations, Margie and Clarice threw fistfuls of gum away from themselves and insisted they all hurry away, but this time Joannah stopped and let them cluster around. She loved the company of kids, their chatter and energy, but back home she hardly interacted with them, and whenever she'd seen them visiting the nursing home, they'd kept to their Barbies or the television screens. These barefoot Romanian children, half of them shirtless, the other half in threadbare dresses or T-shirts with the slogans worn off, pressed their bodies against her, nervous, excited, and muscular like forest creatures. These kids now were touching her bike and tugging at her clothes. One boy coughed raspily without covering his mouth. When a girl with a raised scar on her hand like fried egg white unzipped a saddlebag, Joannah shook her finger in exaggerated disapproval. "*Nu, nu.*" Another boy coughed that same ragged cough. She placed pieces of gum into outstretched hands until she was certain each child had gotten several, and then she stroked their warm, bristly heads, which were mostly shaved, boys and girls alike, probably against lice, according to her sister. She hadn't chewed gum in years, but she was so hungry she unwrapped a soft, pink piece for herself before she set off again, waving to the children and shouting, "*La revedere*," goodbye, feeling as joyful as she ever had in her life. After a pause, the herd of children set out to chase her, their bare feet slapping the asphalt, their hands grabbing her saddlebags, and she sped up, fueled by a fear that they would topple her. She imagined falling, imagined the beautiful faces and bodies swarming over her, devouring her. After a quarter mile, the last runner, a boy of about ten, fell behind her and panted with his hands on his thighs.

JOANNAH'S SISTERS WERE expert travelers, and if she'd listened to them, she'd have brought more to eat. They carried shatterproof jars of peanut butter and zip-lock bags of granola to supplement hotel breakfasts and dinners. They would share their food if she asked, but Joannah didn't want to admit she'd failed to prepare. She'd packed a half dozen energy bars for emergencies, but she'd eaten three of them at the eight-hour Hungarian/Romanian border crossing. "Guns, drugs, Bibles?" the guard had asked. Joannah had smiled, thought he was kidding, until Clarice frowned at her.

By now, her sisters and their husbands might already be in the hotel in Deva, a town built around a steep hill with Dacian and Roman ruins at the top. In the guidebook photo the hill rose out of the center of the town like a lone breast whose companion had shriveled away.

Soon, Joannah found the going difficult. She stopped several times to check her tires and brakes and once even kneeled to feel the road surface with her hand to assure herself it was solid, for it seemed she might be sinking in tar. Only then did she realize she was no longer wearing a helmet or gloves,

both of which she'd left at the café. She would miss the cushioned leather-and-cotton gloves, but going back was out of
the question—she'd gone back for the camera the day before
and found no sign of it. In this country, as in plenty of places
in Chicago, when a thing was gone, it was gone. She imagined the man who'd grabbed her pulling the smooth synthetic
gloves over his hands. As for the helmet, she'd remind her sisters she'd survived biking without one when she was a kid.
These poor Romanian kids didn't even have bicycles let alone
helmets. Joannah spit out her old gum and bit into a new sug-
ary piece, which made her still hungrier. She reached down for
her water bottle and found it wasn't in its cage—she'd left it
behind in the café.

She biked slowly for hours without passing a stream or roadside well. The heat and humidity pressed on her; sweat and dirt
collected on the inside of her elbows, on the back of her neck, in
the creases of her belly formed by her hunching over the handlebars. Plum trees lined the road, stripped of fruit except on
the topmost branches. On the trunks were painted white skulls
and crossbones.

The mystery of the difficult biking lasted until she passed
a chalky blue marker, shaped like a rocket, which read 524
meters. The grade was so shallow and steady that she hadn't
realized she was climbing. She was on her first mountain pass,
high above the flat land of Illinois and on the other side of the
world from her poor lost mother. All her miles along the Chicago lakefront hadn't prepared her for this.

On a bench a quarter mile past the rocket marker sat an
unsmiling round-eyed teenage girl in faded navy blue stretch
pants who watched over two pint jars of cream on the seat
beside her. A cardboard sign behind the jars read *1.25 lei*, about
thirteen cents at the official exchange rate, about a penny at the

black market rate. Just outside Oradea, Bogdan had stopped and paid a girl for the contents of a thick glass jar like these and, after offering it around, drank down the whole thing. When he handed the jar back, yellowish cream coated his lips. Margie had pulled Joannah aside and instructed her to never drink such milk: it was unpasteurized, bacteria laden, and dangerous to adults who hadn't grown up with those microbes. Joannah had licked her own lips after seeing Bogdan's coated lips, and she licked her lips again now.

"Bună ziua," good day, Joannah said, pronouncing it *boo-nah zeewah*, waving to the girl. The girl mouthed, *"Ziua,"* without expression, and Joannah felt she'd been given permission to drop her own cheery pretense. Maybe people here let a person feel melancholy; maybe they didn't say, *You'd be pretty if you smiled.* As Joannah struggled up the road, the girl's eyes stayed fixed on her, as though Joannah were a dull-witted dancing bear lagging behind the rest of her troupe at a circus the girl had been forced to attend. Was this what Joannah had seemed like to her sisters while sitting home waiting for her mother to lose her mind and finally die? She wished she could stop and sit with the girl, but sensed she wouldn't be welcome.

Farther up the mountain, Joannah spotted another woman, maybe her own age, sitting on a log bench breast-feeding a child who looked four or five years old. She wore a red head scarf with a gold pattern on it, but most of her hair hung out the front and curled alongside her face. Her yellow blouse hung off her shoulder, as did another gold-patterned scarf, and she wore a red flowered skirt on top of other skirts—orange ruffles showed below the hem. Her feet were bare. The boy stopped nursing and turned to watch Joannah pass, revealing his round face and his mother's bare breast. The mother tipped her head back, stretched her long neck toward the woods and the sky, lifted a cigarette over the boy's head, and inhaled deeply. Could this black-eyed woman in bright skirts and scarves be of the same world as those gray raking women on the hillsides? The woman exhaled a long stream of smoke as she watched Joannah pass. She wouldn't have dared impose on the pair without an invitation. The boy then slid off his mother's lap, picked up a stone, and tossed it at Joannah—it fell way short. The woman languidly covered her breast and tugged the gold scarf over her shoulders.

When the grade steepened dramatically, Joannah shifted into her granny gear. Though it was afternoon, the sky darkened, and over the course of the next hour, a storm as black as any horror movie backdrop unrolled across the heavens. Switchbacks sent her weaving over the mountainside, took her breath away at each turn. When thunder boomed over the next peak, she recalled a relief map depicting the ridge of Carpathians that lay before her, a terrifying obstacle she hadn't let herself think about. Distant music drifted in and out as she wove upward—a fiddle, a tambourine maybe, echoes of voices. She focused on the intermittent sound as though it were meat smoke from a barbecue. A steak was what she wanted right now. Bloody rare, though her sisters would tell her well-done would be safer. At home she was practically a vegetarian, but her belly was telling her she needed meat.

The top of the pass was indicated by a third blue marker—928 meters—this one stuck in the ground beside a wooden shelter, maybe a bus stop, which was occupied by an old woman and her cow. The sky was now the color of a gray cat, and stray raindrops pelted Joannah's bare legs and arms. She pulled her bike under cover just before the deluge and took a seat on the cement bench beside the woman, who was perhaps her mother's age. Joannah smiled, and the woman smiled back, close-mouthed. *"Bună ziua,"* Joannah said, happy to meet someone who seemed happy to see her.

The woman opened her mouth to reveal a toothless cavern and laughed, maybe at Joannah's pronunciation, maybe at the absurdity of an American showing up on top of her mountain. The old woman's laughter degenerated into coughing. "Kent?" she asked. Joannah shook her head, but if the woman was truly disappointed about not getting cigarettes, she didn't show it. The cow switched its tail at some flies that were also taking cover from the storm. The old woman picked up Joannah's arm and squinted at her blue sport wristwatch, waterproof, for whatever that was worth. She then reached across Joannah's chest and with her knob-jointed fingers handled the gold cross hanging from Joanna's chain. There were no other souvenirs of Transylvania, her mother had said—her grandfather had fled the country with nothing and never went back. Joannah had copied and framed a photo of Dracula's real-life castle from a library book to supplement the family history and put it above the couch where she slept. The rest of her family's blood was Irish.

The boniness of the old woman's hands made Joannah's breasts look absurdly round and swollen by comparison, pornographic, as though they might burst out of her pink sports bra and matching tank top. Joannah dug some gum from her pack and gave it to the woman before reflecting that, without teeth, she couldn't chew it. Then Joannah gave her a toothpick that had a tiny American flag stuck to it. *"Ooo-ess-ahh,"* Joannah said, imitating Bogdan's pronunciation of *USA*. The woman slipped the gifts into a pocket. Her housedress was pale, its pattern worn away, and the bottom of the pockets had been mended with coarse black thread in a way that reminded Joannah of surgical stitches. In response to the gifts, the woman leaned forward, nearly off the bench, and grabbed the cow's udder and jostled it, as if to show Joannah how full it was. Joannah imagined leaning down, closing her mouth around a teat the size of a finger, swallowing mouthfuls of frothy whole milk. Joannah thought that if she hadn't lost her water bottle, she might've asked the woman to fill it up, whatever dangers the fresh milk might pose. Would the woman have some eggs if Joannah followed her home? She'd asked for eggs for breakfast, and Bogdan had made a show of going into the kitchen, but there had been none.

The two women sat silently, the cow's head bobbing between them, rain banging a wild message on the tin roof. When the storm finally began to peter out, Joannah thought she heard a fiddle again. She trained her ears on the sound, and so was startled when she felt the woman's callused hand on her leg. The woman took hold of Joannah's exposed thigh the way she might have inspected a salted ham in a market, and then she slapped Joannah's leg hard enough to raise a handprint. Joannah covered the red mark on her leg with her own hand, unsure what had just happened, unsure if she should be offended. The woman laughed and elbowed Joannah, and then pulled up her threadbare dress to reveal, as though it were the punch line to a joke, a thin, scarred leg, striped with varicose veins. The woman slapped the withered thing and tossed her dress back over it. Beside the old woman's leg, Joannah's plump, muscled thigh looked almost edible.

Joannah was trying to conceal embarrassment when she heard rumbling in the distance. The noise grew louder until it was deafening. Had the old woman not been sitting so calmly, Joannah would have pushed her bicycle into the woods and flattened herself on the ground for the onslaught. Arching up and over the mountain pass, a military convoy of drab green trucks and tank-like personnel carriers appeared. Long-barreled guns stuck out the fronts of the trucks. As the vehicles, probably fifty altogether, passed and turned the corner toward Deva, Joannah saw young men sitting on benches in the backs of the trucks. Despite their deep-set eyes and bulging Adam's apples, these skinny, bristle-headed soldiers reminded her of the children who begged for gum along the road, and Joannah would have liked to touch their bristly heads. The trucks rolled slowly, straining toward the crest of the hill, then, one by one, cut their engines and coasted down, perhaps to save fuel. The old woman's face did not register anything during these five or six minutes, and even after the convoy passed, she only blinked in Joannah's direction. The cow, however, tossed her bony head and pulled against her neck rope.

Dark clouds still loomed overhead, but light had broken through in the west. The woman elbowed Joannah again and pointed at a lone cyclist in a bright orange poncho who was pedaling from the direction of Deva. The cyclist weaved back and forth up the steep grade in an S pattern as he approached. Joannah recognized the green bike with worn tires.

"Bogdan!" she stood to greet him. "What are you doing here?"

"Joannah, you are disappeared," he said, panting. He turned down the hood of the poncho, something he must've borrowed from one of the other men in the group. Sweat and rain had soaked his hair. "You must not to be lost," he said. "I went to this hotel in Deva, but you are not arriving." His canvas sneakers looked waterlogged; the thin, dark dress laces were too short, so he'd skipped half of the eyelets.

"I can't believe you came back," Joannah said, dragging her eyes away from his shoes. "Uphill."

Bogdan's hands, large and square, rested lightly on the handlebars. Those hands would be the envy of the man back in the café. Joannah realized she hadn't looked at Bogdan until now, hadn't realized how big and solid he was. His formidable height and the solid ledge of his shoulders could be an affront to the Great Leader, who, despite his supposed greatness, was a flaccid-looking man with narrow, sloping shoulders. Transylvanian vampires in the books were irresistibly handsome and suave as they drew away your life force, but Ceausescu looked smug in the official photos that hung in every dining room and lobby as he sucked away the freedom of his people and the livelihood of the land. If the Great Leader wanted, he could probably throw Bogdan in jail or have him shot for his fine figure, the same way stepmothers in fairy tales disposed of beautiful daughters. Over the last few days, Bogdan had talked about his university in Bucharest, where he was studying engineering, and about his country's exports—shoes and pesticides—but now Joannah wondered if he had a girlfriend, or maybe a sweet doting mother.

"It is my job for to take care for you," Bogdan said. "In future, you must to stay with the group."

"All right," Joannah said, but she knew she could always find a way to escape the group. "Bogdan, will you tell this lady you can translate? Maybe she wants to say something to me."

When Bogdan spoke to her, the old woman just swatted the air, dismissing the whole prospect of verbal communication. "We must to go," Bogdan said, "and to meet the others of your group." He took off the poncho to reveal his checked button-up shirt, which was too short for his torso and made of a synthetic material that was all wrong for biking. He'd worn the shirt every day so far, and at breakfast it had been wet and clean. Rather than wadding up the poncho, he folded it carefully and tucked it into his improvised front pack, a canvas shoulder bag tied to the handlebars.

"Do you have any food?"

"There is food for dinner at this hotel in Deva at eighteen o'clock."

According to her watch it was four o'clock now. "All right, then. Onward toward a tiny chicken and a dirty bun," said Joannah.

Joannah mounted her bike, waved to the lady with the cow, and coasted down the mountain beside her guide. For the first half mile of curving road, plum trees with skulls and cross-bones blurred past them, but then the grade became gentle, which meant Joannah and Bogdan had to brake only occasionally. Steam rose off the road as the rain evaporated, and Joannah heard a fiddle again, heard it start, stop, and start again.

"I'm fine, you know," said Joannah. "You don't have to worry."

"Yes, I must to worry. These peoples of this region are half-of-gypsies."

"What are *half of gypsies*?"

"They are nothing." As with the rattlesnakes, Bogdan seemed to regret what he had said.

"Will you have to go into the army after college?" Joannah wanted to know about the military convoy, wondered if there was a base near here, but she wanted something other than an official response from Bogdan.

He smoothed his canvas bag against his handlebars with one hand as he steered with the other. "All Romanian mens must to go in this army."

"What about the women?"

"Womens must have five children."

"What?" she asked, thinking she must've misheard, but further conversation was aborted when two boys ran in front of them, waving their hands. They'd come out from behind a patched and unpainted privacy fence, the gate of which now hung open on one hinge.

"You must not to stop," said Bogdan, even as they were both slowing. "Deva is seven kilometers."

"You want to deny these poor kids their gum?"

Bogdan braked precisely beside her and reached over and held her handlebars steady as she dug in her saddlebags. The boys each accepted two pieces of Bazooka and then clutched her front and back wheels and yelled to someone in the distance. Out through the open gate dashed a pair of young women, one in a white blouse and skirt, her dark hair tumbling around a white sash, her belly swollen in what was probably the seventh month of pregnancy. She grabbed Joannah's wrist and started pulling her toward the house. Joannah resisted, managed somehow to not fall forward over her bicycle. She had seen such young women in every town, but they had seemed sad and quiet. This pair was full of life.

"What do they want?" Joannah asked Bogdan.

He inquired in Romanian, and the girl in white blabbed anxiously, gesturing with one hand, still tugging at Joannah's wrist with the other. "She invites us to this party for her wedding," he said.

"A wedding?"

"She says is good luck to have foreign peoples at this party. You won't believe," he continued, "but she is thinking I am foreign man." Bogdan probably did look foreign, a strong young fellow on a Czechoslovakian ten-speed, wearing shorts with cargo pockets.

When Joannah began to get off her bike, Bogdan said, "Joannah, you know we must to meet the group in Deva."

"The group is fine. You go ahead, and I'll catch up with you." Joannah didn't want Bogdan to leave without her, but a wedding party would be worth seeing, even if just to have a bite of food.

"You think nothing bad can happen in Romania?" Bogdan asked. "This is not America."

Well, it certainly wasn't Chicago. Behind and above them lay the ridge they'd crossed. Steaming dark green forest clung to the side of the mountain and continued across the road, and thick gray clouds swirled above, carried by a wind so high they couldn't feel it here. Maybe the pregnant bride, mist rising around her feet, was some kind of half-human, a *half-gypsy*, but Joannah reflected, as a joke to herself, that she had her gold cross to protect her. Having a foreigner in one's home was illegal, Clarice had said, as bad as having a typewriter, but maybe Ceausescu's policy made exceptions for weddings.

"I'm going through that gate to see what's happening," she said. "Don't worry so much."

Bogdan gripped her handlebars again. "I must to worry. You don't know these places of Romania. In old times peoples went into these hills and didn't come out."

"But our grandfathers were from here," Joannah said. "This is our homeland."

Bogdan sighed and swung a leg off his bike.

The young women led them through the gate, and Joannah saw the one-story house built of mismatched planks and plywood stuck together like puzzle pieces beneath a corrugated tin roof. They continued around to the back of the house, into a courtyard of hard dirt and chewed-down grass under a grape arbor covered with a sheet of graying plastic. Here and there water leaked through, though it had stopped raining. She hadn't seen private homes along the route, because they were all hidden behind various walls and fences.

"Do you have something for giving them?" Bogdan asked.

"I have gum and perfume samples."

"Cigarettes or dollars is better, I think."

"I hope there's some food."

"My grandfather has told me of his wedding in these places. He was for three days of feast," Bogdan said. They leaned their bikes against the side of the house. Grape leaves, bunches of pea-size grapes, and colored ribbons hung from the arbor, beneath which forty or so people stood or sat on rounds of fire-wood. The women here resembled those in the fields, but they wore pleated skirts and colored scarves patterned like Oriental rugs, and they were smiling. Many of the men wore their ragged fedoras at rakish angles. She wondered if everywhere behind the walls and fences, the sad-eyed Romanians became lively and joyful. As Joannah and Bogdan entered the arbor, a violinist and a singer took up. The violinist's shirt was unbuttoned to reveal a crop of chest hair tinged with gray, and it made Joannah think of poor, lonely Mr. Masters—she knew she would never sleep with him again. The skinny singer in red and purple skirts rattled her tambourine. As the music resumed, Joannah felt a surge of sadness so forceful she had to look hard down at the wet grass to avoid crying. She looked at Bogdan's shoes with their dark laces, at the bride's bare feet. The music was fast and bright, and yet it felt melancholy, too, so much so that by the end of the song she really was crying. When Bogdan asked what was the matter, she told him she had something in her eye.

A boy in a straw hat brought them each a jar of brownish wine that tasted sweet and strong—wine from plums, Bogdan said. Joannah was thirsty, so she drank hers down and then shook away the shiver traveling up her spine.

"Why do the trees have skulls and crossbones painted on them?"

"You must not to eat fruits with these paintings."

Before Joannah could ask any more, a shrunken woman, the mother of the bride, according to Bogdan, called out to the group and spoke in a nasal singsong. Then an uncle put his arm around the groom and spoke. The groom wore a gray suit of the same bell-bottom, wide-lapel cut as every other suit Joannah had seen in Romania, but this one looked almost new. Only the groom's right eye moved, while the left was tiny and motionless in its socket. The party was instructed to drink their wine, and Joannah found the little boy had refilled her glass. She swallowed, and the alcohol sent poisonous shivers down into her legs. Unlabeled bottles of the cloudy brown stuff were passed around for refills, and then everybody was looking at Joannah. Bogdan suggested she toast the couple and wish them luck, so she held up her wine and shouted, "May you make beautiful children!"

The crowd drank. When Bogdan translated, everyone cheered and drank again. Joannah happened to be standing near the violinist, who put down his instrument, took her face in his hands, and kissed her mouth as though they were lovers. She was shocked by the taste of him—bitter like tobacco and sweetly poisonous like the wine. She found she was not eager to pull away from this man—the kiss felt like a kiss goodbye, and she had to blink back more tears. When he resumed playing, she saw his two front teeth were capped with gold.

A dozen people, adults and children, joined hands, and before Joannah could ask Bogdan if he'd found any food, a young woman pulled Joannah along. More dancers joined hands with them until nearly everyone at the party was racing around, bumping hips and shoulders, ducking beneath arms that were lifted for them. When the line joined its ends to form a circle, the bride and another girl jumped into the center and spun, hands locked, heads tipped back, sweat plastering hair to their foreheads. When they stopped spinning, the two girls collapsed into laughter in each other's arms. Joannah fell away exhausted. She found her wine and finished it; before she even caught her breath, the straw-hatted boy filled her jar again. Joannah noticed the hat had a daisy stuck in its brim.

The pretty girl who had twirled with the bride pulled Joannah aside and said, "Anti-baby?" The rims of her eyes had been darkened a charcoal color.

Joannah shook her head and shrugged. She was breathing hard from the exertion; her belly was shrunken and aching from hunger. Where was the food? Where was the feast?

The girl held out both hands as if to receive holy waters and repeated the phrase more anxiously, "Anti-baby?" When it became clear that Joannah wasn't going to comply, the girl spat at the ground and stomped away in her cracked plastic sandals.

Joannah didn't mind not understanding the people who spoke to her, except the three other women who later repeated the phrase "anti-baby" with varying degrees of urgency. Apart from her hunger, she loved being here with all this energy coursing through her and around her. She found Bogdan chatting with the boy in the straw fedora, whom he introduced as the bride's little brother. "There is most beauty in village," he said in a heavy accent. He held out an arm expansively and slurred something like, "Rominadas arpen peel."

"Are you drunk?" Joannah asked.

"Cerpingly not."

"Then tell me, what is *anti-baby*?"

"Anti-baby is pills."

"Why are these girls asking me for pills?"

"Our Great Leader forbids pills," said Bogdan. "In order that womens can have childrens."

"Birth control pills? But what if they don't want to have children? Children."

"Romanian women wants five childrens. These womens must to be gypsies and mud-jars."

"Mud-jars?"

"Hungerish people."

"Hungry people? I'm the hungriest, Bogdan. Where's the food?" She glanced at her watch. Six-thirty. Her sisters and the men would be eating dinner now.

"From Hungary, this next country." He gestured vaguely in a direction that may or may not have been west and adjusted his glasses. "Romanian womens today are wanting five childrens." He spread out his big, square hand as if to prove the number five.

Joannah imagined giving birth in Romania; she would be lying on a metal table, arms restrained as though she were the mistress of Frankenstein, legs spread wide. Flies would perch around her lashes like ghoulish eyeliner, drinking from her corneas, sucking up her tears before she could weep them. Mr. and Mrs. Great Leader would stare down at her from portraits on the wall as she performed her duty for the state. Bogdan continued to hold up his hand signifying the five children, and Joannah resisted an urge to fold her own fingers between his.

Later, she saw the pregnant bride lean into the groom, pressing him against the ramshackle house. As the two began to kiss, the groom's hands slid along the bride's back, dragging the loose fabric of her blouse and skirt up and down. Joannah felt her own body grow languid, her own lips swell, and she wrapped her arms loosely around herself. The groom's hat fell off, and he did not retrieve it. When the music started up again, the bride dragged the bare-headed groom back toward the violinist and began another circle dance with all those who remained standing, including Bogdan and Joannah. The female singer had gone. Most of the men were now propped against chunks of wood, as the groom's father was, or were passed out flat at the edges of the courtyard, their bodies strewn about like scraps of fat cut from a steak.

"We are too late. The food is all gone," Bogdan reported, when the sun was starting to set. "This boy says that persons from the village are eating all the lamb kebabs for lunch."

"There's got to be something," Joannah said.

Bogdan conferred with the boy, whose eyes suddenly lit up.

"Maybe this boy can find you something. He says he is trying."

The boy returned twenty minutes later, and he was holding out a small cast-iron frying pan, and in it were three miniature fried eggs with shiny yolks the size of marbles.

"Why are they so small?" she asked and blinked, wondering if the problem was in her perception. How drunk was she?

"I'm telling this boy you like eggs. These are eggs from this bird, *graur*. This boy knows where is a nest. I don't know in English. In Russian is *skvorets*."

Any other time Joannah might have questioned eating the eggs, but she scooped the shining fried triplet from the pan and ate it with her hands. The buttery eggs slid into her mouth and down her throat almost without her tasting them, and yet her impression was that they were the best thing she'd ever eaten.

"Delicious!" she declared. "Thank you. I mean, *mulţumesc*."

"This boy says you speak Romanian very well," Bogdan said.

Joannah lifted the boy's hat and stroked his bristly head. She smiled at Bogdan, wondered if together they could have a child like this. When Bogdan's eyes registered alarm, she wondered if he could read her mind. The boy grabbed his hat and ran away, still carrying the empty pan. Afterward Joannah kept feeling the eggs inside her as though they had sprouted feathers.

Her eyes adjusted to the growing darkness, and when the clouds blew past to reveal the bright moon, the foreheads and eyes of the people around her shone. The groom appeared from nowhere and grabbed Joannah and spun her, handling her shoulders and arms and hips, pulling her to him and pushing her away. Her feet moved in synchrony with his, as though they'd danced together a thousand times, as though Joannah had been the one kissing him against the house. When the music sped up, the bride pushed the groom aside and locked hands with Joannah. They spun in the center of the circle until their grip broke and they flew apart. The bride stumbled back, laughing, and reached to pull Joannah up from the ground, but just as Joannah smelled the girl's sweet breath, the groom tugged the bride away with his arms around her swollen middle.

"How you are enjoying Romania?" Bogdan asked when he appeared beside her.

"I am loving Ro-man-yah," Joannah said, imitating his pronunciation, and mopped sweat from her face with the bottom of her pink tank top. "But I'm so hungry. I need a dozen more bird eggs to fill me up. Can we still get dinner at the hotel?"

"I will tell you my grandfather is from these places," Bogdan said.

"Tell me about your grandfather, Bogdan. Was he a vampire?"

"My grandfather is miner of gold from the mountains," he said, pointing up into the air, perhaps toward a mountain. Then he let the finger fall.

When the music started again Joannah turned to look and fell against Bogdan, almost knocking them both to the ground.

Bogdan caught her and held her there, letting her weight rest against his hips.

Joannah looked up into Bogdan's face and saw something new. She felt as though he had just produced for her a platter of prime rib, as though a black-and-white scene had suddenly gone to blood-soaked color. She wrapped her arms around him. She had been unfair in thinking him foolish this morning, for he was clearly wise in his knowledge of English and Romanian, wise in knowing the secrets of this place. His grandfather might have mined the gold for her necklace. She remained pressed against him, but instead of wrapping his arms around her, he just looked at her, astonished, and breathed the three syllables of her name, "Jo-ann-ah." The moon appeared from behind a cloud and revealed that his eyes, through his glasses, were gray-green and out of focus.

The heat of his body made Joannah realize she should not merely have dipped her hands and feet into those Romanian streams—she should have submerged herself and let the cool currents wash over her. She imagined food she'd never ordered in Chicago restaurants: rare rib-eye steaks, a filet mignon wet with juice. She wanted to tell Bogdan about how she loved the women on the hillsides, but when she opened her mouth to speak, she couldn't find words in English any more than she'd been able to yell for help in Romanian at the café. At critical moments there was never anything to say. She'd had nothing to say to her mother in that moment of lucidity when her mother gripped her hand and begged with her eyes to not be sent to a nursing home.

"We must to go," he said. "And I must to do one thing."

She watched Bogdan walk to his bicycle and take something out of his pack. He then embraced the groom and gave him the disposable razor that one of the American men had given him.

Bogdan called it "Zhillette," the first consonant unbearably soft. Joannah gave the bride a twenty-dollar bill and watched her secrete it in her stretched-out bra. Then Joannah knew she could not let the girl enter married life with such a poor bra to hold her beautiful swollen breasts. Joannah slipped the sweaty pink thing out through the armhole of her tank top. The bride clutched the fabric and kissed Joannah's cheek.

"We must to go," Bogdan said. "These people are waiting for us in Deva."

"Is the kitchen still open?"

"Much food is in Deva. Eggs for breakfast. From chickens."

"And tomorrow we'll go to *Dra-cool-ya's* castle."

"Is three days by bicycle," Bogdan said.

She swallowed the last of her wine, rubbed her finger along the bottom of the glass to get the dregs—solid food, she told herself, delicious.

"I have to give her something else," Joannah said. She was fumbling to unclasp her gold chain when Bogdan grabbed her hand and pulled her toward their bicycles leaning against the house. As she followed him out the gate and toward the road, the fiddle started up behind them again, sadder and slower than before.

In the daylight, the woods on the other side of the road had looked fresh and lush, inviting. Now the densely leafed branches seemed to forbid entry, and the whole forest was inhaling and exhaling like some root-bound leviathan regaining its strength after a fierce battle. Wood smoke from a cookstove chimney swept through the air on the wake of the great creature's breath, and the smoke mingled with the smell of Joannah's sweat. She leaned against the skull and crossbones on a plum tree and watched the clouds. She searched for a plum, but there were none.

"Will we die from drinking wine made of poison plums?"

"Our grandfathers are of this place. We are strong."

"It was the best wine I ever tasted."

"Jo-ann-ah, sleepink hotel-um," Bogdan announced just before he toppled onto the roadside. Joannah pushed her bike toward him along the shoulder, pressing a wiggly tire print into the dirt until the bike slipped sideways to the ground.

She let her bike fall into the ditch, rousing a black-and-white chicken that fluttered, clucking, beneath a wooden fence and into the adjacent courtyard.

Gravel dug into her forearms as she lay on her stomach beside Bogdan a few inches from the road. In the dim strobe of light and dark, as the moon was revealed and then covered again by clouds, she noticed one of Bogdan's buttonholes had been carefully enlarged and re-sewn with coarse dark thread. She thought of the dozens of shirts at home in her dresser, a waste when she only needed the shirt on her back. What would it matter if she had to wash it every night? Her arms were covered with goose bumps from the cooling night air.

Running her hand across Bogdan's chest was like biking uphill, each rib a switchback, and she found herself breathing hard at the effort of moving from one to the next. In the distance, she made out the rumbling of trucks.

Bogdan began whispering. Long sentences in Romanian, sentences that grew louder to cover the sounds of the approaching convoy. He was whispering a story she would understand if she listened carefully enough. His arms eased to life and wrapped around her. He rolled his body over hers, over again into the drainage ditch so that she lay on her back beneath him, her bike at their feet. His glasses fell beside her head onto the warm muddy grass, but in the shadow of his face she couldn't make out his eyes at all.

"Tell me in English, Bogdan," she whispered.

"I'm saying to you, Jo-ann-ah, these childrens from this forest are living with wolves. My grandfather is telling me this before he dies, and I am forgetting this story until I'm seeing this boy with his flower in his hat. Once I was such a boy, and I came to these woods to visit my grandfather, and I am learning about these wolves. I'm saying to you, Jo-ann-ah, this milk from these wolves is strongest milk, so these childrens are strong, and they protect these places. You see, Jo-ann-ah, even the Great Leader fears if these childrens of wolves comes to Bucharest." Bogdan reverted to Romanian, but inserted her name more frequently into the sentences, "Jo-ann-ah," as if those were the sounds that could invoke a spell that could drown out the trucks.

Her gold chain slithered away under her armpit. She wished for a bottle of plum wine so she could tip it to her mouth and let it slosh down her throat and onto her cheeks and neck. She hummed along to the violin tune in order not to hear the wheels approaching on asphalt, but the rumbling grew so loud that their voices and the violin were drowned out. Joannah stretched up and her teeth clacked against Bogdan's, smooth as hard candies, smooth as polished bones. Vehicles without head-lights approached and passed like phantoms. As the convoy rolled past them, vehicle by massive vehicle, Bogdan's hands moved over her breasts, around her back, along her thighs. The earth swelled around her. Just as she was about to howl, Bogdan covered her body like the lid to a box, and she reached up and covered his ears with her hands.

His hands moved over her like dozens of grasping hands, and then his skin was many bodies of hungry skin against hers. From now on she knew she would eat anything he put in front of her—sour sheep cheese, pork fat, warm raw cream. She would no longer kill the life in the water with iodine pills, but would drink *apǎ* however it arose from the earth. The heat and pressure of his mouth on her neck told her about the children conceived in such moments, children of drunkenness and raucous joy, survivors of the regime. As trucks and personnel carriers strained up the mountain past them, Joannah knew she wanted to give birth to such children, wild creatures who drank wolves' milk and grew stronger than dictators. Children who could run like deer and hide deep in the woods, until it would be safe and wise to emerge.

Natural Disasters

We have already donned our blindfolds to grope in draw-string bags, to have our fingers stuck into the ick of Nutella spread on a disposable diaper. We have sucked luke-warm hot chocolate from baby bottles and have tasted mashed food from little jars without labels. We have picked tiny gold safety pins out of rice and lifted cotton balls from a bowl with a spoon. Some have played "tinkle in the pot," in which a woman squeezes a quarter between her knees as she walks to the center of the room and tries to drop it into a jar. Two of the women created a three-foot-high cake out of disposable diapers, and this structure presides over us like a creepy-puffy baby-powder grandmother, and finally it is almost the time in my baby shower when everyone gathers around and watches me open gifts. And then we will eat, and then, only then, will these people go home. My cousin Nancy and her best friend have brought their infant boys, and I am mesmerized and horrified at how casually they handle their darlings.

Yesterday my summer vacation from teaching high school

English began, and I've been looking forward to focusing more on Baby, but a shower was not my idea. My sister Gail, who is a dear pest, and my husband, who is conveniently out of town, have been colluding against my having any time to myself. Both of them have expressed concern at the grim mind-set I some-times slip into. I'm keeping as physically fit as possible, but still I keep falling into a funk and brooding about the future. I can happily contemplate my baby daughter as a toddling toddler with a silky fountain of hair spraying up from her sweet head; I can imagine her warm little body on my lap as she follows along with her pointer finger when we read the lines of *Green Eggs and Ham*; I see her as a kindergartner pulling on shiny rain boots (maybe polka-dotted ones) and then running away from me toward her teacher. What I'm having a rough time with is seeing myself with a tiny, helpless baby.

"If you weren't pregnant, Barb, I'd get you back on your anti-depressants lickity-split," Gail said this morning. When she got here and found me wearing black, she marched me into my room and found a purple sweater for me to put on with my jeans.

Ever since the tinkle-in-a-jar game, I've had to pee, and so I struggle up from my seat and down the hall. I strained my Achilles tendon last time I did prenatal yoga—the teacher keeps reminding me a yoga class is not a competition—but I don't want to let on to my sister. When I get back, the women are telling stories.

"When I was in labor for Luke, I begged the nurse to kill me," my cousin Nancy says, glancing down at the boy flopped across her lap. "I grabbed her pen and tried to stab myself in the chest with it. So they insisted on an epidural."

"I was in labor for twenty-six hours with my first," says my best friend from high school. We haven't kept in touch, but it's nice to see her freckled face again. She has three children, all apparently healthy and happy, and she seems not to have lost her mind at all. "They wanted to do a C-section, but I said, *Hell, no. After all this, I'm pushing this thing out myself.*"

I don't fear giving birth. I'll make it through that exercise just fine, as I've made it through more than a dozen marathons and a couple triathlons, as I got through earning my master's degree in one year while teaching full time. I've been out winter camping in below-zero weather with my husband, and together we've hiked up mountains with heavy packs in hundred-degree heat. My body will come through for me, and I have little doubt that I will give birth to something like a perfect child. That's not the problem.

Also, I have enjoyed being pregnant, have enjoyed doors being opened for me, seats being found for me in restaurants, my husband cooking all manner of weekend breakfasts tailored to my tastes. For months, other women have ignored the frown I'm told I wear perpetually, and they've smiled at me anyway. Being pregnant has not been a problem, for I know Baby is safe so long as she is inside me.

A siren sounds just as I am returning to my chair, and I fall heavily onto the cushion in such a clumsy, comical way that the women around me laugh.

"It's just a test," my sister says, speaking loudly and authoritatively enough that we can hear her over the siren, which emanates from the fire station a quarter mile away.

"They test the siren on the first Saturday of every month. This is the third Saturday," I say as the mournful sound echoes inside me. "And it's three o'clock. The test siren is always at one."

Somebody looks up the weather on a smartphone (my sister tried to make everybody put them away during the party) and finds that a tornado was sighted just sixteen miles north of here. My heart pounds as I study the hallway through which the tornado's winds will tear. Books about composition theory and French philosophers and even the Nancy Drew mysteries I've saved since childhood are missiles poised to fire. That floor-to-ceiling bookshelf I built last year is all edges, sharp corners, and metal screws. I must remember to ask David to bolt it more sturdily to the wall studs before Baby is born, and perhaps we can secure each shelf of books with a bungee cord across the front.

The bedroom door is closed, but atop my dresser are my old Kappa Delta Pi honor society pins, hair ties and barrettes, race medals, lapis lazuli earrings that hang down to my shoulders, corks from wine I drank in France—any of those could blow down in a tornado's winds and slither toward Baby's throat to stab or choke her. On my husband's dresser are shoelaces, tie clips, cufflinks, and more medals. On his desktop in our shared office are rubber bands and paper clips galore. He has thus far not imagined his lifestyle poses any danger to Baby.

We all move to the basement, negotiate the steep stairs with the wrapped packages. I sit on the only comfy chair, while others sit on cushions they've dragged down; my sister perches beside me on her knees on the rug.

"I wish I had a bomb shelter," I say. "Or one of those survivalist pods."

Everyone except my sister laughs, but I'm trying to recall whether the siren cutting out means the danger has passed or if it means the fools at the firehouse think we've been given warning enough.

"Take a deep breath, Barb. You're going to be fine, we'll all be fine," my sister whispers. She is holding out a box wrapped in lavender teddy-bear paper. Ten other women and one seven-year-old girl stare from a semicircle around me. The two baby boys are gazing at their mommies now, begging for protection, no doubt. My sister leans in again and whispers, "If it comes any closer, we'll go sit against the west wall, but the chance of getting struck by a tornado is tiny." She holds her finger and thumb an inch apart.

So is a baby tiny, I think, tiny and helpless.

"There was a tornado here in 1980," I remind my sister. She's right that we're doing all we can, but after Baby is born, I won't take a chance. I'll build a kind of bunker below the level of this basement. I'll stock it with baby food and enough pure water to keep Baby nourished for weeks if necessary in case of natural disaster. So long as it's not a flood, in which case the unfinished attic would be a better place to hunker.

Last weekend I told my sister that an earthquake struck southwest Michigan in 1947, and she accused me of being paranoid. I told her she could look it up online, see old black-and-white photos of cracked plaster and toppled chimneys. At this moment, it is far too easy to imagine my new baby crawling through glass shards while I am trapped under a fallen beam.

"Here's your first gift. It's from Maxine." To get my attention, my sister pokes me in the belly with the corner of the lavender teddy-bear box, and I shoot her a glare. I smooth my hand over my belly and accept the thing.

There's a comforting daydream I've had lately: a cushioned world without edges, a world of foam rubber, cotton balls, warm air of optimal humidity, a world in which walls are covered with quilted fabrics, soft and washable, or coated with a high-density gel like you find in those shock-absorbing bicycle seats. If only there were a way to make walls bend and curve in response to pressure, so the walls of baby-safe rooms could gently enfold bodies. Give me sagging Claes Oldenburg typewriters capable of producing only nursery rhymes and simple, hopeful sentences, beanbag chairs plump with Styrofoam balls.

In tornadoes such furnishings would blow about harmlessly. In case of flood, Baby and I would use the pieces as rafts.

The lavender teddy-bear box is nearly weightless, and I rest it on my knees as I remove a long purple snake of ribbon. What are these women thinking? Such a thoughtless object could travel into Baby's mouth, down Baby's esophagus until it clogged. I stuff the thing into the paper bag beside me—there will be no more ribbons after this baby is born. I remove the box lid to find a newborn's snowsuit, yellow.

I hold the snowsuit up to show the women the darling duck embroidered over the heart, and my best friend from high school says, "You're sure going to need that suit this winter. I feel lucky my babies were born in spring, so all those early doctor appointments were in the warm weather."

"Thank you, Maxine. It's really nice," I say to my aunt, who is only ten years older than me. She has two teenage boys as well as the seven-year-old girl who is sitting beside her now, vigorously working her finger around in her nose.

"Look at that sky!" says Cousin Nancy, pointing at the little slider basement window. She loosens her grip on her baby to such a degree that I want to thrust my arms under hers to catch him when he falls. The spot of sky I can see is undeniably the gray-green color that bystanders report before a tornado demolishes a trailer park. There is a trailer park a half mile down the road.

The snowsuit is cute, but it isn't waterproof and doesn't look warm enough to protect against frostbite. Cold and snow like we had last year could imprison us in our home and cause us to miss scheduled vaccinations, and the ice-covered roads could even render me unable to rush Baby to the doctor for a choking or bleeding emergency. I can't imagine how to protect her if we have to leave the house in winter, especially since David will probably be at work or out of town when trouble strikes. Despite my generally good balance, a slippery spot on a walkway between the house and the car might result in my slamming to the pavement on top of Baby. Perhaps David can rig up some battery-operated space heaters to warm the walkway between the house and garage.

"You shouldn't use that in a car seat," Cousin Nancy says. "They're saying now that it's dangerous to have kids dressed in fluffy fabrics. The fluff compresses in an accident, leaving the straps too loose."

"Really?" I ask.

"And kids can overheat," my freckled former best friend says. "You don't want to cook your baby. The little ones can't let you know they're too hot."

If I wrap her for protection against the weather, then I risk cutting off her air supply. I squeeze the puffy fabric in both hands and try not to cry. As soon as these people leave, I'm going to look up the safety information regarding snowsuits. If Baby is not safe in something so soft, then where can she be safe?

The next gift is a monitor that allows David and me to listen to what's happening in the baby's room—as if I'll let her out of my sight! For this, I thank my sister, who helped David and me find this house, which is turning out to be ill-suited for a child, with its freestanding garage, its tile and hardwood floors, and steep basement steps down which a baby could tumble. Baby reads my mind and shifts in my belly.

"I'm so sorry," I say, putting my hand on my stomach. I am considering not having this baby at all, but may keep her inside me indefinitely

The women all smile, except Cousin Nancy, who tilts her head at me in puzzlement, maybe waiting to hear what I'm so sorry about. I wish she'd just pay attention to the squirming boy on her lap. Next I open the envelope containing the gift from my seven-year-old cousin, and find a package of a dozen of those child-safety plugs that prevent kids from sliding keys into sockets. I look around and imagine every wall-mounted outlet hissing with vipers of electricity. And in the kitchen, the appliances! Dear God, the oven is a crematorium, the refrigerator—I can hear it humming from down here—is a suffocation chamber. Give me stoves with smooth, flameless burners made to warm food only to the temperature of breast milk, hot water heaters set to tepid. Cousin Nancy's best friend puts her infant on his blanket at her side, as though nobody could accidentally step on him, as though there's no mildew in the basement rug.

The tornado siren sounds again, and this time everybody jumps a little. My sister checks her phone and says, "There's been a sighting of another tornado ten miles from here. But it's north of us. Nothing to worry about, Barb."

By the time the siren peters out, I feel exhausted. Fifteen minutes after that, as I'm numbly opening the last package, the sun shines through the basement slider window, and my sister announces that the warning has passed, that now it's just a tornado *watch* for the rest of the afternoon, as if that's fine with her. We all trek back up the steep stairs. After the gifts are passed around again and admired, everyone sighs in relief, and folks fill plates with snacks, pretending the world is a perfectly reasonable place to raise a child. Somebody brings me quarter sandwiches without crust and little balls of fruit scooped out of a watermelon carved like a cradle—inside it is a grapefruit made to look like a baby head with halved grapes inset for eyes. Really it looks like an alien invader. Finally my aunt brings me a cupcake with a naked baby made of marzipan curled atop it as though asleep.

Because I am readjusting myself, I accidentally knock away

the cupcake, whacking it like a softball into the three-tiered diaper cake, which falls over with a whoosh.

"You're going to be glad to have those diapers," my sister says. "For emergencies. Sometimes you won't want to bother with cloth diapers." She has railed against cloth diapers from the start, and at another time I would have argued with her, but I am starting to appreciate the padding in those diapers, which might be perfect for covering hard surfaces. While everyone is eating, I study the booty and sense a kind of violence in the brash primary colors before me: the plastic blocks from my neighbor Suzanne, the star-shaped sun catcher, and even that stuffed fish mobile my friend Jenny showed up with. I don't like their cartoon separation of blues, yellows, and reds. Colors should blend into one another the way they do in rainbows, which show the storm is over. Let reds dissolve into purples which blend through a thousand blues to blue-greens, to true green.

Without warning, my seven-year-old nose-picking cousin casually plops an infant boy onto my lap, and I grab hold. He is a warm, soft blob, utterly helpless. And surprisingly heavy. The greatest danger for babies, I realize, is gravity. Gravity is the problem I must solve before this baby leaves my body. Once I find a way to free Baby from the terrible pull at the center of the planet, she will float through rooms and glide helmeted through bumper-car doorways as if swimming. Thus ungrounded, Baby will be safe even from strikes of lightning.

I wrap my arms around the plump creature and hold him securely against my belly, but he soon begins to struggle. When he starts to cry, the other little boy cries, and then I begin to cry, too. I can no longer trust this strong body of mine that I have worked so hard to maintain, especially my big, solid bones—ribs as inflexible as jail bars, sharp elbows and scapulae, axe-blade pelvic bones, long, hard femurs. And what about this spine against which Baby will continue to be pressed, as if crucified, for another month? I am thinking I could make incisions in my skin and slide these bones out to make of myself a vessel of all-enveloping softness. And that way, if a tidal wave engulfs this neighborhood, we might bob and flow atop the currents together, like jellyfish.

The Fruit of the Pawpaw Tree

Susanna O'Leary had long tended the biggest garden in Potawatomi, Michigan, and she planned to keep on, one way or another, even if she had to do it without the Ford tractor. That tractor had given forty-five years of faithful service, but the unholy heat had plain worn out the old engine. This summer's heat and drought were also causing the pumpkins to ripen early, and when you hefted one of those big fruits by the stem, you found it almost as light as a gourd. The cucumbers and zucchini were shriveling, and the tomatoes clinging to scorched vines were small and strong-flavored. Susanna spent summers in her garden and barnyard and during the school year worked as a junior high school cafeteria lady, which meant that in a week and a half she'd be hellaciously busy with feeding lunch to two hundred kids and then coming home to can tomatoes and to freeze beans. But there was no law saying a woman couldn't work hard.

The heat had settled into the walls and the floors of Susanna's rambling one-story house and had taken its toll on the occupants, rendering everyone as slow-moving as snakes. Three of Susanna's grandchildren, ages four, five, and seven, who lived in her house, spent a lot of time lying in the shallow creek letting the current run over them while their ma worked as a receptionist in a cool dentist's office a few miles away

Susanna was sitting at her desk this afternoon with her feet up, reading a magazine article about a garbage collector in Egypt, swatting occasionally at a housefly, and pressing a mason jar of iced tea to her forehead, trying to gather her energy for Junebug's next bottle-feeding. A floor fan blew hot air across her in what felt like slow motion.

When Larry slogged into the room wearing his towel like a skirt on his skinny-legged way from the bathroom to the back porch where he slept, she felt like tripping him just to make something happen. Larry's neck was long and thin, and his Adam's apple protruded to an alarming degree.

"Hope you didn't use all the hot water," she said, her standard refrain, but even her words felt slow and burdensome.

"I took a cold shower," he said and clutched at his towel as though he couldn't trust it to stay up. Larry's parents had kicked him out, and in a moment of weakness, Susanna had taken pity on this kid and let him move in with nothing more than the first week's rent. She liked him well enough, but was determined not to let on.

"Why aren't you at work?" she asked.

"I was late again." He stood there dumbly, his curly black hair hanging across one eye. "I just can't get there at five in the morning, so Theo fired me. I don't know what's the matter with me."

"If you don't know, then nobody knows. But you're two weeks behind on rent, and I'll have to kick you out if you don't pay." She tried to hide the sympathy she felt, sympathy she would never have extended to her own children, though they'd been ambitious, responsible youths. Maybe it was that Adam's apple that made her feel strangely tender toward him.

"I'm looking for another job," he said and sighed.

"Don't you have to leave the house to look for a job?"

"It's so hot riding my bike," he said. "I've been trying to talk my uncle into taking me on as an assistant. He's in heating and cooling. You might have seen his van. Wendell's Heating and Cooling."

"We could use some of that cooling about now."

"I seen in that hall closet you've got a big central air unit," Larry said. "I guess it doesn't work."

"Hasn't run for twenty years, and it's not going to start anytime soon. I can't afford to have it fixed when people don't pay rent."

"I could call my uncle, see if he can come over and check it out."

"Just get a job and pay your rent."

"His wife divorced him last year, and now he's sleeping in a tent over by Old Douglas Road. He cooks his food on a campfire."

Susanna watched the housefly land on the edge of her desk, and she slowly raised the flyswatter and whacked it, causing Larry to jump a little. She put down the swatter and wiped a bandanna all over her face and then applied the iced tea again, but the cubes had melted. Nobody'd had a good night's sleep in weeks.

When the ducks erupted into loud quacking and yakking, Larry started so vigorously that he almost dropped his towel. The donkeys' braying had terrified him his first morning here, when he thought the wheezy honking might be coming from swamp monsters. The kid had so far proved himself to be as hopeless as Junebug the donkey or Bullet, her son Jeffrey's old blind 4-H horse, who spent his day grazing and turning in circles trying to catch sight of whatever showed in his remaining sliver of peripheral vision.

When Susanna could put it off no longer, she carried the bottle of mare's milk through the gate into the barnyard, and the three-month-old donkey ran straight at her. Junebug didn't stop when he reached her, but lowered his head so that it landed solidly in her stomach, knocking her off balance. She stuck the thumb-size nipple in his mouth before he could bite her.

At a few days old, the baby donkey had seemed dull, and the mama donkey wouldn't let him nurse, and so Susanna thought it might be wise to let this one fade away and start again from scratch. Back when she had been struggling to feed and clothe five kids, she would have let nature take its course, would have left the baby to gradually grow weaker and then die, figuring if the mother didn't want to feed it, then neither did she. However, her daughter Marika had visited and cried at how sweet he looked, and everybody came over and took his picture. They fussed over Junebug's fluffy hair. The whole world went on and on about how she had to save this creature.

Susanna had felt bullied when she first picked up the leggy little foal, leaned him against the side of the barn, and force-fed him milk she'd reconstituted from an expensive mare's milk powder. She repeated this every few hours, around the clock, for the first few weeks. He never did learn to drink milk from a bowl the way the instructions on the milk bag claimed he would; two mornings in a row it appeared the baby had finished his bowl of milk, but when Susanna checked on him the next night, she found a twenty-pound possum stretching up on hind legs, supping there. When the baby was a few weeks old and able to eat some milk pellets, she built a crawl pen with a doorway too low for the mama donkey to enter, but the boy wouldn't go in and eat his pellets unless Susanna pushed him in and latched the gate, and if she didn't let him out again he spent the night he-honking for his ma.

Now that she had gotten him down to one bottle-feeding a day, he seemed to be developing a problem in his left rear leg—he stepped only on the tip of the hoof of that foot and sometimes jumped around on three legs. She'd assumed at first it was an abscess that would resolve with some soaking, but a week of Epsom salts hadn't helped. Marika kept begging her to drive the donkey down to the veterinary clinic at Three Rivers for X-rays.

X-rays, thought Susanna, with exasperation. X-rays for a donkey! Used to be you had animals at your own convenience. Take cats. You had a bunch of cats people dumped at your place, and then every couple years most of them got distemper, and it was terrible to see them die with their eyes gummy, and the kids got upset, but then the strongest survived, and if you had only one cat left, then you had yourself one hell of a cat. But nowadays you had to get even the strays neutered and spayed and vaccinated. This was nonnegotiable ever since Marika got herself onto the Humane Society board of directors. Currently Susanna had three of these pampered felines in the house and two neutered feral cats in the barn. Used to be people drowned cats they didn't want. Used to be if you had a pony or donkey that couldn't walk anymore, you called some guy who came over and shot it in exchange for the carcass, which he fed to his hunting dogs.

Now Susanna had a donkey that had grown to a hundred ten pounds of hand-fed trouble, and nobody would even share her fantasies of roasting it on a spit. All those sleepless milk-filled nights wasted, and she'd paid seventy bucks for milk powder and twenty-five for the pellets for this creature. If she continued on this path, not only would there be the fee for each X-ray, but there was the trouble of transporting him halfway to Indiana in the back of her truck.

"This damned donkey gets cuter every day," said Lydia, her neighbor and daughter-in-law, seeming to appear out of nowhere. "How's my favorite living plush toy?"

"Take him. He's yours," Susanna said. "Seriously. Take him."

"You know I can't," Lydia said. She stuck out her lower lip and blew air upward over her face so her blond bangs fluttered. "I never thought I'd look back fondly at being in jail, but at least it was air-conditioned."

Lydia fingered the moonstone she wore on a gold chain around her neck. It was the size of a radish. She was married to Jeffrey, Susanna's middle son, and lived just a half mile away. Her sentence of a year in county jail for selling pot had just wrapped up a couple of weeks ago.

"You are building up some serious karma taking care of this baby. Your aura gets brighter every day, Susanna."

"Sounds like more damned heat to me."

"I did the tarot for you before I came over, and it foretold of an opportunity for great joy."

When Susanna let go of the donkey, it moved around and bit at the seat of her jeans, the way a normal baby donkey might bite his mama and receive a kick in the head for it. Susanna smacked him, but the donkey figured she was being affectionate and nosed her some more.

"Was that bite in the ass supposed to be joyful?" Susanna asked Lydia.

"I brought the kids. They ran down to the creek to cool off. I hope you don't mind," Lydia said. "I need to leave them here for a few hours while I visit my ladies at the nursing home." Lydia did hair and nails at a half dozen nursing homes in town, as well as at the Blossom Salon in Kalamazoo.

A few hours for Lydia usually meant all day, so Susanna would have to feed six grandchildren lunch and supper instead of the usual three. While she was summoning the energy for a cranky response, a big pine tree by the driveway exploded into thousands of pieces before her eyes. She fell against the rail fence and held her breath, unsure of what she'd just seen or what she might see next.

Junebug the donkey tore across the barnyard, ran to his mother, who kicked him.

"What the fuck?" Lydia said and wrapped her fingers around the moonstone, pushing her knuckles into her breast.

Junebug returned at a jog and stood stiff-legged at Susanna's side. The chickens were squawking in their chicken yard, and Susanna could hear that the creek had erupted into quacking and duck-yakking. Bullet was turning circles frantically in the pasture, trying to see what had happened. Rachel's yellow Lab loped over and started barking at the debris.

When Susanna could breathe again, she stepped through the rail fence and walked to where the pine tree had stood moments ago. There she found a waist-high stump surrounded by tooth-picks. The whole midsection of the sixty-foot-tall pine tree had been reduced to smithereens, and the splinters of wood were bone dry and warm to the touch. The upper limbs lay across the driveway. One had fallen onto the engine compartment of Susanna's broken-down Ford tractor, adding insult to injury. Another branch had fallen onto Larry's bicycle and knocked it over.

"Well, that was something different," Susanna said. Sweat poured anew from her face, neck, and armpits. Her limbs felt shaky. "Something I've never seen before."

"I think it was a sign," Lydia said. She hugged Susanna and walked down the driveway toward home, without her children.

A sign of what? Susanna wondered. She'd known trees to explode from lightning strikes, but never from plain old heat. Her own body was strangely warm these days, more than could be accounted for by the temperature, truth be told, worse than when she'd gone through her change. Maybe it was the blood pressure her doctor had warned her about, or the cholesterol, and maybe she was going to burst apart the same way the tree had done. When she went into the house, she saw a number five blinking on the answering machine, but didn't push the *play* button, which might mean listening to somebody's complaints.

"Larry!" she shouted onto the porch. "Call your goddamned uncle."

THE MORNING EXPLODED with the sound of ducks quacking and yakking in the creek running below Susanna's bedroom window. The noise woke her from a dream of tilling next year's garden. In the dream, she had harnessed Junebug and his ma, Jenny, to pull the rotovator, and as quickly as the blades broke up the soil, tomato and bean plants sprang up. She laughed aloud, laughed as she hadn't in ages at such an absurd thought, that the new donkey could be worth a damn. She folded her arms behind her head and wondered what the ducks might be going on about. Were snapping turtles snapping up their ducklings?

Those ducks were her summer alarm clock, but in the darker months she was forced to go mechanical; she was no more attuned to a five a.m. schedule than poor Larry was.

"Damn noisy ducks," Susanna said, as she did every morning. She would miss those ducks when they disappeared in autumn, but from her ex-husband she'd gotten the habit of lying in bed cursing them this way; though her husband had been gone ten years, she was a woman of habits. "Get the hell out of here, go south, fly off to the nature center, won't you?"

"Dumb ducks," said another voice, quietly.

"What?" Susanna sat up, blinked to make sure she was awake.

"Dumb ducks," said a man's voice. "Like you said."

"Is there somebody in my bed?" Susanna's bed was bigger than a king-size, so big that the mattress was a special order, and new sheets were expensive.

"It's just me," said Wendell Wagner, Larry's uncle, who'd been working on the air-conditioning late last night. Susanna had gone to bed as the man had still been puzzling through an ancient manual he'd found under the dusty unit. He told her that if the coolant had leaked out it would be a problem, because the refrigerant she would need was now illegal. Though she'd said Larry had to pay the man, when she saw what a hard worker Wendell was, she figured she could offer him a post-dated check, one he could cash after she got her first paycheck from the school. Maybe she could make up for the expense this winter by skimping on fuel oil—she'd tell everybody to keep warm by remembering the summer heat.

"You told me I should stay the night if it got too late," Wendell Wagner said. She now saw him in her peripheral vision as a little range of foothills over on the far side of the big bed. When her kids were little, she'd always had to keep them from jumping around on the bed, and now the problem was just as bad with the grandkids. Not only did they jump on it whenever she left the door unlocked, but they enacted battles and built forts in and around and under it.

"Well, I certainly didn't mean you should sleep with me. I meant the couch in the living room," she said. She had encouraged him to stay, hoping he would work all night if that was what it took to fix the old machine. At seven p.m., before he arrived, the radio announced that six people at the Kalamazoo County Fair had had to be rushed to the hospital for heatstroke.

"I put a pillow out there on the couch for you, Mr. Wagner."

"Call me Wendell. I must've walked in my sleep."

"You're starting to remind me of your nephew Larry." She turned her head enough to see he'd carried that pillow with him and had it under his head now.

"Oh, Larry's a good boy."

"Wendell, between you and me, that boy's dumb as a stump."

"He's a late bloomer, and I want to give him a chance, same as you did. It's awful nice of you to rent him a room," Wendell said.

"I didn't want to, but my daughter told me to take pity."

"You strike me as a woman who doesn't do anything she doesn't want to."

"Well, there's a pretty good chance I'm kicking him out."

"And I believe if you want to kick him out, you will. That's the kind of woman you are, a woman who knows her own mind."

Susanna had survived without her husband for ten years by sticking to her routines. She'd honestly planned to never lie down with one of them cheating, troubling sons of bitches again, but here she was, lying with a fellow in the very bed her husband had built, with him telling her what kind of woman she was. Her husband had used black walnut wood and got the idea of hitting the headboard with a chain to make the bed frame look old, and then he'd shellacked it. He probably built a bed for that gal at the bottle gas company, too, in their new place, thirty miles south of here, halfway to Indiana.

"Now I remember why I came back here," Wendell said.

"That big yellow dog was lying on the couch, taking up all the space. That's why."

"You could've pushed him onto the floor. He's used to it."

"That's a mighty big yellow dog you got. I wasn't sure which end of him to push. And I figured if I pushed one end of him off, by the time I got over to push the other end, he'd've pulled himself back up again."

Susanna realized they were not just telling facts here. Wendell had gotten her laughing last night, and she'd made him a pot of coffee. Hot coffee in this heat! He'd claimed it made him sweat and so cooled him down. Also claimed it didn't keep him awake.

"That dog does something that drives me crazy," Susanna said. "I'll put a cast iron pan on the floor for him to lick clean, and if I don't pick it up right away, he carries it out into the woods, so I have to go find it. He can carry a pan weighing ten pounds. But he provides a real service around here, that dog does, by eating all the food my grandkids drop on the floor."

In fact, Wendell had followed the sound of Susanna's snoring to her bedroom, and he had climbed into the enormous bed slowly and quietly, so as not to disturb her, and he'd stayed way over by the far edge. Wendell would never have dared climb into a regular bed with a woman, but he figured that in a bed this size a woman might not even notice him.

The ducks struck up another round of quacking and fussing.

"You're not naked, are you?" Susanna asked.

"I don't think I am." Wendell lifted the blanket. "Nope, I'm definitely not naked."

"Good thing," Susanna said and snorted. There was no law that she couldn't try some talking herself. "'Cause if my grandkids had come in here and found you naked, they'd do terrible things to you."

"What kind of terrible things, Susanna?"

"Oh, one fellow who crawled in my bed, they stole his trousers and filled them up with stinging nettles. The way he howled after putting on those pants, you'd've thought cannibals were cooking him." She felt a little proud of this invention.

"I still got on my trousers," Wendell said. "My shirt, too. I'm not one bit naked, Susanna. That's not anything to worry about."

"Another sneaker, oh, they drug him out of my bed and tied him up between my two donkeys," Susanna said and smiled to herself. "Those donkeys pulled on him until he got to be a very tall man."

"I'm already over six foot," Wendell said and turned toward her in the bed, smiling as much as he dared. "Do you prefer a tall man, Susanna?"

"No reason you should care what I prefer," she said, lacing her fingers over her stomach. When she took a good look at Wendell Wagner, she saw his long body and bearded face were dappled with sunlight. He was nearly as skinny as Larry, and half his face and neck were covered by his curly gray beard.

Susanna's husband had been a very tall man, six-foot-six, which was why he thought he needed a big bed like this, though Susanna suspected he was just trying to sleep farther away from her, giving himself the opportunity to steal away at night without her hearing. Though she'd hated his sneakiness, she didn't really blame him for leaving. They hadn't had much in common anymore besides the kids, and grandkids weren't something he'd been interested in. He'd wanted her to sell this old place, go travel around the country. He'd gotten tired of a woman who wanted to garden all summer. Over the years, she'd realized he was better suited to the woman from the bottle gas company, who took long summer vacations with him.

A dog barked outside the house. The rooster crowed in the

chicken yard. The dog paused as if listening to the crowing and then barked again. The ducks started up quacking and yakking again.

"But since you ask," Susanna said, lifting her sheet for a moment of cool, "I prefer a man who's not a lying, cheating, sly-acting son of a bitch."

"Should I get up and let the dog in?" Wendell asked.

"Naw, don't worry. Somebody else'll let him in." Susanna didn't want Wendell to leave just yet. "I heard my grandkids up and around."

"You think I ought to go out the window?" Wendell said. "So your grandkids don't see me?"

Susanna pretended to consider the offer. "No, you'd better not. If you go out the window, you'll make them ducks crazy, wake up everybody in the neighborhood. And those kids'll see you anyhow. They don't miss a thing."

"I'll stay right here with you, then."

"Doesn't seem like you fixed my air-conditioning. It's already ninety degrees in here."

"I'm afraid that old machine is kaput, Susanna. I'm speaking as a professional."

"Larry thinks you can work miracles."

"I can," Wendell said. "But I work them when I least expect it. Listen, somebody's yelling in your kitchen. Sounds like some of them kids might be fighting."

Susanna turned her head and listened, until she heard what sounded like a box of cornflakes hitting the wall and busting open. A chair tipped over, and somebody started to cry. She shook her head. Only now did she remember that Lydia had left three extra kids there for the night, so breakfast would be more riotous than usual.

"Oh, that's just how those kids eat breakfast," she said. My daughter Rachel yells at them, but I don't mind a little back-and-forth. Gets the blood moving." In fact, as recently as yesterday morning she herself had yelled for them to shut up, but she'd done it without thinking, like scratching an itch. Maybe she just liked to join in their rowdy conversation.

"Listen to them donkeys he-hawing in the barnyard," Wendell said. "They do that every morning?"

Susanna liked having the sounds of her place pointed out to her. She was so used to the donkeys and ducks and kids that they'd blurred into a background racket.

"They figure I ought to be out feeding them instead of lying here talking to you," Susanna said. "I got to feed the little jackass up there with a bottle. Another thing my kids got me into."

"And you don't want to do it?"

"Larry says you're sleeping in a tent somewhere."

"For the next few weeks anyhow, or so long as the fruit's ripening in my pawpaw patch. It's a pleasure sleeping on the hill at night. Coolest place in town."

"Well, all my rooms are full, so I got no place for you here."

"Oh, don't worry about me. I got a little bed in the back room of my shop," he said. "But you ought to come out and join me in the cool night air and see my pawpaw trees. If I don't stay out there, the squirrels are going to eat my pawpaws, so I guess I won't be able to come over and sleep with you anymore for a while."

"Well, I don't remember asking you." Susanna wiped the sweat off her forehead with a bandanna from the nightstand. She had truly believed Wendell Wagner was going to fix the air-conditioning—that showed what a fool she was. They both listened to the sound of the barking dog and the shouting children. When something heavy hit the floor in the living room, the barking and shouting went silent, and then it all started up again, louder. They heard the front door open and close three times. Heard the storm door bang shut three times. Susanna normally would've gotten out of bed to stop all that going in and out.

"You know, I've never had a pawpaw," she said. "I've heard of them, but I've somehow never had one. Never even seen one, truth be told."

"Well, they're fine tasting and they're a mystery, too, a tropical fruit growing right here in Michigan, tropical as your banana. Sometimes they get ripe in late August, and sometimes it's not till November. This year I figure it's going to be early because of the heat." A horn blared in the driveway. Wendell Wagner recognized the two-tone blast from his Ford Econoline work van. He asked, "Would those kids be getting in my truck?"

"You didn't leave it unlocked, did you?"

"I believe I left it unlocked. You don't think they'll get in the back and mess with my tools, do you?"

"I sure hope you didn't leave the keys in the ignition."

Wendell felt his pocket and was relieved to find the wad of metal. "My keys are right in here."

"Good. It'll take my grandson Tommy at least ten minutes to hot-wire it."

The truck's horn sounded again, a sustained blast this time, like somebody leaning on it, and soon the ducks were going wild in the creek. By the time the horn stopped and the ducks quieted down, the donkeys were he-honking again to be fed.

"Maybe I can take a look at that old Ford tractor you said has got a worn-out engine. My dad had an old 8N most of my life, and I worked on it with him. Maybe it's just a head gasket."

"You can't fix my air-conditioning, so why should I think you can fix my tractor? And I've got no money to pay you."

254 BONNIE JO CAMPBELL

"Maybe I'll just do it in my spare time," Wendell said. "If you don't mind it taking a while. Maybe you'll have a few tomatoes for me."

"Tomatoes don't look so good this year, unless you want them sun-dried on the vine."

"Maybe you can give me some tomatoes next summer. It might take me all winter to fix that tractor."

"You really going to give Larry a job?"

"You really think he's too dumb to work?"

Susanna realized she wasn't helping herself by criticizing Larry. If somebody gave him a job, he could pay rent.

"He's an okay kid, I guess, so long as somebody's telling him what to do."

"I figure he could run errands, clean parts for me, change filters." Wendell could imagine Larry assisting him in working on Susanna's tractor between furnace jobs. Wendell imagined taking a break now and again to drink some coffee with Susanna and study the Ford manual—he could send Larry to borrow the manual from his neighbor Joe, who had a tractor of a similar vintage. "You ever drink coffee in this bed? This bed would be a nice place to eat breakfast. Or play cards."

"Why'd your wife kick you out, anyhow?" Susanna asked. "Are you damaged goods?"

"Claimed she couldn't stand my snoring anymore. She was my second wife, and we were only married three years. For the last two years she made me sleep on the couch. Then one day she said she couldn't stand to look at me ever again."

"Hmmm. Well, I didn't hear you snoring," Susanna said, re-weaving her fingers over her chest. She'd always enjoyed disagreeing with snooty women. "And I guess I never liked quiet anyway."

"When I'm sleeping in my tent, I can hear coyotes. Frogs and crickets can be awful loud, too."

"I don't get much quiet around here. And if there's coyotes yipping, it's too noisy to hear them." Since Rachel brought the yellow dog around, Susanna hadn't heard the coyotes, but she didn't want to give Wendell the satisfaction of saying how she missed them.

"Put that pipe wrench down, Sara," said a boy's voice. "You're going to knock a window out."

Wendell held his tongue. He had collected those tools over his whole thirty-year career, and he didn't want to lose them, but he didn't know if he'd ever get into such an interesting situation with a woman again.

"Ow!" shouted a kid. "I'm going to tell Granny you hit me."

"I'm a little fearful of your grandchildren. There's so many of them."

"Just six or seven." When Susanna tiptoed out of bed in her long T-shirt, Wendell wondered if he was supposed to get up, too. She locked the bedroom door and then crept back to her side of the bed. As soon as she got under the sheet again, somebody jiggled the door handle and whined.

"Granny, open up," said a kid, jiggling harder. "Do you got the air-conditioner man in there with you?"

"Locked it just in time," Susanna whispered.

Another girl's voice sounded outside the door. "Tommy hit me. I'm going to hit him back with this pike wrench." Something banged heavily against the lowest wooden panel of the door.

"You're so stupid, you don't even know what it's called," said a third kid with an authoritative voice. "It's not a pike wrench. It's a pipe wrench. For pipes. You think you're going to hit a fish with it or something? You're retarded."

"Shut up, Tommy!"

"I believe she's got one of my big wrenches," Wendell said.

"Granny, Tommy said I'm retarded," the smaller voice whined, but when Susanna didn't respond, she added, "I'm going to hit *you* with it, Tommy," and the tool clunked against the door again. Footsteps sounded down the hall and there was another sound, this time of the heavy tool crashing into a wall.

"Granny, are you in there?" said a new little girl's voice. "We can't find the air-conditioner man, but his truck's here. Tommy says the man drowned in the creek."

"You don't think they'll throw my tools in the creek, do you?" Wendell whispered. "I don't want them to rust."

"You got any kids? Grandkids?" Susanna asked calmly.

"My two daughters live in California. Hardly ever come home to visit. I've been thinking of taking a trip out there, if I can get a break between heating and cooling seasons." He was sitting up a little now, propped on pillows. "My oldest is having a baby, my first grandkid."

"You'll probably move out there, then," Susanna said and felt a pang of something like regret. "It's never quiet with kids around."

"Oh, I've got some things I'm interested in around here," he said. "I don't want to move anywhere else."

Though she wasn't looking at him, she could almost feel him wink, and it made her blush as she hadn't in years.

"I guess you don't remember," he said, finally getting to a subject he'd been saving. "But we met once before."

AFTER WENDELL PACKED up his tools and left, Susanna drank iced coffee in her hot kitchen and then spent an hour in her garden picking tomatoes. She tossed the split ones into five-gallon pails to feed to the chickens and pigs; a decade ago she would have cursed herself for such waste. She experienced a twinge of guilt over the state of her garden, but only a twinge; the heat had made weeding toilsome, and the jungle might be considered shameful, but the overgrown pokeweed and burdock had shaded her tomato vines and protected them somewhat from the sun, and truth be told, the vision of the neglected garden made her feel cheerfully liberated this morning, like the ladies who burned their bras in the old days. When she finished, she stood beside the trunk of the exploded pine, among the wood chips and splinters, listening to the roar of cicadas and crickets. In this kind of heat at least she didn't have to worry about mosquitoes.

"My uncle said he's going to hire me," Larry said later when he passed her in the kitchen. He was wearing his bath towel like a skirt again, but now he was grinning.

"I told him he was a fool if he did," Susanna said. She continued slipping skins off the blanched tomatoes and dropping them into jars, but she couldn't stop smiling. A dozen years ago, Wendell's hair had been as black as Larry's. Now she remembered the man clearly.

Though Susanna was way too busy to visit some guy's pawpaw patch, she kept looking at the map he'd drawn for her. He'd made a stick figure with motion lines to designate a quarter-mile walk along a path. It would be a moonlit night, he said, but still it might be better for her to get there before it was dark. She'd been shaking her head no all the while.

TWELVE YEARS AGO, as Wendell Wagner told the story, he had been sitting in the open side door of his work van, eating a sandwich in the parking lot of Gil's Potawatomi Grocery, preparing for a one o'clock service call. A woman with wavy chestnut hair had pulled up beside him in a flatbed truck. She'd gone into the store, and when she came out and got back into the truck, it wouldn't start and lost power with each attempt. She opened the truck's hood, put her foot up on a landscape timber she was using for a bumper, and gazed inside. When he got out and stood beside her, he felt a jolt pass between them, a shock so powerful he feared the truck had an electrical problem. In the back of the truck was about a half ton of manure, and it was starting to smell.

"I've got cabbage rolls in the oven," she'd said as he approached. "I hate for them to burn."

"My ma called them things *pigs in a blanket*," Wendell had said when he found his voice. Then he'd helped her jump the truck with the cables she produced, and she'd said thank you and driven away. He'd thought her a fine woman, and he would have liked to converse with her, ask her about the load of manure and about the cabbage rolls to see if she put chili sauce on them the way his ma did, but she'd been in a hurry. He'd been a married man back then, and his wife had been sick and he'd been busy taking care of her anytime he wasn't working, leaving little time for talking to interesting people.

While her jars of tomatoes boiled, Susanna fixed up some more milk powder and went to feed the baby donkey. She moved out of the way just in time so Junebug banged into a fence rail instead of her belly. He looked up, stunned for a moment, before grabbing hold of the big nipple and sucking. Susanna inspected the long fuzzy ears for mites. She glanced around to make sure nobody was watching, and then she buried her hands in the plush baby-fur on his chest and belly, rested her cheek against his sweet, fuzzy neck. As much as she didn't like to admit it, she had changed over the last few years.

Other than the occasional rooster, she was not inclined to butcher her own livestock—she would happily eat meat from plastic packages. She didn't really want to let this donkey die, and she didn't even wish for the demise of the spoiled cats, truth be told. Like Wendell had said, she was a woman who did what she wanted now. She wasn't as poor as she used to be when the kids were all at home, and even if Larry never paid his rent, she wouldn't go hungry. But if she wanted to kick him out, she would.

Maybe she'd spent too much time with her New Age daughter-in-law, and that was why Susanna now considered that Junebug might be a reincarnation of her old friend Tom Taylor, who had been killed on the train tracks—Tom Taylor had limped on his left leg, too, and he was as stubborn as they came. Or maybe the baby was the last residue of her ex-husband, a stumbling ass unrivaled when drunk. Maybe she was no longer even holding a grudge against the man. She worked a few burrs out of the hair on Junebug's chest. When the milk was gone, she climbed onto a fence rail and watched the little guy buck and fart across the barnyard toward his humorless mama.

Maybe by being a damned fool for all the needy creatures, Susanna had formed some new kind of energy field. Maybe her tractor would start right up now if she cleared away the shreds of broken pine tree.

After Wendell told the story, she had indeed remembered him jumping her car, though she'd been in a hurry that day, cooking cabbage rolls and doing six other things. He didn't have a beard then, only a mass of curly black hair that fell in his eyes. His Adam's apple had been so sharp-looking, though, she'd thought it might hurt him from inside out. Something about her faulty memory made her remember him as wearing nothing but a towel, though he'd been out in public, so that was absurd. Though her truck had been old and rusted, he'd said something like, "Don't tell me a good solid Ford truck like this has let you down."

She hadn't had time for nonsense back then, hadn't even had the desire to puzzle out what he was trying to say. She remembered only that when she'd met his gaze, his shaven face had assumed a peculiar mixture of surprise and terror. Susanna had otherwise seen that look in the eyes of horses who'd run wild for a few years, horses who'd gone hungry and uncared-for, horses who'd almost forgotten they were domestic animals until you caught and saddled them.

He'd offered to test her alternator if she wanted to come to his place, but she said no, thank you, and drove home. A few weeks later she'd had to replace the alternator. And she had forgotten Wendell, more or less. But all these years later, she had taken in Larry for no good reason.

She was far too busy to go see Wendell Wagner, but after forty-eight jars of tomatoes were lined up on the counter in the hundred-degree kitchen, she put some crackers and cheese and tomatoes in a grocery bag and headed across town with the hand-drawn map.

She'd known about pawpaws from books and songs, but she'd never actually seen one until Wendell pointed out a plum-size peanut-shaped fruit the color of a d'Anjou pear dangling from a low branch.

"Can't we pick it?" Susanna asked. They were sitting at a picnic table beside his tent.

"You can't pick a pawpaw, woman. That's sacrilege. You've got to wait for just the right moment. When it's ripe, it'll fall."

"But you said it might take months," she said. "Can't we shake the tree, at least?"

"Shaking the tree, now, that's a gray area. Let's wait a little longer." He'd shaken this very tree plenty, but with Susanna here, he could wait for things to happen in their own time.

"It's a little cooler here, like you said." Susanna took a deep breath and exhaled for a long time. The cicadas and crickets were as raucous as Susanna's grandkids at breakfast.

THE THIRD MORNING after the third night she spent with Wendell in his tent, they heard a thud in the grass nearby. Wendell scrambled out with his pants in his hand. Susanna took her time dressing, and when she found Wendell he was still naked, sitting on the picnic table, but he'd finished cutting away the bruised green skin from the first pawpaw of the season. He handed her a peeled fruit the color of acorn-squash meat and closed up his pocketknife.

When she bit into the yellowish fruit, it gave only the gentlest resistance. The texture was that of custard. Susanna savored the sweet, dense flesh, found the mellow flavor resembled mango, but it didn't have the tropical fibers, and it resembled banana, too, and also made her think of pears fried in brown sugar and butter, something she'd never eaten, but might, now that she'd thought of it. The grasshoppers rattled in the long grass all around them, and cicadas hissed from the trees.

"Thank you for this," she said. Her sixty-third year had started with her doctor telling her she had high blood pressure and high cholesterol and was at risk for osteoporosis. Susanna had not been expecting that she would wake up one day and find life had gotten easier, that coffee would smell better, that tomatoes would peel with less effort, that she'd feel like jogging to the barnyard with the bottle of mare's milk instead of walking, that she'd want to sleep in a tent and cook on a campfire. She noticed how intently Wendell was watching her, and she said in a measured way, "This is something new, all right, something different. I've never tasted anything like this before."

She took another bite and wondered how on earth she had lived without this fruit all these years. The half dozen seeds disbursed evenly throughout the body of the fruit were smooth as magic beans against her tongue. Susanna thought about that radish-size moonstone Lydia was wearing, the way she smiled when she touched it. If Susanna could string a handful of these glossy, walnut-dark seeds into a necklace, she might wear it. She might reach up and touch the seeds to remind herself of this sweet taste.

"Are you serious about taking a look at my tractor?"

"As serious as the day is long," he said.

She didn't know if Wendell had any more idea than she did about overhauling a tractor engine. There was no law, though, that said she couldn't give a man a chance.

ACKNOWLEDGMENTS

THANK YOU, Heidi Bell, Carla Black Vissers, Andy Mozina, Lisa Lenzo, and Susan Blackwell Ramsey for sharing your time and wisdom during the creation of this book. Thank you, Bill Clegg, for helping conceive this collection, and thank you, editor extraordinaire Jill Bialosky, for its care and feeding. Kellie Wells weighed in early on the whole shebang, Alicia Conroy gave profound feedback on a late draft, and Margaret DeRitter helped me get the commas in the right places. Assorted kind souls helped me with one or more of the stories, including Diane Seuss, Heather Sappenfield, David Long, Steve Amick, Darrin Doyle, Jamie Blake, and Mimi Lipson.

It takes great friends, fellow writers, and supporters galore to make a writing life, and my crew includes the folks at W. W. Norton (thanks especially to Erin Sinesky Lovett) the brand new Clegg Agency (shout out to Chris Clemans), dynamic booksellers across the country (much appreciation to Dean Hauck of Michigan News Agency), clever librarians (thanks, Marsha Meyer for making so much happen at Portage District Library), Alison Granucci of Blue Flower Arts, and the good and kind publicist Sheryl Johnston. The John Simon Guggenheim Memorial Foundation provided generous support during 2012.

Though this work is entirely fictional, some stories have been inspired by folks in my hometown of Comstock, Michigan, especially Susanna, Sheila, and Thomas Campbell. And thank you, Darling Christopher, for everything, always.

"Sleepover" appeared in *Southwest Review* as winner of the World's Best Short Short Story contest. "The Greatest Show on Earth, 1982: What There Was" (formerly "What There Was"), "Children of Transylvania, 1983," and "Daughters of the Animal Kingdom" appeared in *The Southern Review*. "Mothers, Tell Your Daughters" appeared in *One Story*. "Somewhere Warm" and "Playhouse" appeared in *Third Coast Review*. A version of "Blood Work, 1999" appeared in the final issue of *Story* magazine. "My Dog Roscoe" originally appeared in *Witness* magazine, and a version was reprinted in *Dog Is My Co-Pilot* (Crown Archetype). "A Multitude of Sins" was published in *Boulevard* under the title "Home to Die." A version of "To You, as a Woman" appeared under the title "Candy" in *Ontario Review*. "Natural Disasters" appeared in *Mid-American Review*. "Tell Yourself" appeared in *Kenyon Review Online*. A version of "The Fruit of the Pawpaw Tree" appeared as "September News from Susanna's Farm" in the final print issue of *TriQuarterly Review*.

MOTHERS, TELL
YOUR DAUGHTERS

Bonnie Jo Campbell

READING GROUP GUIDE

MOTHERS, TELL YOUR DAUGHTERS

Bonnie Jo Campbell

DISCUSSION QUESTIONS

1. Many women in these stories experience some sort of physical violence, trauma, or abuse, and a few go on to commit violent acts themselves. How do you think violence shapes these characters? In interviews, Bonnie Jo Campbell has said that she sees her characters as survivors rather than as victims. Is this an important distinction?

2. In "Tell Yourself," "Daughters of the Animal Kingdom," and the title story, "Mothers, Tell Your Daughters," we see mothers concerned that their daughters will make the same mistakes they made. Do you think certain female intergenerational struggles are destined to be repeated? Are there some that can be transcended?

3. The female protagonists in *Mothers, Tell Your Daughters* continue to love the very men who have abused or betrayed them. How do they reconcile both aspects of their relationships?

4. Many characters have complex relationships toward motherhood. How does motherhood shape their experiences? Does Campbell give any special insight into what it means to be a daughter?

5. Does the author make us feel sympathy for characters who are difficult to like or understand? If so, how does she do this? For example, in the story "To You, as a Woman," we see an example of very bad parenting.

Sign up for our newsletter and giveaways at
bit.ly/wwnorton-reading-group-guides.

6. *Mothers, Tell Your Daughters* has first-, second-, and third-person narrations. How do you think these different voices influence the way we understand these stories?

7. The stories take place in largely rural or postindustrial settings. How does location shape the lives of the characters? How does their level of education and economic status affect their lives?

8. Sexual coming-of-age figures largely in many of the stories and leads many of Campbell's women into trouble. How do the characters change in regards to innocence, power, and agency? What types of lessons do they learn?

9. In the title story, "Mothers, Tell Your Daughters," the narrator's daughter is a professor of women's studies and has perspectives that stand in opposition to her mother's. Do you see differences between an academic perspective on women's struggles compared to the points of view of Campbell's characters?

10. The women in Campbell's stories have a diverse range of backgrounds. What aspects unite them?

11. Though all the stories are told from a female point of view, they often center on contentious relationships with men. How might the stories be different if told from the men's perspective?